THE DEVIL'S HUNT

THE DEVIL'S HUNT

P. C. Doherty

ST. MARTIN'S PRESS ☙ NEW YORK

Library of Congress Cataloging-in-Publication Data

Doherty, P. C.
    The devil's hunt / P. C. Doherty.
        p.   cm.
    ISBN 0-312-18084-5
    1. Corbett, Hugh (Fictitious character)—Fiction.   2. Great
Britain—History—Edward I, 1272–1307—Fiction.   3.
Oxford (England)—History—Fiction.   4. Middle Ages—
Fiction.   I. Title.
PR6054.037D48   1998
823'.914—dc21   97-43668
                                                   CIP

First published in Great Britain by HEADLINE BOOK PUBLISHING, a
division of Hodder Headline PLC

First U.S. Edition: March 1998

10   9   8   7   6   5   4   3   2

To my 'Beloveds'
Ekene, Ebele and Victor Jr
and their parents
Victor and Christine Ikwuemesi

Prologue

'Brutal, sudden death!' Father Ambrose, Parson of Iffley church, had proclaimed, 'Shall be sprung like a trap upon every man living upon the face of God's earth.'

Piers the plough boy, leaning against a pillar of the parish church, had listened to the sermon half dozing or casting lustful, hot-eyed stares at Edigha, the blacksmith's daughter. Now, later that same Sunday, Piers was to have his heart's desire. He'd met flaxen-haired Edigha beside the village well. They'd stolen out of the village, down the beaten track, past the gallows and into the field of ripe corn. Edigha had giggled and pulled at Piers's hand.

'I shouldn't really go!' she whispered, her blue eyes bright with merriment. 'Father will expect me!'

'Your father's damping the ashes down in his forge,' Piers retorted, grinning with a display of cracked teeth. 'Whilst, Edigha my love, the flames in my belly burn hot for you.' He said the words proudly, repeating what he'd heard the travelling minstrels say to a tavern wench in the Goat's Head tavern after he'd come from ploughing the previous Monday. Piers's short but eloquent speech had the desired effect. Edigha giggled again and trotted along beside him. Keeping their heads bowed, they moved through the sea of waving corn. Rabbits and mice, alarmed by their approach, scuttled for shelter, whilst above them wood pigeons fled like darts from the shadow of a hovering hawk. Piers

1

stopped and looked up at them. For some strange reason he recalled Father Ambrose's words: the hawk hung against the blue sky, motionless, waiting, watching, before its killing plunge. Piers shivered.

'What's the matter?' Edigha pressed herself against him. 'Have the fires gone out?' She wrapped her arms around his waist, slipping one hand down to brush his groin. 'We have to be back by sunset,' she whispered.

Piers stared at the sun now setting in a glorious ball of fire, lighting up the sky with red-hot sparks. He turned, the breeze ruffling across his brow, and stared across at the small copse.

'There's something wrong,' he whispered. 'It's so silent.'

'You are frightening me,' Edigha teased back yet she caught his mood. A tryst with Piers was what she had wanted but now, out here in the open, the corn swaying about her in the whispering wind, she was not so sure. She gazed across at the trees. It would be dark and cool in there, and her stomach jerked as she realised they would have to return the same way. If anyone saw them there would be teasing and whispering in the Goat's Head and around the village well for weeks to come.

'Can't we go back by the trackway?' she muttered.

'We'd be seen.' Piers grasped her hand.

He made to run forward but then he recalled the ghoulish stories: Ralph, the reeve, standing in the tap room, a tankard in his hand, describing in hushed tones the severed corpses recently found in the woods around the city.

'Bleeding like stuck pigs they were,' Ralph had warned. 'Blood bubbling out like wine from a broken jar: their heads wrapped by hair to the branches above.' Ralph had shaken a warning finger. 'It's those bloody ne'er-do-wells!' he ranted. 'Those so-called scholars from the town with their airs and graces.'

Everyone had nodded. Oxford was strange: a town with its own rights and privileges; with its own peculiar smells and sights. All towns were bad enough with their swaggering merchants and sharp-eyed traders but Oxford, with its scholars, many of them strangers from other parts and even from foreign countries across the seas, was worse than Sodom and Gomorrah, or so Father Ambrose said. Whilst the scholars with their bird-like talk and gaudy raiment, were devils incarnate. Now and again some of them came out to Iffley, strutting like peacocks, their knives and swords pushed in their belts. They'd eye the girls and look for anything they could steal. Naturally these same students now took the blame for the hideous corpses found in the countryside around the city .

'If they're going to commit hideous murders,' Bartholomew the miller had growled, 'they should do it within their own walls.'

'But why?' Father Ambrose had intervened. 'I've heard that the corpses belonged to beggars. Some people claim they were used,' his voice fell to a whisper, 'for foul, Satanic rites.'

'Piers! Piers!'

The ploughboy broke from his reverie.

Edigha was playing with the laces of her bodice and lust flared again in his belly.

'Come on!' he muttered thickly. He gently touched the generous swell of her breasts, his fingers fluttering down around the slim waist. He pulled her close. 'You are so giving!'

'I'll be your wife, won't I?' Edigha enjoined, her blue eyes holding his. 'You said so. I'll be handfast as your wife. At the church door before All Hallows?'

Piers stooped to kiss her but then jumped, his head snapping back as he looked up. A speck of blood splashed on his face, a feather drifted down: the hawk had plunged to

3

make its kill. Piers didn't wait any longer; Edigha might change her mind. They hurried on through the corn, stopping now and again to hug and kiss, Piers's sweaty fingers scrabbling at Edigha's bodice, tugging at the cords. At last they reached the edge of the wood and ran into its cool green darkness. Piers pulled Edigha down on top of him. She giggled and resisted, then broke free and ran on. Piers sighed. Girls always did that, turning their courting into huntsman's bluff. Piers got up and chased after her, catching her in a small glade. He sighed with pleasure: her hair had broken loose and was hanging down, a mass of gold on either side of her red, sweaty face, her blue eyes were bright. He grasped her hand, pulling her to him, and they walked between the trees. He began to kiss her, relishing the sweet smell of her skin, licking at the sweat which laced her throat. Suddenly Edigha went rigid. She pushed him away and stepped back, staring at something behind him. Edigha's face was white, her eyes screwed up, her mouth opening and closing in terror, whilst strange sounds gurgled from the back of her throat.

'What is it, love? What is it?'

She half raised her hand. Piers turned slowly as if he knew what he was going to see. At first he could see nothing untoward, but then he looked up. From an old oak tree a branch jutted out like a spear and, on its end, lashed by its hair to the branch, was a severed head. Piers took a step closer: the eyes were half-open, the grey cheeks sagging, the mouth gaped bloody like that of a slaughtered animal. The neck was cut and ragged, still caked with gore. Piers's mouth went dry. His legs began to tremble. Edigha seized his hand, and they both turned and fled from the terror in the woods.

In Sparrow Hall, near Turl Street in Oxford, Death had also sprung like a trap. Ascham the archivist knew he was going to die. He lay, his legs bent in pain, his mouth opening and shutting. He tried to force a scream but he knew it was useless. No one would hear; the doors and windows were closed. His death had come spinning through the air, the crossbow quarrel taking him full in the chest.

Ascham knew he was dying. He could taste the iron, salty tang of blood gurgling at the back of his throat. Stabs of pain went through his body. He closed his eyes, whispering the words of the Confiteor, seeking God's absolution: 'Oh, my God, I am sincerely sorry for these and all the sins from my youth . . .' His mind wandered even as his body trembled with pain. Images from the past came to him – his mother bending over him, the shouting of his brother, his early days in Oxford, jaunty, full of life. The girl he met and would have married, sad-eyed and moist-mouthed when he turned and walked away; Henry Braose; his great friend, scholar, soldier and founder of this very Sparrow Hall where he now lay dying. So much evil now! Resentment, fury and hatred. The Bellman proclaiming the Devil's malice, trying to destroy everything Henry had built up.

Ascham opened his eyes. The library was dark. He tried again to scream but the sound died on his lips. The candle, flickering under its metal cap on the table, shed a small pool of light and Ascham glimpsed the piece of parchment the assassin had tossed on to the table. Ascham realised what had brought about his death: he'd recognised the truth but he'd been stupid enough to allow his searches to be known. If only he had a pen! His hand grasped the wound bubbling in his chest. He wept and crawled painfully across the floor towards the table. He seized the parchment and, with his dying strength, carefully hauled himself up to etch out the letters – but the pool of light seemed to be dimming. He'd lost the feeling in his legs, which were stiffening, like bars of iron.

5

'Enough,' he whispered. 'Ah, Jesus . . .'

Ascham closed his eyes, coughed and died as the blood bubbled on his lips.

Chapter 1

The outlaw standing in the gallows cart moved his head as the chafing rope gripped his neck. He hawked, spat and glared defiantly at Sir Hugh Corbett, former courier and clerk of the Secret Seal but still the powerful lord of the manor of Leighton in Essex. Beside Corbett was the man who had hunted him down, caught him and brought him to trial in Sir Hugh's court: Ranulf-atte-Newgate, formerly Clerk of the Chancery of the Green Wax, Corbett's henchman, bailiff and chief steward. The outlaw licked his chapped lips and glared hatefully at Ranulf.

'Well, come on, you red-haired bastard!' he shouted. 'Hang me or let me go!'

Corbett pushed his horse forward.

'Boso Deverell, you are an outlaw, a wolf's-head, a thief and a murderer! You have been found guilty and sentenced to hang!'

'Go to hell!' Boso retorted.

Corbett ran his fingers through his hair: he stared at Father Luke, the village chaplain, who was standing beside the cart.

'Have you shriven him, Father?'

'He's refused confession,' the dusty-faced priest replied, his eyes hard, seething with fury.

Father Luke glanced up at the lord of the manor, studying Corbett's sallow, clean-shaven face; the black hair streaked with grey; the sharp nose above thin lips. Father Luke held Corbett's eyes: he knew this clerk, hard on the outside but soft within.

'You are not going to pardon him, Sir Hugh?' he whispered. 'Or lessen his punishment?' The priest gripped the reins of Corbett's grey roan. 'He killed two women,' the priest hissed. 'Raped them and then slit them from neck to crotch as if they were chickens.'

Corbett nodded and swallowed hard.

'And that's just the start of it,' the priest continued remorselessly. 'He's responsible for other deaths.' Father Luke pointed at the few villagers who had assembled just after dawn to witness royal justice being done. 'If you show mercy,' the priest declared, his hand on Corbett's knee, 'every wolf's-head—' He threw his hand dramatically out towards the forest. 'Every wolf's-head will learn from it.' The priest's eyes brimmed with tears. 'I don't want to bury any more of my flock. I don't want to have to tell husbands, fathers, lovers that their women were raped before their throats were cut! Hang him!'

'Do you want his life so badly?' Corbett replied, his eyes never leaving those of Boso.

'God does.' Father Luke turned to the outlaw. 'Are you ready to die, Boso?'

The outlaw coughed, brought his head back and spat, catching the priest on the side of the face. Ranulf pushed his horse up.

'How many did you kill, Boso?'

'More than you'll ever know.' Deverell's eyes shifted back to Corbett. 'It's a pity you were at home, lord of the earth! Otherwise I'd have come calling on that flaxen-haired wife of yours!'

Corbett pulled his horse's head around. He glanced at the villagers, their grimy, brown faces passive; his stewards and bailiffs stood slightly apart from them. Corbett drew his sword and held it up, clasping his fingers round the cross-piece.

'I, Sir Hugh Corbett, the King's loyal servant, lord of Leighton Manor, by the power granted to me of axe, rope and tumbril do sentence you, Boso Deverell, to be hanged immediately for the diverse and horrible crimes of murder, rape and theft!'

As Corbett's death sentence rang out, a strange silence descended upon the crossroads; even the birds in the trees and the rooks circling above the gallows fell silent. Corbett looked at the priest.

'Father, say a prayer. Ranulf, hang him!'

Corbett turned his horse away and rode back along the track, waiting round the bend behind a fringe of trees. He closed his eyes, gripping the pommel of his saddle. He heard the creak of wheels, followed by a murmur of approval.

'God have mercy!' Corbett whispered.

He hated hangings! He knew Boso had to die but it brought back memories: the rain-soaked forests of Scotland with corpses hanging by the score as Edward's troops crushed the Scottish rebels under Wallace; fields blazing in sheets of flame; villages covered by a thick, heavy pall of smoke; wells choked with corpses; women and children dying in ditches.

'Thank God!' Corbett breathed. 'Thank God! I'm not there!'

'It's done.'

Corbett opened his eyes and saw Ranulf-atte-Newgate, his long, red hair hidden under a hood, his white face solemn though the green eyes reflected a task well done.

'It's over, Master. Boso's gone to hell. Father Luke's pleased and so are the villagers.' Ranulf straightened up and stared up through the overhanging branches. 'By dusk the news will be all over Epping. The other wolf's-heads will learn to leave Leighton alone. And you'll keep your promise, Master?'

Corbett took the leather gauntlets from his belt and put them on.

'I'll keep my promise, Ranulf. Within a week, I'll issue a Commission of Array. You can take every able-bodied man into the forest and hunt down the rest of Boso's followers.'

Ranulf smiled.

'Are you so bored?' Corbett asked.

The smile died on Ranulf's face. 'It's been three months, Master, since you left the royal service. The King has written to you five times.' He saw the flicker of annoyance on Corbett's face. 'But, yes, I am bored,' he added hastily. 'I liked being a royal clerk, Master, busy on the King's affairs.'

'As in Scotland?' Corbett snapped.

'That was war, fighting the King's enemies on land and sea – we took an oath.'

Corbett studied Ranulf; his henchman was no longer a stripling but an ambitious clerk. Sprung from the gutters of London, Ranulf had educated himself, and was now skilled in French, Latin and the art of drafting and sealing letters. To put it bluntly, Ranulf hated the countryside and loathed farming, and he was growing increasingly restless. Corbett put his gloves on slowly.

'I could write letters,' he offered. 'The King would take you back in his service. You could hold high office, Ranulf.'

'Don't be stupid!'

Corbett grinned. He leaned over and grasped Ranulf's wrist.

'When the King's forces sacked Dundee,' he said, 'I saw the corpse of a woman with a child in her arms who could have been no more than three years. How in God's name, Ranulf, were they the King's enemies?'

'So you think the King should retreat? Give up his claims to Scotland?' Ranulf pulled back his hood and scratched his head. 'Some of the Royal Justices would rule that as treason.'

'I just think there's a better way,' Corbett replied. 'The wars have exhausted the treasury. Wallace still leads the rebellion: the King should sit down and negotiate.'

'Then why not tell the King that?' Ranulf replied. 'Why not return to the royal service? Make it clear you will do anything but wage war in Scotland?'

'Now you are being stupid.' Corbett gathered the reins of his horse. 'You know, Ranulf, that where the King goes, his chief clerk must follow and that's the end of the matter.'

Corbett edged his horse forward. Ranulf cursed, pulled up his hood and followed him.

They were scarcely through the gates leading up to the manor house when Corbett sensed something was wrong. A thatcher, with bundles of straw on his back, stepped to one side and shouted excitedly, pointing up the path. Corbett rode on. Suddenly a figure seemed to leap out of nowhere, jumping up and down, waving his hands. Corbett reined in and stared down at his master of horse, Ralph Maltote, who knew everything about horses but little about human nature. Maltote's round, boyish face was red and sweaty. He gasped for breath as he clutched the reins of Corbett's horse.

'Oh, don't say another mare's in foal,' Ranulf murmured. 'It's the only time you become excited, Maltote.'

'It's the King.' Maltote wiped his mouth on the back of his hand. 'Sir Hugh, it's the King. He's here with the Earls of Surrey and Lincoln and others. Lady Maeve is entertaining them. She sent me on.'

Corbett leaned down and patted him on the shoulder.

'Well, at least it's not a mare in foal, Maltote – that would be too much excitement in one day.'

Corbett rode on, Maltote trotting behind him. They rounded the bend in the trackway and paused: the broad, pebbled path leading to the main door of the manor was now thronged with men-at-arms, retainers, knight bannerets, all wearing the gorgeous livery of Edward of England. Horses milled about beneath broad banners and pennants bearing the golden, snarling leopards of the Plantagenets, quartered to display the arms of England, France, Scotland and Ireland. Chamberlains and household officials were shouting, trying to impose order. Sumpter ponies were being untethered, carts and covered wagons pushed hither and thither.

'Where Edward goes,' Corbett sighed, 'chaos follows.' He dismounted, throwing the reins of his horse at Maltote. 'Ranulf, you had best join us.'

He walked up, threading his way through the bustling throng. Now and again one of the knights would catch his eye and greet him, and Corbett would reply. He climbed the steps and pushed through the half-open door. His baby daughter Eleanor was just inside, jumping up and down like a grasshopper, the image of Maeve, her blonde hair falling in tresses to her shoulders. The little girl's face was bright with excitement at the doll, a gift from the King, clutched in her hand.

'Look! Look!' She danced towards Corbett. 'Look, a goll!'

Corbett crouched down. 'Eleanor, stay still.'

The small child jumped even more, in and out of his arms, pressing her hot, sticky face to his.

'It's a goll! It's a goll!'

Corbett stared at the costly toy dressed in silken taffeta.

'You are right.' He sighed, grasping his daughter's hand. 'It's a goll and reminds me of some of the ladies at Edward's court.' He glanced up at the girl's nurse, hovering close. 'Keep her safe,' Corbett whispered. 'And watch the soldiers!' He grinned at the perplexity in the nursemaid's berry-brown face. 'You will receive many invitations for a kiss, Beatrice,' he murmured. 'But any girl who survived Ranulf...'

The nurse's eyes took on a more knowing look. She glared furiously at Ranulf.

'Yes, now you've got the right idea,' Corbett declared. 'And the Lady Maeve?'

Beatrice pointed to the door now guarded by two men-at-arms with drawn swords. Corbett went across, the man-at-arms opened the door and he entered his main hall. Just inside the doorway clustered a group of knights and royal officials. Corbett paused to greet them.

'Sir Hugh?'

A tousled-haired, ink-stained clerk pushed his way through. Corbett shook the hand of Simon, one of Edward's personal clerks. Simon nodded towards the dais where the King and his two earls sat, paying court to the Lady Maeve, still not aware of Corbett's arrival.

'It's good to see you, Sir Hugh.' Simon licked his lips. 'The King's in a good mood – he has received welcome news from Scotland – but his leg hurts and the wound in his side, where he cracked his rib, still pains him. His moods can change at the drop of a coin.'

'So he has not changed at all?'

Corbett pushed his way through and made his way along the hall. At the table, on the dais, three grey-haired men dressed in travel-stained clothes, their cloaks swung arrogantly around them, only had eyes for Maeve. She sat, queen-like, in Corbett's chair, her silver hair gathered neatly under a jewel-encrusted wimple, her ivory-pale face slightly flushed as she listened to some story from Henry de Lacey, Earl of Lincoln. On her other side, Edward was urging de Lacey on.

'Come on, Henry!' The King pounded the table. 'Tell her what the friar told the abbess.'

'Sire!' Corbett called out. 'You are not corrupting my wife with your camp-fire stories?'

The King's head swung round, Maeve looked up.

You look so beautiful, Corbett thought. He noticed her hand resting on a slightly swelling stomach, her fingers running along the golden cord pulled up over her waist.

'Hugh!' She would have risen but the King gently forced her back.

'You should have been here, Corbett.' The King rose and stretched his massive, thickset body, clawing at the iron-grey hair that framed his face.

You look old, Corbett thought. The King's face was greyish as if covered in a fine dust, the beard and moustache were unkempt. His heavy-lidded eyes seemed to droop even further as if Edward wanted to protect his soul from any man seeing into it. Corbett bowed.

'Sire, if I had known you were coming . . .?'

'I sent a bloody messenger!' The King glared at his servants at the far end of the hall.

'My Lord, he never arrived.'

'Then the silly bugger got lost.' The King wiped his hands on the front of his gown. 'Or is in some tavern with a wench. Just like you, eh, Ranulf?' The King forced a smile and he came round the table. 'I've been flirting with your wife, Corbett. If I wasn't married, I'd kill you and take her myself.'

'Then two good men would die violently,' Maeve replied coolly from behind him.

Edward just smiled slyly and extended his hand for Corbett to kiss. Hugh knelt, and the King pushed his hand against his mouth so the ring scored Corbett's lip.

'There was no need for that,' Corbett whispered as he rose.

'I've missed you,' the King hissed, towering above him. 'Ranulf!'

Again his hand was extended. Ranulf kissed the ring quickly and stood back before Edward could do further harm. The King glimpsed the anger in Corbett's eyes. He stepped down from the dais and put his arm round Corbett's shoulder, forcing him to walk with him down the hall.

'I missed you, Corbett.' His grip tightened, pulling Hugh closer so he could smell leather, sweat and the faint cloying perfume of the King's clothes. 'I send you letters but you don't reply. I invite you to council meetings but you don't come. You are a moody, snivelling bastard.' Edward's fingers dug into Corbett's shoulders.

'What are you going to do, your Grace?' His former principal clerk replied. 'Talk to me or choke me?'

Edward smiled lazily, his hand falling away. He had opened his mouth to speak when the door was flung open and Uncle Morgan ap Llewellyn, dressed rather ridiculously in Lincoln green, with a brown military cloak swirling around him, crashed into the hall, spurred boots jingling. One of the spurs caught in the rushes. Uncle Morgan stumbled and Corbett bit his lip to stop himself laughing.

'Bloody rushes!' Morgan swore and immediately began to kick at the offending floor covering. His face was dirt-stained, and large damp patches of sweat were visible on his chest and shirt. He took his cloak off and threw it on the table. 'Hugh, can't you afford Turkish rugs . . .?'

Morgan suddenly realised whose presence he was in. He almost hurtled towards the King, going down on one knee, brushing back his sweat-soaked hair.

'Sire, I did not know you were here,' the Welshman gasped. 'I was out hunting . . .'

Edward grasped Morgan's hand, pulled him to his feet and embraced him.

'I wish I had been with you.' Edward planted a kiss on Morgan's cheeks, then pushed him away. 'These young dogs don't hunt like us, Morgan. They are getting soft!'

Corbett closed his eyes and prayed for patience. The King, as usual, was being charming to people he need not be. Now he would only set Morgan off and provoke his famous lecture on how soft both Corbett and everyone else had become.

'Sire, I have said that myself.' Morgan lifted a stubby finger, his rubicund, friendly face breaking into a knowing smile. 'Too soft, not like in Wales, eh, Sire? When you hunted me and I hunted you.'

Oh God, Corbett quietly prayed. Oh please, don't start him off!

'Listen.' The King grasped Morgan affectionately and winked at Corbett. 'My retinue's outside – lazy buggers the lot of them! Ensure they have something to eat and drink, and teach them a little discipline.'

Maeve's uncle drew himself up, chest puffing out like a wood pigeon, head going back, overjoyed to be given such a responsibility. He spun on his heel and headed like a whippet for the door.

'Dearest Morgan,' Edward breathed.

'Dearest Morgan,' Corbett whispered back, 'is a bloody nuisance! By day he lectures me. By night he drinks and tells everyone the saga of his life!' Corbett glanced over his shoulder, hoping Maeve had not heard. 'But he's a good man,' Corbett added. 'He loves Maeve and Eleanor – although he and Ranulf are both bred for mischief.'

Edward linked his arm through Corbett's and walked him further down the hall.

'A good soldier,' Edward said. 'Cunning and astute. He fought long and hard before he took the royal pardon. Like so many! All gone!' Edward turned. 'All gone, Hugh! Burnell, Peckham, my brother, Edmund . . .'

16

Now the tears will fall, Corbett thought, he'll brush them gently from his eyes and clutch my arm.

'I'm lonely,' the King said hoarsely. 'I miss you, Hugh.' He brushed his eyes and clutched Corbett's arm.

'You have other clerks,' Corbett retorted. 'Sire, I cannot go on campaign again. I still have nightmares: the land a sea of fire; towns full of screaming women and children.'

Corbett had decided to play the King at his own game but Edward's eyes became bright with pleasure.

'The war in Scotland is over, Hugh. Wallace has been captured. The Scottish lords are suing for peace. I don't want you in Scotland, I want you in Oxford.' The King turned and looked up the hall where de Warrenne and de Lacey had returned to their teasing of Maeve. 'You have heard the news?'

'Aye,' Corbett replied. 'A journeyman came here last week bringing parchment and vellum. You refer to the rumours about corpses being found? About the traitorous proclamations from someone calling himself the Bellman?'

'Beggars,' the King interjected. 'Poor beadsmen. Many of them gather at St Osyth's Hospital near Carfax. Four have been found with their heads sheared off their shoulders and tied like rotting apples to the branches of a tree.'

'In the city itself?'

'No, outside. Sometimes to the north, sometimes to the west.'

'Why should someone kill a poor beadsman?' Corbett asked.

He noticed how Ranulf, at Maeve's invitation, had now joined her on the dais. Corbett said a quick prayer: Ranulf was as attracted to baiting de Warrenne as a bee to honey and the old earl was famous neither for his good looks nor his patience.

17

'I don't know,' Edward retorted. 'Although the last one was Adam Brakespeare. You remember Adam, Hugh?'

The King gestured Corbett over to sit on a bench. The clerk recalled a thin whippet of a man with tawny hair and a nut-brown face. A master-of-arms, Brakespeare had been with them in Wales. On one occasion, when the elusive Welsh led them into ambush, Brakespeare had pulled Corbett from a stinking marsh as the arrows fell like rain around them.

'Adam was a soldier.' Corbett played with the ring on his finger. 'He was one of your favourites. There was even talk of knighting him?'

'When the army of Wales disbanded,' Edward replied, 'Adam returned home. He gambled rather stupidly and lost everything. He drifted, a landless man, until he became ill and petitioned the Chancery for help. By the time the petition reached me, Brakespeare was dead. His was the third corpse they found outside Oxford.'

'And the Bellman?' Corbett asked.

Edward's face tightened. 'Ah, yes, the Bellman.' The King's lips curled like a snarling dog. 'He's a writer, our Bellman. He issues proclamations and letters from Sparrow Hall invoking the ghost of the dead de Montfort.' Edward's voice rose, silencing the cheerful chatter at the top of the hall.

Corbett slowly edged away as the King plunged into his own nightmare.

'De Montfort! De Montfort!' The King's fist came smashing down on the table. 'Always bloody de Montfort! He's dead! Don't they understand that? I trapped him at Evesham, Hugh. I cut his army to bloody ribbons. I saw him die.' Froth bubbled on the King's lips. 'He's not even buried,' the King rasped. 'There was nothing left of him.' He turned his red-flecked eyes to Hugh. 'I killed him, Corbett, him and his entire, traitorous family. I cut his body to ribbons and fed it to the dogs. Now the bastard's back.' He thrust his hand inside his gown and drew out a scroll of parchment and tossed it at Corbett. 'I've threatened Sparrow Hall,' he said. 'Even though it was founded by my good friend Braose. They are to put their own house in order or I'll close it down myself. I sent a letter to Copsale, the Regent of the hall. He died in his bed. I sent a similar request to Ascham, the librarian and archivist, and he was murdered. I'll burn the place down!' the King swore.

Corbett played with the parchment.

'Don't do that, Sire,' Corbett advised. 'Don't lash out. Oxford has its own way of retaliation. They'll think you are frightened, trying to hide something. Moreover, although the Bellman says he dwells at Sparrow Hall, you don't know if that's true.'

The King grasped Corbett's hand. 'Go back there, Hugh,' he begged. 'You are my best hunting dog. Get in there and search him out. Avenge Brakespeare's death. Find me the Bellman!'

'I have left the royal service.'

The King dug into his pouch. He brought out the secret seals and ring of office and pushed them into Corbett's hand.

'Here's your fresh commission. Do this for me, Hugh. I'll stand godfather to your next child.'

Corbett knew he could not refuse. The King was no longer play-acting. He was begging and, if refused, would turn vindictive. Uncle Morgan, Maeve, Eleanor, Ranulf and Maltote would all feel the full lash of his fury.

'I'll go.'

'Good!' Edward beamed and brought his hand down heavily on Corbett's shoulders. 'That's my good lurcher, my sharp-eyed mastiff! That's what they call you, Corbett, do you know that?' Edward's sudden pleasantness was shot through with a touch of malice. 'They call you the King's dog.'

'I am the King's loyal subject,' Corbett replied.

The King pushed his face towards him. Corbett smelt his wine-drenched breath.

'I know, Hugh. There's nothing wrong with being a mastiff amongst a pack of curs – I told them so. Go to Oxford and find out who culled those poor beadsmen but, remember, I want the Bellman. I want to hang him myself!' The King got to his feet. 'I'll be leaving within the hour but Simon will remain. Now, I just hope that bastard de Warrenne hasn't finished my story. Have you heard it, Hugh? About the abbess, the friar and the box of figs?'

The King was gone within the hour in a flurry of hugs, kisses and promises of royal favour. The royal party mounted their horses and galloped off raising clouds of dust, the King yelling that he would be at his palace of Woodstock, 'Where he would reside "to keep an eye on matters".'

Corbett gave a sigh of relief and hugged Maeve. They returned to the hall where Corbett broke his fast. He then ordered the room to be cleared so that only Maeve, Ranulf and an anxious-looking Simon remained.

'Are you going to Oxford?' Maeve asked tartly.

'It seems I have to.'

Simon smiled wanly. 'Oh, thank God, Sir Hugh. A refusal would have put the King in a terrible rage. He spent yesterday kicking his clerks off their stools for the slightest mistake.'

'So, you accepted the Seal and ring?' Maeve persisted. 'Is that what you want?' Maeve pursed her lips in a gesture of annoyance before she burst out laughing. 'I am not a fool, Hugh. If you disobeyed, the King on this occasion . . .'

'Do you want me to go?' Corbett stretched over and patted her stomach.

'Yes, I do,' Maeve retorted. She nodded at Ranulf who was sitting in cat-like silence. 'For a start, it would be nice to see a smile on Ranulf's face, and you're bored as well, Hugh. After all, as Ranulf remarked, one sheep does tend to look like another.'

Corbett squeezed her hand. He pulled out the roll of parchment the King had given him. He undid this carefully and studied the clerkly hand.

'It's written in chancery script,' he murmured. 'So it could come from the pen of any trained scribe.'

'If it was a royal scribe,' Simon retorted morosely, 'he'd be hanged, drawn and quartered. Read it, Sir Hugh.'

'"To the Mayor, Burgesses, Chancellor of the University of Oxford and to the Regents of the Halls,"' Corbett began, '"The Bellman sends fraternal greetings. Once again I raise a clamour, bringing to attention the abuses of our King and his Council of nobles.

Item:– There should be a parliament at least once a year, at which the King should listen to the petitions of his good burgesses and citizens.

Item:– Holy Mother Church should not be taxed, nor its revenues disturbed, without the agreement of a Convocation of the Clergy.

Item:– The King dissipates his wealth in a futile war against the Scots whilst closing his eyes and ears to the manifold abuses of his officials at home.

Item:– The King should confirm the clauses of Magna Carta and the privileges of the University . . ."'

The proclamation went on, listing real or alleged abuses but it was the final paragraph that caught Corbett's attention.

'Remember,' it began, 'in your prayers, the saintly

Simon de Montfort, Earl of Leicester, brutally killed by this same king. The Earl's measures, published here in the city of Oxford, would have established good governance of this realm. Given at Sparrow Hall on the feast of St Bonaventure, the 15th of July 1303, and ordered to be proclaimed throughout the City and University of Oxford, signed, THE BELLMAN OF OXFORD.'

Corbett studied the manuscript closely. The vellum was of good quality with the edges precisely cut, the ink was mauve, the letters clearly formed, the phrases neatly set out. It bore no other mark except the sign of a bell at the top: this had been pierced by a nail where the notice had been pinned to the door of some church.

Corbett passed the manuscript over to Maeve. She studied it and then pushed it across to Ranulf.

'What does it mean?' she asked.

'Almost forty years ago,' Corbett began, 'Simon de Montfort, Earl of Leicester, led a rebellion against the present king and his father. De Montfort was a brilliant, charismatic leader. He didn't bother with the nobility but appealed to the burgesses and the citizens of cities like Oxford and London. He won their support, as well as that of many of the clergy who sit in their own parliament called Convocation. De Montfort was the first to expound the theory of a Parliament where the commons and nobles could meet in separate sessions to present petitions to the King as well as seek agreement before they were taxed.'

Maeve shrugged. 'But that is just.' She screwed her eyes up. 'Didn't one of Edward's judges say that what affects all must be approved by all?'

'Oh, Edward agreed: he took on the idea himself. Parliaments are regularly called although they don't command the same importance de Montfort wanted to give them.' Corbett played with the blackjack of ale a servant had poured him. 'What de Montfort wanted,' he continued, 'was for Parliament to control the King and all royal officials but, more importantly, de Montfort wanted to control Parliament.'

'But why is the King so frightened of such an idea, from a man who was killed almost forty years ago?' Maeve asked.

Corbett shrugged. 'Because de Montfort was almost successful and, if he had been . . .'

'And if he had been,' Ranulf interrupted, 'De Montfort would have become King and Edward . . .'

'Edward –' Corbett finished the sentence for him, '– would have disappeared into some castle where he would have met with an unfortunate accident. There would now be a new royal line and that is the nightmare still haunting the Crown!'

Chapter 2

Corbett studied the Bellman's proclamation once again.

'How long have these been appearing?'

'Over five months,' Simon replied. 'At first we thought it was some scholar's madcap scheme. Then the King's Council tried to hush matters up but the proclamations became more frequent. The King wrote to the Regent, John Copsale, who wrote back claiming all innocence. A month ago Copsale who was in his fifties, was found dead in his bed. The physician said he had died from natural causes, but since then the Bellman has grown more vindictive.'

'And how are matters at Sparrow Hall now?'

'As in any college, Sir Hugh, there are tensions, rivalries, petty jealousies. Lady Mathilda would like more royal patronage: the other Masters find the Braose family irksome. They don't like the name of the hall and would prefer to change it as well as the statutes drawn up by Braose when the college was founded.'

'Why?'

'Sparrow Hall is seen as a royal foundation, built on the blood of a man, de Montfort, whom many now see as a saint. Copsale believed it important for the Hall to have more self-determination, especially for a college in Oxford which prides itself on its history and its independence.'

'Was de Montfort from Oxford?' Maeve asked.

'De Montfort had a great following in the University,'

Corbett replied, 'amongst both the Masters and students. More importantly, the Earl raised troops there for his civil war. He also held a great Council in the city where he issued the *Provisions of Oxford*, a scheme to take over the royal Council and Government.'

'And, of course,' Ranulf added, 'Oxford is the gateway to the kingdom. Scholars come there from all parts of the country as well as from abroad. The Bellman's treason is like a pestilence, it could spread and cause further unrest.'

'And the King doesn't need that,' Simon interjected. 'Taxes are heavy, the royal purveyors are collecting provisions. The great earls want to return to their manors. It's a fire which might quickly spread.' Simon gestured at the proclamation. 'I have a sack of these: I'll leave them with you. But, before you ask, Sir Hugh, we have no evidence as to whether the writer is a Master or a scholar at Sparrow Hall. Of course, the King sent down his justices – but what could they do? The Masters and the scholars protested their innocence and cried harassment.'

'Why doesn't the King,' Maeve asked, 'just close down Sparrow Hall?'

'Oh, the Bellman would love that,' Corbett answered. 'Then the entire University as well as the city would see the King conceding defeat. It would be embarrassing in the extreme: Sparrow Hall was founded by Lord Henry Braose, one of Edward's principal captains, who fought resolutely against de Montfort. Braose was given some of the dead earl's lands and revenues, and he used these to buy buildings in Oxford, near St Michael's Northgate. The Hall itself – and I remember it well – stands on one side and, across the lane, there's the hostelry where the scholars stay: a large five-storey house with gardens and courtyards.'

'If the Hall was closed –' Simon tapped his fingers on the table '– the Bellman would indeed laugh. Many see

Sparrow Hall as cursed, founded and built on the blood of the so-called great Earl. They even say his ghost haunts the place seeking vengeance.'

'Who are the Masters there?' Corbett asked.

'Well, Alfred Tripham is the Vice-Regent. Until Ascham's and Copsale's deaths there were eight Masters. Now Tripham is in charge with five others: Leonard Appleston, Aylric Churchley, Peter Langton, Bernard Barnett and Richard Norreys, the Master of the Hostelry. Henry Braose's younger sister, the Lady Mathilda, also has a chamber in the Hall.'

'That's unusual! – for a woman to be given residence in an Oxford Hall?'

'Lady Mathilda,' Simon replied, 'is a good friend of the King. She's constantly petitioning the Crown for further recognition of her dead brother and extra grants to enlarge the Hall.' Simon pulled a face. 'But the Exchequer is exhausted, the treasury's empty.'

'And no one at the Hall knows anything about the Bellman or about Copsale's death?'

'No.'

'And Ascham?' Corbett asked.

'He was the librarian and archivist,' Simon replied. 'A great friend of the founder. Five days ago, late in the afternoon, Ascham went into the library. He locked and bolted the door, and the window was shuttered. He lit a candle but we don't know whether he was working or looking for something. When he failed to arrive at the buttery, the Hall bursar, William Passerel, went looking for him.' Simon shrugged. 'The doors were forced and Ascham was found lying in a pool of his own blood, a crossbow quarrel in his chest. But he didn't die immediately.'

The clerk pushed back his stool, opened his pouch and passed across a piece of parchment. Corbett unrolled it.

'"The Bellman fears neither King nor clerk,"' he read aloud. '"The Bellman will ring the truth, and all shall hear it."'

The message was written in the same script as the proclamation.

'Turn it over,' Simon remarked.

Corbett did so and noticed the strange symbols daubed in blood. 'P A S S E R . . .' He spelt out the letters.

'Apparently,' Simon explained, 'Ascham wrote that in his own blood as he lay dying.'

'But that's almost the name of the bursar you mentioned at the hall?'

'Yes, William Passerel,' Simon replied. 'But no action can be taken against him. For most of that day, when Ascham died, Passerel was in Abingdon on official business. He returned and went straight to the buttery, and then decided to look for Ascham who was his friend.'

'And the library was sealed?' Corbett asked.

'The door leading to the passageway was locked and barred from the inside. The garden window was shuttered. There are no other entrances.'

'Yet,' Corbett said, studying the scrap of parchment, 'someone not only shot Ascham but was able to leave this note? And Passerel the bursar still remains free?'

'Oh yes, there's no evidence against him. Passerel can prove he was in Abingdon. Servants attested that when he came back he went straight to the buttery.' Simon gave a lop-sided smile. 'There's one further problem. Passerel's eyesight isn't very good. He also suffers from the rheums in his fingers. He could not hold or pull back a crossbow winch. Nor is there any explanation of how he could enter and leave the library, locking the windows and doors from the inside.'

'The King and his council have discussed this?'

'Oh yes, Edward and his principal henchmen have spent

hours on the matter. They have even got a spy in Sparrow Hall. I don't know who it is.' Simon licked his lips. 'The King said the spy would make himself known when you arrived in Oxford . . .'

Corbett tapped the parchment against the table. 'Why now?' he murmured. 'Why does this mysterious writer called the Bellman appear, writing and posting his proclamations attacking the King? What does he hope to gain?' He glanced at Simon. 'There's no evidence of interference by the King's enemies either here or abroad?'

Simon shook his head.

'And the writing?'

'As you can see,' Simon replied, 'it's in a clerkly hand. Those proclamations could be the work of you, or me or Ranulf.' He smiled ruefully. 'Clerks are ruthlessly trained in the same style of writing.'

'No threats have been made, there's been no attempted blackmail?'

'No.'

'And you think Copsale's death and Ascham's were the work of the Bellman?'

'Possibly.' Simon spread his hands. 'But, there again, the antagonism between these Masters is so intense, that Ascham may have been killed for other reasons and his death made to look like the work of the Bellman.'

'And the beggars who have been found dead?'

'Ah, that's a tragedy.' Simon sipped from his blackjack of ale. 'The corpses are always found outside the city, with the head sheared off and tied by the hair to the branch of some tree. There are two other things common to the deaths. Firstly, the corpses all belong to men, old beggars. Secondly, they are always found near a trackway leading to or from the city.'

'Are the bodies marked?'

29

'One had been killed by an arrow – again a crossbow bolt, fired at close quarters. It went clean through the body. Another had been struck on the back of the head by a club or mace. The rest appeared to have had their throats cut.'

'And they were all from the hospital of St Osyth?'

'Yes, it's a charitable foundation near Carfax, the crossroads in Oxford.'

'Could it be the work of some gibbet lord?' Ranulf asked. 'The magicians and warlocks who always lurk around cities like Oxford?'

'No, there's plenty of them about but, there's no mutilation, no clear reason for such deaths.'

'Is there any connection between these deaths and the Bellman?' Maeve asked, fascinated by the task entrusted to her husband. She had forgotten the twinges in her belly and her determination to settle accounts with the reeve whom, she believed, was helping himself.

'None,' Simon replied. 'Except in the case of the old soldier, Brakespeare. About two days before his corpse was found, he was seen begging in the lane between Sparrow Hall and the hostelry. However, apart from that –' he got to his feet '– I can tell you no more.' He looked at the hour candle burning on its wooden spigot near the fireplace. 'I must go. The King told me to join him at Woodstock.' His voice became more pleading. 'You will go, Sir Hugh, for all our sakes?'

Corbett nodded. 'Ranulf, make sure Simon is fed and his horse ready.' He rose and took Simon's hand. 'Tell the King that, when this is finished, I'll see him at Woodstock.'

Corbett sat down and waited till Ranulf had taken Simon out of the hall. Maeve grasped his hand.

'You should go, Hugh,' she said softly. 'Eleanor is well. Oxford is not far away and the King needs you.'

Corbett pulled a face. 'It will be dangerous,' he

murmured. 'I can sense that. The Bellman, whoever he may be, is full of malice. He hides behind the customs and traditions of the University and could do the King great damage. He will do his best not to be caught for, if he is, he will suffer a terrible death. Edward hates de Montfort, his memory and anything to do with him.' He glanced at his wife. 'Two years ago, during the council meeting at Windsor, some poor clerk made the mistake of mentioning de Montfort's *Provisions of Oxford*. Edward nearly throttled him.' Corbett put his arm round his wife and drew her closer. 'I'll go there,' he continued, 'but there'll be more deaths, more chaos, more heartache and bloodshed before this is over.'

Corbett's words were prophetic. Even as he prepared to leave for Oxford, William Passerel, the fat, ruddy-faced bursar, sat in his chancery office at Sparrow Hall and tried to ignore the clamour from the lane below. He threw his quill down on the desk, put his face in his hands and tried to fight back the tears of fear pricking his eyes.

'Why?' he whispered. 'Why did Ascham have to die? Who killed him?'

Passerel sighed and sat back in his chair. Oh why? Oh why? The words screamed within him. Why had Ascham written his name, or most of it, on that document? He had been in Abingdon the day Ascham had been murdered. He had only returned a short while before. Now he stood accused of murdering the man he had regarded as a brother. Passerel stared up at the crucifix fixed on the white-washed wall.

'I didn't do it, Lord!' he prayed. 'I am innocent!'

The sculpted, carved face of the Saviour stared blindly back. Passerel heard the hubbub in the street below grow. He went to the window and peered out. A group of scholars, most of them from the Welsh counties, now thronged below. Passerel recognised many of them. Some wore gowns bearing a crudely sewn sparrow, the badge of the Hall. Their leader, David ap Thomas, a tall, blond-haired, thickset, young man, was busily lecturing them, his hands flailing the air. Even the blind beggar, who usually stood on the corner of the alley with his pittance bowl, had gathered his clammy, dirty rags about him and drawn closer to listen. Passerel tried to compose himself. He went back to the list he was compiling of Ascham's personal effects: the scarlet gown with tartan sleeves; the green cushions; the silk borders; mazers; gilt cufflets; silver vestments; saucers; dishes; pater nosters; amber beads and breviaries. For a while, despite the distraction of the growing clamour below, Passerel worked on. However, as the clamour grew to shouts and yells of defiance, he heard his own name called. He stole furtively to the casement window and stared out. His heart sank and beads of sweat turned his skin clammy. The crowd was now a mob. They were shouting and yelling, shaking their fists: their leader, David Ap Thomas, standing with hands on hips, glimpsed Passerel peeping through the window.

'There he is!' he yelled, his voice ringing like a bell. 'Ascham's assassin, Passerel the perjurer! Passerel the murderer!'

The words were taken up: fistfuls of mud and ordure were hurled at the window. A brick smashed through the mullioned glass. Passerel whimpered, gathering his cloak about him. He jumped as the door was flung open. Leonard Appleston, Master of Divinity in the hall, lecturer in the schools, burst in. His square, sunburnt face was ashen, his mouth tight with fear.

'William, for the love of God!' He grabbed the bursar by the arm. 'You must flee!'

'Where to?' Passerel's hands fluttered.

'Sanctuary,' Appleston replied. He grasped the bursar and pulled him closer. 'Take the back stairs, quickly. Go!'

Passerel looked round the chamber at his books, his beloved manuscripts. He, a scholar, was being forced to flee like a rat up a drain. He had no choice. Appleston was already bundling him out of the room, pushing him along the gallery. In the stairwell he passed Lady Mathilda Braose, her thin, waspish face startled; beside her was the deaf mute Master Moth who followed her everywhere like a dog. She cried out but Appleston pushed Passerel past her. The bursar, fear now lending him speed, scurried through the kitchen and the scullery, out across the urine-stained hall. A mangy cat slunk up, its back arching. Passerel lashed out and looked back through the gateway. Appleston was standing at the door urging him on.

'Why should I flee?' Passerel's lower lip quivered. 'Why should I?' he shouted.

He heard a sound at the mouth of the alleyway and looked up. His stomach clenched in fear. A group of students had gathered there. Passerel hoped that, in the poor light, they might not see him. He flattened his bulk, closing his eyes, praying to Saint Anne, his patron saint.

'There he is!' a voice cried. 'Passerel the murderer!'

The bursar fled down the alleyway. He stopped at the end. Which way should he go? Down Bocardo Lane? Perhaps reach the castle? He heard the sound of pounding feet and changed direction. He ran as fast as he could, pushing his way past students, merchants, knocking aside children playing with an inflated pig's bladder. He gasped with relief when he saw the lych-gate of St Michael's Church. Behind, shouts of 'Harrow! Harrow!' echoed as the hue and cry was raised. He thought he had outwitted his pursuers until a clod of earth sped past his head. Passerel hurried on through the cemetery and threw himself through the doorway of the church. He slammed the door behind him, pulling across the bolt.

'What do you want?' a woman's voice sang out above him.

Passerel, drenched with sweat, peered into the darkness. He stared up at the light flickering through a slit in a wooden partition above the door. At first he thought he'd heard a ghost until he realised there was an anchorite's cell built just above the main porch. Passerel heard the sound of shouts and blows from outside.

'I seek sanctuary!' he gasped.

'Then ring the bell to your left,' the anchorite ordered. 'And hurry! The church has a side door and they'll cut you off!'

Passerel groped in the darkness and pulled at the rope. Above him the bell began to toll like the crack of doom.

'Run!' the anchorite shouted.

Passerel needed no second bidding. He fled up the nave, slipping and slithering on the smooth, greystone floor. He reached the oaken rood screen, heavy and squat. He stumbled through the entrance into the sanctuary and grasped the altar. The bell, still rolling from the force of his pull, clanged on. Passerel, weeping like a child, crouched in the darkness. He stared up at the red sanctuary light, a little lamp within a red glass bowl, which flickered on a shelf beneath the silver pyx holding the host. The side door opened with a crash. Passerel whimpered with fear.

'What do you want? What do you seek?'

Passerel screwed up his eyes: a cowled figure stood in the entrance to the rood screen. A tinder was lit and a candle bathed the sanctuary in a pool of light. The face above it was gentle with straggly, spiked hair, and sad eyes in a wrinkled ageing face. Passerel sighed with relief as he recognised Father Vincent, the priest of St Michael's.

'I seek sanctuary,' Passerel whimpered.

'For what crime?'

'For no crime,' Passerel said. 'I am innocent.'

'All men are innocent,' the priest replied, 'in the eyes of God.' He lit a candle on the altar as well as two large ones on the offertory table near the lavabo bowl. 'Stand up! Stand up!' Father Vincent ordered. 'You are safe here!'

Passerel did so, trying to keep his legs from trembling.

'I am Master William Passerel,' he announced. 'Bursar of Sparrow Hall. They have accused me of the murder of Robert Ascham the archivist.'

'Ah!' The priest came closer. He lifted his hand around which was wrapped a string of polished, black rosary beads. 'I have heard of Ascham's death and that of the Regent Sir John Copsale. They were both good men.'

'No man is good!' the anchorite shouted from the back of the church.

'Shush, shush, Magdalena!' the priest answered. 'Sir John Copsale gave generously to our alms box. I have heard of Ascham's death and the doings of the Bellman.'

The priest's voice, like every sound, echoed round the church – small wonder the anchorite could hear it.

'The Bellman came here!' Magdalena boomed. 'Pinned his proclamation to the church door he did. Creeping he came: mouse-eyed and close-mouthed. A goblin of wit!'

'Shush! Shush!' The priest brought his hand down on Passerel's shoulder. 'Your pursuers have gone. I heard the bell toll and came out. Bullyboys, the lot of them.' He added, 'Swaggering swains, empty vessels always make the most sound.' The priest smiled. 'I ordered them out of God's acre. They had no right to bring their violence here but they are keeping watch on the lych-gate and around the cemetery. If you leave, they will kill you.' The priest drew himself up, eyes wide. 'That's what happened to the last man who fled here. He came and went like a thief in the night. They caught him near Hog Lane and chopped his head off.'

Passerel moaned in fear.

'However, you are safe here,' the priest added kindly. 'Look.' He grasped Passerel by the arm and led him across to a recess in the wall. 'This is the place of sanctuary. I'll bring a bolster, some blankets, wine, bread and cheese. You can stay here for forty days.' He watched as Passerel clutched his stomach. 'If you have to relieve yourself, go out at the side door. There's a small drain near one of the graves. But mind your step.' He chuckled. 'Don't fall in and take no light with you.'

Passerel sat down in the recess. The priest padded away. He returned a little later with a cracked pewter cup, a jug of watered wine and a trauncher of bread, strips of dried bacon, cheese and two rather hard manchet loaves. Passerel ate hungrily, listening to the priest chatter as he returned with a roll of blankets that smelt of horse piss.

'There!' Father Vincent stood back and admired his handiwork. 'Keep the sanctuary clean.' He pointed at the red winking lamp. 'The Lord sees you and Holy Mother Church protects you. I'll shrive you before morning Mass and you can be my altar boy. I'm giving a sermon tomorrow. It's a very good one, on the dangers of riches.'

'What does it profit a man?' Magdalena's voice boomed down the church. 'To gain the whole world but suffer the loss of his immortal soul.'

'Quite, quite.' The priest began to douse the candles. 'I'll leave one alight.' He reached down and grasped Passerel's hand. 'Goodnight, brother.'

Father Vincent went out under the rood screen. Passerel heard the side door close and he leaned back with a sigh. What could he do? he wondered. Surely master Alfred Tripham, Vice-Regent of Sparrow Hall, would help? He would petition the Sheriff for assistance. Passerel gnawed at his lip. Nevertheless, his life was over. He had been happy at Sparrow Hall with his books and manuscripts, and studying the accounts in his little money chamber. Now it was all gone in the twinkling of an eye. What would happen to poor Passerel now? If this nonsense continued he would be given a choice: either to surrender himself to the Sheriff's bailiffs or to leave Oxford and walk to the nearest port and take ship to foreign parts. Passerel scratched his chapped legs and ruefully decided he would be dead of exhaustion before he reached the city gates. And outside? Those students would be waiting for him.

'On your knees and pray to God!' Magdalena's voice echoed down the church. 'Pray that you be not put to the test!'

'Shut up!' Passerel whispered.

He put his face in his hands and tried to make sense of the chaos and tragedy seething around him. He recalled Copsale being found dead in his bed. The Regent had always had a weak heart: had he died in his sleep? And Ascham? Passerel remembered opening the door to the library and finding the archivist lying there, the blood like spilled wine soaking his robes; the crossbow bolt in his chest. Yet the window had been shuttered, the door had been bolted. Why had Ascham been murdered? What had he meant by his mutterings about 'dear little sparrows' or something like that? What had he hoped to find amongst the writings of de Montfort's adherents, so much rubbish from decades before? And what of Ascham's belief that someone at Sparrow Hall wished to destroy the work of its founder, Henry Braose?

Passerel took his hands away and looked around. It was growing darker. The solitary candle wavered and bent in some draught, its flickering flame brought out the garish painting on the far wall, which portrayed a group of demons, hollering like hounds after some poor soul. Passerel saw little comfort there. He lay down on the slab, groaning at its hardness, recalling his own soft, high bed. He heard a sound. The side door opened – someone was coming in. Passerel stiffened. Someone was slithering quietly towards the sanctuary. He kept still, watching the entrance to the rood screen. He heaved a sigh of relief as he glimpsed a pair of shadowy hands place a wine jug and cup down. A friend from Sparrow Hall? The footsteps receded, and the side door quietly closed. Passerel got up and walked across. He picked up the jug and sniffed at it. The claret it contained was rich and thick. Passerel's mouth watered. He poured himself a generous cup and drank quickly.

'This is the House of God and the Gateway of Heaven!' the anchorite shouted. 'A Place of Terrors!'

Passerel, emboldened by the wine, lifted his head.

He was about to fill the cup again when pain seized his belly, as if someone had thrust a knife into his innards. Passerel staggered forward, the jug and cup falling from his hands and shattering on the ground, ringing like a bell along the deserted nave. Passerel clutched at his stomach. He opened his mouth to scream but gagged on the bile at the back of his throat.

'It is a terrible thing indeed,' the anchorite intoned, 'for a sinner's soul to fall into the hands of the living God!'

Passerel, his face soaked in sweat, eyes popping, stretched his hand out towards the anchorite's light. The waves of pain stretched up through his belly along his gullet. Closing his eyes, William Passerel, former bursar of Sparrow Hall, slumped in death before the sanctuary screen.

As Passerel died before the high altar of St Michael's Church, the old beggar Senex – for that was the only name by which he was known – tried to flee from the death pursuing him. He couldn't run very fast: a suppurating ulcer on his right shin made him wince every time he brought his foot down. Senex shuffled on, staggering blindly through the darkness, straining his ears, listening for any soft footfall.

'Oh please!' Senex whispered.

He sat down, crouching like a dog, arms wrapped tightly round his chest. If he stayed here, silent as a statue, perhaps he would not be found. Senex recalled a rabbit pursued by a weasel he had once seen in a field. The rabbit had stayed frozen beside a tussock of grass. Senex closed his eyes: he didn't know how old he was and he had given up trying to guess. Life was never good but nothing had prepared him for this. He should never have come to Oxford. If he had stayed in the countryside sleeping in barns and begging at cottagers' doors, he would have been safe. Yet last winter had been severe so Senex had wandered into Oxford and made his way to St Osyth's Priory, his hands and feet covered in burning chilblains and blisters. The good brothers had tended to his every wound except for the ulcer on his shin, which they had been unable to cure. Senex had grown accustomed to the city: the jostling noise, the arrogant, swaggering students: the grand Masters in their furred robes. Oh, he had eaten well: last Midsummer's Day he'd even been given a shilling to buy sweetmeats for himself and his comrades at St Osyth's. Senex opened his eyes and listened, he stared back through the darkness: all he'd wanted was a piece of cheese and a pot of ale. Senex shivered as he recalled the whispers around St Osyth's about those other inmates who had disappeared, their headless corpses found in lonely woods. He now knew the reason why and he quietly cursed. He thought of a prayer, a short one, taught him many years ago when he and Margaret, his elder sister, had tramped the lanes begging for bread.

Senex whimpered like a dog. Margaret was gone: she'd

died of a fever in the ditch, many years ago. He'd covered her corpse with bracken. Surely Margaret in heaven would help him now? Poor, old Senex would never hurt a fly. The beggar man stared into the gloom. He'd been told that it was a game. Perhaps he could win, for the first time in his life? Senex began to crawl forward on all fours, going back along the way he had come, keeping close to the mildewed wall. He reached a corner and turned: he could see a chink of light in the distance but then he heard that whistle again, low yet clear, like a man calling his dog. Senex listened intently. Was someone lurking there? He turned and scampered away, back to the place he'd left, his hand catching the grey ragstone wall. There must be a way out surely? He would not be trapped like old Brakespeare had been. Senex stopped, fingers to his lips – Brakespeare had been a soldier and he'd been caught! Senex stopped and sniffed the air; he could smell faint cooking smells; bacon and freshly cooked meat. Senex's stomach growled. He licked dry lips. If he kept going ahead perhaps he'd be safe? He reached the corner and, after crouching, ran on blindly. He froze at the stealthy patter of feet behind him. Someone was in hot pursuit. Senex reached a wall, he scrambled up, looking for an escape but could find no way. He turned. He should have gone right! He heard the whistle again and the pinprick of a torchlight grew as the figure carrying it drew closer. Senex put his hands up.

'Oh, please no! Please no!'

He heard the click and, before he could move, he took the crossbow bolt full in his stomach. Senex crouched down, his fingers curling in pain, grasping the dirt. He couldn't move. He tried to edge forward but then he saw the boots. He looked up and, as he did, the great two-handled axe took his head off, clean and sheer.

The next morning, just after dawn, journeyman Taldo,

making his way out of Oxford towards Banbury, came across Senex's corpse. It lay beneath an old holm tree and, from one of the branches stretched across the path, hung the old beggar's severed head.

Chapter 3

On the day after Taldo had hurried back to Oxford to report his grisly findings to the sheriff, Sir Hugh Corbett, Ranulf and Maltote entered the city. An early downpour of rain had drenched the streets and cleaned the runnels and alleyways, dulling the rotten odour from the middens. Corbett, his cowl pulled back, let his horse find its way through the dirty packed streets of the university town. They'd entered by the south gate but, instead of going straight towards the castle or Sparrow Hall, Corbett took Ranulf and Maltote along the byways and alleyways so they could grasp the feel of the city. Corbett himself felt a little nostalgic. It had been years since he'd returned: now, the sight, sounds and smells brought back the glorious days of his youth. A happy, carefree time when Corbett had lived in shabby apartments and thronged with the rest of the bachelors, students and scholars down to the bleak rooms of the Schools to hear the Masters lecture on rhetoric, logic, theology and philosophy.

Corbett found his return eerie: despite the passing of the years, nothing seemed to have changed. Peasants from the outskirts of Oxford tried to force their way through with heavy wheeled carts or sodden sumpter ponies laden with produce for the city markets. As he passed the open doorways of shabby tenements, Corbett glimpsed children and beldames warming their knees before the fire, and sullen lamps glowing in the darkness. On every street the houses huddled on either side, interspersed by a tangle of alleyways and trackways still rough and slippery after the rains. Nevertheless, as always in Oxford, the streets were thronged. Merchants in fur-lined robes marched purposefully in their high, leather Moroccan boots. Servitors went before them to brush aside screaming children or barking dogs. Franciscans, Dominicans and Carmelites made their way to their respective houses: some walked in devout silence, others were as noisy and chattering as magpies. On a corner a gong cart, full of dung and ordure from the sewers, was now being used as a punishment post. A fellow who had sold faulty cloth had been forced to stand waist-deep in the dung whilst lashed to the wheels were other traders found guilty by a Pie Powder court of selling rotten meat, tawdry goods or trying to break the price code set by the market beadles. Next to this, a dog-whipper, the cage on his cart full of fighting, snapping curs, was formally arresting a lean-ribbed mongrel whilst a group of scruffy urchins screamed abuse and claimed the dog belonged to them. The dog-whipper, his sulphurous face ablaze with fury, cursed and yelled back.

Corbett sighed and dismounted, telling Ranulf and Maltote to do likewise. They took a short cut up Eel Pie Lane which led them on to the High Road. Here Corbett ran into roaming bands of scholars, wags, braggarts, hedge-creepers and rascals from the University, all dressed in their tawdry finery: the short gowns of the bachelors, the tattered hose and shabby jackets of the commoners. The air rang with the noise of different accents and tongues as students spilled out of the Halls or the lecture chambers of the schools. Lost in their own world, the scholars shouted and sang, pushed and shoved each other, totally oblivious of the good citizens and burgesses of the city. These passed the scholars with muttered curses and looks of disdain. Here and

there some Masters or lecturers strutted like geese, heads
swathed in woollen hoods lined with silk, which proclaimed
their status and importance. Behind them beggar scholars,
youths unable to pay the fees, staggered along carrying
books or other baggage for their masters. Beadles and
proctors, the disciplinarians of the University, also strode by
wielding lead-tipped, ash cudgels. As they passed the
students fell silent, though their presence did little else to
curb their high spirits and boisterousness.

Corbett paused, wrapping the reins round his hands,
staring up and down the High Street. This had changed:
there were more houses on either side, so densely packed
that their gables met to block out the light. Pushed in
between these, were the cottages of the poorer folk, padded
with reeds, straw or shingles which the rain had turned to a
soggy mess. The market stalls on either side of the High
Road had now re-opened after the downpour and were
doing a busy trade. Jostled and pushed, Corbett had to move
on. Behind him Ranulf lifted one boot and groaned: the
mud and dirt were ankle-deep and he looked pityingly at a
group of urchins who, despite the weather, were playing in
mud half-way up their legs. Ranulf bit back a curse. He
would have loved to have roared his irritation at Corbett
trudging so stoically ahead of him but the noise was growing
more deafening. Corbett abruptly turned left, going down a
sordid alleyway. It was quieter here and, when he led them
into the yard of the Red Lattice tavern, Ranulf sighed with
pleasure. He joyously threw his reins at a surly ostler who
came out quietly cursing at these new arrivals who'd disturbed his rest.

'Something to eat and drink,' Ranulf murmured, rubbing
his stomach, 'would satisfy the inner man.'

'Just a little wine,' Corbett retorted. Ignoring Ranulf's
black looks he led them into the musty taproom. They

stood by the door drinking quickly before going back into the streets.

'What are we doing?' Ranulf pushed alongside Corbett. 'Where are we going, Master?'

'I want to show you the city,' Corbett retorted. 'I want you to feel it in your brain as well as your belly.' He paused and beckoned his companions closer. 'Oxford is a world unto itself,' he explained. 'It is a city made up of small villages which are the Halls or Colleges. Each stands in its own ground and has its own workshops, dorters, forges and stables.' He pointed down the street where Ranulf and Maltote could glimpse a great metal-studded gate in the high curtain wall. 'That's Eagle Hall and there are numerous others. Each has its own privileges, traditions and history. They take students from France, Hainault, Spain, the German States and even further east. The Halls dislike each other; the University hates the town; the town resents the University. Violence is rife, knives are ever at the ready. Sometimes you may have to flee and –' he added, '– to know in which direction you are fleeing, could save your life.'

'But you are the King's clerk,' Maltote spoke up, stroking the muzzle of his horse. 'They'll obey the King's writ?'

'They couldn't give a fig,' Corbett replied. 'Let's say we were attacked now, who'd come to our assistance? Or later stand up as a witness?' He punched Ranulf playfully on the shoulder. 'Keep your cowl pulled, your face down and your hand well away from your dagger.'

They went along the High Street and stood aside as a church door opened: scholars, in shabby tabards tied round the waist by cords and leather straps, burst out from the noonday Mass. As Ranulf whispered, the service seemed to have had little effect on them. The scholars jostled and shoved each other, bawling raucously, some even sang blasphemous parodies of the hymns they had just chanted.

Despite the wet and the jostling crowds, Corbett persisted in showing his two companions the layout of the city. At last they returned, past the Swindlestock tavern, making their way gingerly around the gaping sewer in Carfax and into Great Bailey Street, which led up into the castle.

'Why are we going there?' Maltote asked. 'I thought we were for Sparrow Hall?'

'We have to visit the Sheriff,' Corbett explained over his shoulder. 'Sir Walter Bullock.' He grinned. 'And that will be an experience in itself. Bullock is as irascible as a starving dog.'

They crossed the moat, really nothing more than a narrow ditch, its water covered with a black slime on which a cat's corpse, soggy and bloated, floated lazily beneath the drawbridge. A guard dressed in a dirty leather sallet slouched against the wall beneath the portcullis, his sword and shield lying on the ground beside him. He hardly looked up as they entered the inner bailey. The castle yard was busy: a group of archers shot lustily at the butts; a group of ragged-arsed children, armed with wooden swords, attempted to fight a strident goose; women stood round the well, slapping cloths on the side of the great tuns which served as their bowls. No one took any notice of the new arrivals except a relic seller dressed in garish rags who'd been touting his wares and now came across, a piece of wood in his hand.

'Buy a piece of the juniper tree.' He pushed the blackened piece of wood almost into Ranulf's face.

'Why?' Ranulf asked.

The fellow bared his mouth in a horrid display of crumbling teeth. 'Because it's the very tree,' he whispered, 'that protected the baby Jesus when Mother Mary took him into Egypt, away from Pilate's fury.'

'I thought it was Herod?' Ranulf retorted.

'Yes, but he was helped by Pilate,' the relic-seller gabbled.

47

Ranulf took the piece of wood and studied it carefully.

'I can't buy this,' he said. 'It's not juniper, it's elder!'

The rascal's mouth opened and closed. 'God bless you, sir, I was in confusion myself. You are sure?'

'Certainly,' Ranulf replied, handing it back.

'Then that's what it is,' the relic-seller whispered and, turning round, walked over to a group of castle scullions. 'Buy a piece of elder!' he shouted. 'The very tree on which Judas hanged himself!'

Corbett grinned; he was about to ask Ranulf how he could tell the difference between juniper and elder when a prod in his back made him turn around.

'What do you want?'

The serjeant looked Corbett over from head to toe.

'What do you want?' he repeated. 'And where did you get those horses?'

Ranulf stepped between his master and the serjeant and stared at the man's dirty, unshaven face.

'We want the Sheriff,' Ranulf replied. 'Sir Walter Bullock. This is Sir Hugh Corbett, the King's principal clerk from the Office of the Secret Seal.'

The serjeant hawked and spat. 'I couldn't give a bugger if he was from the Holy Father!'

He bawled across at a groom to come and take their horses and, snapping his fingers, told Corbett and his companions to follow.

They found Sir Walter in his chamber above the gate house. It was a stark room with coloured cloths hung against the wall like rat banners. The fat, balding Sheriff was eating from a dish of eels, beside him on a trauncher were several apples and some cheese. Short and thickset, Bullock was dressed in jerkin, hose and shirt, his war belt and leather riding boots thrown on the straw-covered floor beside him. As the serjeant ushered Corbett and his companions in, slamming the door behind them, the Sheriff raised his clean-shaven face bright as a brass pot.

'What do you want?' he asked, his mouth full of eels.

'That's what the ignorant bastard downstairs asked me,' Ranulf retorted.

Bullock sat back on his stool and nodded towards the arrow slit window.

'If it was big enough, you'd leave through that!'

Corbett sighed and pulled from his wallet the King's seal and tossed it on the table. Bullock swallowed his mouthful of food and picked it up.

'You know what that is, Master Bollock?' Ranulf taunted.

'My name's Bullock.' The Sheriff pushed back his stool and got up, licking his fingers and wiping them on a dirty napkin. He went and stood before Ranulf, hands on hips. 'My name is Bullock,' he repeated. 'And do you know why, sir? Because I am like one: stocky, addle-pated and foul tempered.' He poked Ranulf in the stomach. 'Now you look like a fighting boy, but that doesn't concern me. I've pulled bigger things out of my nose!' He turned abruptly to Corbett, his hand extended. 'I am sorry, Sir Hugh. The King sent a cursitor, we've been expecting you.'

Corbett grasped the Sheriff's hand. He noticed how the man's eyes were dark-ringed with exhaustion.

'You look tired, Master Sheriff?'

Sir Walter waved to a bench near the wall. 'If I lie down, Sir Hugh, I'd never get up. Would you like some wine? Something to eat?' He looked slyly at Ranulf. 'Maybe a bucket of water from the well to cool you down after your long, hot journey?'

Ranulf grinned at this little fighting cock of a man. 'Sir Walter, I apologise.'

The Sheriff shook Ranulf's hand then picked at his teeth. 'Bugger this for a soldier's life!' he growled.

He waited until Corbett sat down then pulled his own stool across. He ticked the points off on his stubby fingers.

'The King's at Woodstock breathing down my neck. There's a parliament summoned to sit at Westminster: I'm under orders to get the right man elected. There's some charlatan selling rats' teeth to children. The garrison hasn't been paid for four months. I am running short of supplies. There are three felons in the Bocardo,' he added, referring to the town gaol, 'whose necks I am going to stretch before dusk. A tavern wench was ravished in the Chequers tavern. I've got a boil on my arse. I haven't slept for two nights and my wife's kinsfolk want to come and stay till Michaelmas.' He sniffed. 'Now, those are only the minor matters.'

Corbett smiled. He dug into his purse and handed two gold coins over.

'I don't take bribes, Sir Hugh.'

'It's not a bribe,' Corbett replied. 'It's your wages. I'll tell the Exchequer.'

The coins disappeared in the twinkling of an eye.

'The Bellman?' Corbett asked.

'I don't know who he is,' the Sheriff replied. 'All I know is that every so often, one of his proclamations is pinned on the doorway of some Hall or church.'

'Didn't you fight at. Evesham for de Montfort?' Corbett asked abruptly.

Bullock's gaze fell away. 'Yes, I did,' he replied as if to himself. 'I was young, an idealist, stupid enough to believe in dreams. Now, Sir Hugh, I am the King's man in war and peace. I'm no traitor. I do not know who the Bellman is or where he comes from. Oh, I have trotted down to make my inquiries amongst the empty heads of Sparrow Hall, but I might as well whistle across a graveyard as expect a response!'

'And the corpses round Oxford?'

Bullock shrugged. 'You know as much as I do, Sir Hugh. Poor men; heads taken off and strung up by their hair to a tree. I have had my men out. They've scoured the woods and fields. There's something going on.' He paused and scratched the mole on his right cheek. 'Oxford is a curious place, Sir Hugh. In the churches they sing the *Salve Regina* and venerate the Body of Christ. At night, in the taverns, they lose their souls in wine and debauchery. Beyond the walls, in the lonely places – well, to cut a long story short, on the Banbury road my men talked to a forester. He led them to a glade deep in the trees. There's a rock, a huge boulder, as if Satan himself thrust it up from hell. Someone had used it as an altar; there were marks of fire, blood-stains and, in the branch of a tree, an animal's skull.'

'Warlocks?' Corbett asked.

'Wizards, warlocks, and witches?' Bullock sniffed. 'That's all there was. The local peasants or farmers are innocent: they've neither the time nor the energy for such nonsense.'

'And you think it's connected to these deaths?'

'Possibly.' Bullock wiped his mouth on the back of his hand. 'I'd love to find the killer. I hope it's some arrogant popinjay of a student. By the way, another corpse was brought in this morning: an old simpleton called Senex. He was found like the others –' Bullock smiled grimly '– with one exception: the old man's hand was tightly clenched. When I prised the fingers open, I found dirt, pebbles and, more importantly, a button.'

'A button?' Ranulf queried.

'Yes, of metal, embossed with a sparrow, the escutcheon of Sparrow Hall. What is more,' Bullock continued, 'as you know, Sir Hugh, these buttons are only worn on the gowns of Masters or certain rich scholars. Most of the rest are clothed in nothing better than sacking.'

'So, what do you think?' Corbett asked.

51

Bullock got to his feet. 'My view is that there is a coven of warlocks in the hall who follow the Lords of the Gibbet. The deaths of these old beggars are linked to some loathsome practices but I have no proof or evidence. The old man may have picked the button up whilst he was being hunted or, in his death struggle, plucked it from someone's coat. However, his is not the only corpse we have this morning.' Bullock slurped from his wine goblet. 'An evening ago, just before Vespers, William Passerel the bursar was hounded from Sparrow Hall by a mob of students. It's common knowledge that Ascham, who was well loved, wrote most of Passerel's name on a scrap of parchment as he lay dying in the library. Now Passerel fled, and took sanctuary in St Michael's Church. Father Vincent, the parish priest, gave him sanctuary, food and drink. The mob dispersed, but later on, someone entered the church and left a flagon of wine and a cup near the rood screen door. Passerel drank it; but it contained an infusion of poison. He died almost immediately.'

'How do you know that?' Corbett asked.

'St Michael's has an anchorite, a mad, old woman called Magdalena. She saw the person steal into the church, a mere shadow. She glimpsed Passerel drinking and then heard his death screams.' Bullock moved to the door. 'Come on, I'll take you down to the corpse chamber!'

The Sheriff led them down, out of the gate house, across a still busy yard. They went down a long, narrow staircase which led into the cellar and dungeons of the castle. It was as black as night, only occasional pitch torches provided pools of dancing light. Bullock took them along the dank, musty passageway, round a corner to a room at the far end. He pushed the door open, and they were assaulted by the sour air inside; fetid, soggy straw covered the floor. The squat, tallow candles and smelly oil lamps placed on ledges gave the vaulted room a macabre atmosphere. As Corbett's eyes grew accustomed to the light, he saw two tables, like those found in a slaughterhouse, on each of which lay a corpse. One was covered by a sheet, bare feet protruding beneath: the other was naked except for a loin cloth; the man bending over it was dressed like a monk in a cowl and gown. He didn't look up as they entered but kept dabbing at the corpse's face with a cloth.

'Good day, Hamell!'

The man turned, pulling back his hood, and leaned against the table. His face was a cadaverous yellow, long like that of a horse, with mournful eyes and slobbering mouth. His upper lip was covered by a straggly moustache, cut unevenly at one end. He gazed blearily at the Sheriff.

'This is Hamell, our castle leech.'

'And a drunken sot,' Ranulf whispered.

'I'm not drunk.' Hamell staggered towards them. 'I've just taken a little cordial. This is a filthy business.' He breathed strong ale fumes in Corbett's face. 'You've come to claim the corpse?'

'He's the King's clerk,' Bullock explained.

'Oh, Lord save us!' Hamell slurred. 'So the King wants the body, does he?' He staggered back towards the corpse, the wet rag still clutched in his hand. 'Dead as a doornail, this one is.'

'What caused it?' Corbett asked, coming up behind him.

'I'm not a physician,' Hamell slurred.

He pointed to the purple scratches on the man's stomach, chest and neck: the face was a liverish hue, the eyes popping, the mouth half-open, the swollen tongue thrust out.

'He consumed deadly nightshade,' Hamell explained. 'I've seen cases before – people who have taken it accidentally.' He gestured at Corbett to go to the other side of the table. 'But the face and swollen tongue –' he pointed to the discoloration of the skin '– means he drank a lot. It's easily done,' he added. 'Particularly if it's stirred into strong wine.'

'And there are no other wounds?' Corbett asked. 'Or marks?'

'Some scratches,' Hamell explained.

'And the other corpse?' Corbett asked.

Hamell turned and pulled back the sheet. Corbett flinched. Ranulf cursed and Maltote was promptly sick in the corner. Senex's corpse was a dull white like the underbelly of a stale cod but it was the head, severed from the bloody neck, and placed beneath one of the arms, which rendered the whole scene ghastly.

'I haven't sewn it back yet,' Hamell explained cheerily. 'I always do that.'

Bullock, hand to his mouth, also turned away.

'And make sure you do it properly this time,' he growled. 'Last time, you were so drunk, you sewed it on back to front!'

Corbett looked at the severed neck and the dark blood encrusted there, and recognised the sheer cut of a sharp axe brought down with great force.

'Cover it up!' he ordered.

Hamell did so.

'What was found in his hand?'

The leech pointed to the side of the table. Corbett, bringing a candle closer, carefully scrutinised the dirty pebbles, then picked up the brass button, the shape of a sparrow clearly etched on it.

'Can I keep it?' he asked.

Bullock agreed. Corbett examined Senex's hands: the cold, chapped fingers and the jagged, dirty nails. He noticed the palm of the right hand was much dirtier than that of the left. He then examined the knees, remarking how grubby they were.

'He must have been crouching,' Corbett explained.

'Kneeling on soil or dirt. His killer stood over him. He brought the axe back, and that's probably when the button fell off. Poor Senex, scrabbling about, clutched it even as the axe fell.' Corbett put the button into his pouch. 'Ah well, God knows, Master Sheriff, I have seen enough!'

They left the chamber. Maltote had now composed himself, though his face was as white as a ghost. They walked back up into the castle bailey. The serjeant who had accosted Corbett was waiting for them.

'You have more visitors, Sir Walter, from Sparrow Hall: the Vice-Regent. Master Tripham and others have come to claim Passerel's corpse.' The soldier pointed to a cart standing near the gateway.

'Where are the visitors?'

'I put them in the gate-lodge chambers.'

Sir Walter rubbed his eyes. 'Come on, Sir Hugh.'

They returned to find three people waiting for them. Master Alfred Tripham, the Vice-Regent, was sitting on a bench and didn't bother to rise when the Sheriff and Corbett entered the room. He was tall with an austere, clean-shaven face under a mop of silver hair. Deep furrows were scored around his thin-lipped mouth. He was dressed in a costly, dark-blue robe, his hood, cowl and gown were embroidered with silk edgings of a Master. Lady Mathilda Braose was sitting on the Sheriff's stool. She was short and thickset, her steel-grey hair and plain face shrouded by a dark veil. A grey cloak covered a burgundy-coloured dress buttoned high at the throat. She had lustrous brown eyes but these were shadowed with dark rings and the petulant cast to her lips gave her sallow face a sneering, arrogant look. Richard Norreys, who made the introductions, was a much more jovial, pleasant man: round-faced with a neatly trimmed moustache and beard, his mop of red hair had greying streaks. He had a firm handshake and seemed eager to please.

'We waited here,' he declared in a sing-song accent, 'because, Sir Walter, we were told you would return shortly. But if I had known you had such illustrious visitors...' Norreys's protuberant blue eyes blinked. He licked his lips as if choosing his words carefully.

'Oh, stop grovelling, Norreys!' Lady Mathilda pushed the plate of eels away from her. 'Sir Walter, we have come to collect Passerel's corpse. He died a dishonourable death. We wish to give him honourable burial.'

Bullock didn't answer her but picked up the plate of eels, leaned against the wall and started eating. He didn't bother to look at Tripham, and Corbett sensed the bad blood between them. Lady Mathilda glanced at Corbett slyly, dismissing Ranulf and Maltote standing behind with a contemptuous pull of her mouth.

'So, you are the King's clerk? Corbett, yes?'

Sir Hugh bowed. 'Yes, my lady.'

'I have heard of you, Corbett,' she continued, 'with your long, snooping nose. So the King's dog has come to Oxford to sniff amongst the rubbish.'

'No, madam,' Ranulf spoke up quickly. 'We have come to Oxford to catch the Bellman, an attainted traitor. We will take him to London so he can be hanged, drawn and quartered at the Elms near Tyburn stream.'

'Is that correct, Red Hair?' Lady Mathilda whispered mockingly. 'You'll catch the Bellman and hang him.' She snapped her fingers. 'Just so?'

'No, madam,' Corbett replied. 'As you say, I'll forage amongst the rubbish and drag him out, as I will the assassin responsible for the deaths of Ascham and Passerel and, perhaps, the cold-blooded killer of old beggar men.'

'What's that?' Tripham rose to his feet. 'Are you saying they are one and the same?'

'He's a good dog.' Sir Walter grinned, popping a piece of

bread into his mouth. 'He's already been sniffing amongst the rubbish.'

'Lady Mathilda! Lady Mathilda! Master Tripham!' Master Norreys came forward, hands flapping. He remembered himself and wiped the palms of his hands against his woollen tunic. 'Sir Hugh is the King's clerk,' he continued. 'We've met before, sir.' He went up to Corbett. 'I was with the King's armies in Wales.'

Corbett shook his head. 'Sir, there were so many and it was so long ago.'

'I know, I know.' Norreys pulled back the sleeve of his gown and showed the leather wrist guard. 'I was a speculator,' he explained.

Corbett nodded. 'Ah yes, a scout!'

'Now the Welsh are at Sparrow Hall,' Tripham intervened. He forced a smile as if apologising for his previous bad manners. 'Sir Hugh, whatever you think, you are most welcome. The King has insisted that we show you hospitality. Richard Norreys here is Master of the hostelry. He will ensure you have good food and are well housed.' He hitched his robe round his narrow shoulders. 'And tonight, Sir Hugh, be our guest at Sparrow Hall. Our cooks are trained in the French fashion. Master Norreys, you too can join us.' He blew his cheeks out and turned to where Sir Walter still leaned against the wall. 'Sir, you have Passerel's corpse?'

The Sheriff continued to chew slowly. He put the bowl back on the table, licked his fingers and nodded at Corbett. He was about to lead Tripham out of the chamber when there was a knock on the door. The young man who slipped into the room was fresh-faced, his black hair carefully oiled and tied behind him. He was dressed in the clothes of a student commoner, a brown woollen jerkin, with hose of the same colour pushed into boots, the belt round his waist carried a dagger slitted through a ring. He had an ordinary face except for his eyes, which were bright, watchful and anxious until Lady Braose beckoned him over. He trotted across like a lapdog and stood behind her. Corbett watched curiously as Lady Mathilda made signs with her fingers. The young man nodded and gestured back. Lady Mathilda's face softened, reminding Corbett of a doting mother with a favoured child.

'This is my squire,' she announced proudly. 'Master Moth.' She smiled at Corbett. 'I am sorry if I was brusque, sir, but when Master Moth is not with me –' her eyes slid towards the Sheriff '– I become afeared for him.' She patted Master Moth's hand. 'He's a deaf mute; he has no tongue. He can neither read nor write. An orphan, a foundling, who was left at Sparrow Hall. He's the son I never had but wished I could.' She turned and made more signs. The young man responded and pointed at the window. 'Master Sheriff,' Lady Mathilda snapped. 'It's time we were gone before our cart goes without us! Sir Hugh?' She rose. 'You'll be our guest tonight?'

Corbett nodded.

'And I suppose the questioning will begin?'

'Yes, madam, it will.'

Lady Mathilda grasped Moth's arm and hobbled towards the door.

'Come on, Master Sheriff,' she snapped. 'You wish us gone and so do we!'

Sir Walter bade his farewells to Corbett and followed, shouting over his shoulder that, if Corbett wished to speak to him, he knew where to find him. Corbett waited until their footfalls faded in the distance.

'A pretty pottage, eh, Ranulf?' he asked. 'Hate and resentments all round.'

'Does anyone in Oxford, Sir Hugh, love anyone else?'

Corbett smiled wryly and moved to the window. He stared down into the castle yard and glimpsed Sir Walter and his party making their way to the corpse chamber whilst Lady Braose sent Moth scurrying to fetch the cart.

'I thought it strange,' he murmured. 'Do you realise, Ranulf? A bursar at Sparrow Hall was chased by a mob of students and forced to take sanctuary in a church where he was later poisoned, but no one asked why. No one showed any grief. Oh, they came to collect the corpse but they acted as if they'd returned for some forgotten baggage. Now, why is that, eh?'

'Perhaps Passerel was disliked?'

'I don't think so.' Corbett licked his lips and realised how hungry and thirsty he had become. 'Come, we'll break our fast in some tavern and then go to the hostelry to see what awaits us.'

'You have not answered your own question, Master?'

Corbett stopped, his hand on the latch of the door.

'I wager a tun of wine to a barrel of malmsey that, before long, Passerel will be depicted as a murderer, maybe even the Bellman and – if we are foolish enough to swallow that – that the Bellman will remain silent until we are out of Oxford.'

Chapter 4

Two hours later, as the rain clouds began to gather, Corbett and his party arrived at Sparrow Hall in Pilchard Lane. The college itself was a gracious, three-storeyed building with a grey slate roof capping yellow sandstone bricks; it boasted a fine main door with a large oriel window above it. The other windows were square and broad, with coloured glass filling the mullions. The hostelry on the other side of the lane was more nondescript. Apparently, its founder had bought three four-storey mansions, each with a brick base, the upper storeys of plaster and wooden beams, and had connected the houses by makeshift wooden galleries. The hostelry lacked the grace of the Hall; some of the windows were shuttered, and others were covered by horn paper.

Corbett, Ranulf and Maltote went down a side lane and into the rear yard, its chipped cobbles covered in mud. This housed stables, forges and store rooms. Scholars, in various forms of dress, lounged in the open doorways. An ostler came across to take their horses. As Corbett dismounted, the scholars took a deeper interest in them, clustering together, whispering and pointing. A brick flew well above their heads and a voice in a Welsh accent shouted, 'The royal dogs have arrived!'

Ranulf's hand went to his dagger. The yard fell silent. More students now thronged about. A tall, thickset, young man, languidly pushing back a mop of hair from his ruddy face, sauntered across. He was dressed in the garb of a commoner: tight-fitting hose, soft leather boots, a white cambric shirt covered by a robe which fell just above a protuberant codpiece. He wore a broad leather war belt round his waist, from which a sword and dagger hung, pushed through rings. As he sauntered over, others followed.

The ostler hastily led the horses away, whilst the students ringed Corbett and his companions.

'It's a fine day,' Corbett declared, throwing his cloak back over his shoulders so the students could see his sword. 'Shouldn't you be at your studies? The Trivium, the Quadrivium, Grammar and Logic? In the immortal words of Aristotle: "Seeking truth and turning the will to good".'

The leader of the scholars stopped, nonplussed. He would have liked to have quipped back in the time-honoured fashion. Corbett wagged a finger at him.

'You have been neglecting your horn book, sir.'

'That's correct,' the young man replied languidly, his voice betraying a soft, Welsh accent. 'Hall life has been disturbed by the comings and goings of inquisitive, royal clerks.'

'In which case,' Ranulf spoke up, stepping forward, 'you can join us at Woodstock to debate the matter in front of His Grace the King.'

'Edward of England does not concern me,' the fellow replied, grinning over his shoulder at his companions. 'Llewellyn and David are our Princes.'

'That's treason,' Ranulf retorted.

The student leader took a step forward. 'My name is David Ap Thomas,' he declared sternly. 'What's the matter, clerk, don't you like the Welsh?'

'I love them,' Corbett replied, putting a restraining hand on Ranulf's shoulder. 'I am married to the Lady Maeve Ap

Llewellyn. Her Uncle Morgan is my kinsman. Yes, I have fought the Welsh; but they were resolute fighters – not bullyboys.'

The scholar stared at him, surprised.

'Now,' Corbett retorted. 'Either stand out of my way, sir . . .!'

'Leave him be, ap Thomas!' a voice shouted.

Richard Norreys shouldered his way through the crowd. The scholars dispersed, not because of Norreys's arrival, but due to Corbett's claim to kinship with one of the leading families of South Wales. Norreys was apologetic as he led them across the yard into the downstairs parlour of the hostelry. The passageway was rather dirty, its whitewashed walls marked and stained, but the parlour itself was comfortable. The sandstone floor was scrubbed, and tapestries, shields and weapons hung on the walls. Norreys ushered them across to a table, flicking his fingers at a servitor to bring goblets of white wine and a dish of sugared almonds.

'I must apologise for Ap Thomas.' He breathed heavily as he sat down at the table beside Corbett. 'He's a Welsh noble and likes to play the part of the swaggart.'

'Are there many Welsh here?' Ranulf asked.

'A good number,' Norreys replied. 'When Henry Braose founded the Hall and bought this hostelry, special provision was made in the Foundation Charter for scholars from the shires of South Wales.' Norreys smiled. 'Henry felt guilty about the Welsh he killed but . . . don't we all, Sir Hugh?'

For a while they discussed the King's campaigns in Wales. Norreys recalled the mist-filled valleys, treacherous marshes, sudden ambuscades and the soft-footed Welsh fighters, who would steal into the King's camp at night to cut a throat or take a head.

'You served there long?' Corbett asked.

'Aye, for some time,' Norreys replied. He spread his

hands. 'That's how I received preferment here. A benefice for services rendered.' He looked at the hour candle burning on its nook beside the fireplace. 'But come, Sir Hugh, we are expected at the Hall at seven o'clock and Master Tripham's a stickler for punctuality.' He got to his feet. 'I have chambers for you,' Norreys continued. 'Two chambers on the second floor.'

He led them out and up a wooden staircase. Now and again they had to pause as students rushed by, horn books in their hands, sacks or bags slung over their shoulders.

'The afternoon schools,' Norreys explained. He then began to describe how Braose had bought three great mansions with cellars and chambers and united them to form the hostelry.

'Oh yes, we have everything here,' he said proudly. 'Garrets for the commoners, dormitories for the servitors, chambers for the bachelors. All those who have the money to pay.' He glimpsed Maltote perspiring under the weight of the heavy saddle bags he carried. 'But come on, come on.'

Norreys led them up to the second gallery. The passageway was dull and damp, the walls mildewed. He pushed open the doors of two rooms; both were no more than austere monastic cells. The first had two truckle beds; the other, Corbett's, a mattress on the floor. It also possessed a table, chair, chest, two candlesticks and a crucifix on the wall.

'It's the best we can do,' Norreys mumbled. He glanced shamefacedly at Corbett. 'Sir Hugh, you are not really welcome here, you must know that.' He hastened on, 'If it grows cold, I can have braziers brought up. For heaven's sake, watch the candles, we live in mortal fear of fire. The refectory and tap room are on the ground floor, though Master Tripham will probably invite you to eat at the Hall.'

'If we could have some water?' Corbett asked. 'My companions and I would like to wash.'

Norreys agreed and left them.

Muttering and cursing under their breath, Ranulf and Maltote made themselves as comfortable as possible. Corbett placed the few possessions he had brought in a small battered chest under the arrow slit window. His writing bag he hid under the bolster of his pillow before he went to see Ranulf and Maltote. He stood in the doorway and grinned: Maltote was already fast asleep on his bed, curled up like a child; Ranulf squatted to the side of him, glowering at the wall.

'Don't say you wish you were back at Leighton,' Corbett teased.

'I can see why you told us to bring little or nothing of value,' Ranulf replied without turning his head.

'At Oxford,' Corbett said, 'students are not thieves, they are like jackdaws. If they want something, they take it. I began my first Trinity term here in one set of clothes and finished it in another.'

A servant brought up two pewter bowls and jugs of water. Corbett returned to his own chamber. He washed his face and hands, rested for a while and was drifting off to sleep when he was roused by the harsh ringing of a bell. He rose, put his sword belt on and decided to wander around the hostelry. The sprawling mansion immediately reminded Corbett of the maze in Queen Eleanor's garden at Winchester: there were passageways and galleries, stairways and steps leading hither and thither, past chambers, offices, store rooms – a veritable warren. It was none too clean, reeking of burnt oil and boiled cabbage. He went down to the refectory, a long, white-washed chamber with tables and benches placed along the walls. A few students lounged there, arguing loudly, whilst others lay fast asleep on the rushes in the corner. A servant came over and asked if he wished something to drink but Corbett refused. He went along a passageway and stopped before a great, iron-studded door. He tried the handle but the door was locked.

'Can I help you?' Norreys came running up, a bunch of keys jangling in his hand.

'I'm fascinated by your hostelry, Master Norreys. It's a veritable warren.'

'It could be better,' Norreys replied. 'But the Masters of the Hall are reluctant to spend more silver.' He pointed to the door. 'That leads to the cellars and store rooms. It is kept firmly locked, otherwise the students would steal wine and beer and help themselves to the stores. Do you want to go down? I must warn you, it's no better than the hostelry itself and you'll need a candle.'

Corbett shook his head. 'What were these houses before?'

'They belonged to a wine merchant. One of the houses was used for storage, and the merchant and his company lived in the other two. And there's the yard and the cellars beneath.'

'No gardens?'

'Oh no, the price of land is rising, Sir Hugh. Five years ago Master Copsale sold the garden plots to the City Council.'

Corbett thanked him and returned to his own chamber. Ranulf and Maltote were awake. After they had unpacked their belongings, they dressed and followed Corbett out of the hostelry into the lane. They paused as a friar hurried by pushing a wheelbarrow, with a sheeted corpse lying in it. Beside the friar went a young boy, struggling to keep a candle alight: at every step the altar boy took, a bell, slung on a cord round his waist, tinkled as a warning. Corbett blessed himself and stared up at the windows of the Halls opposite. The sky was still overcast and he glimpsed the glow of candles. Three debtors, chained together and released from the city prison, hobbled along, begging bowls in their hands. A drunken bailiff swayed behind them; he cursed and yelled as a group of children knocked against him in pursuit of a little monkey dressed in a small jacket and a bell cap. They were throwing sticks and stones and, in turn, were chased by the relic-seller whom Corbett had met earlier at the castle. Corbett tossed a coin into one of the beggars' bowls and waited for the mêlée to pass before making his way across and up the lane. He pulled hard at the bell outside the main door of the Hall: this was swung open, and a smiling Master Moth beckoned them in. Corbett was immediately struck by the contrast between the Hall and the hostelry: here, bright oaken wainscoting covered most of the walls, above this hung coloured cloths and tapestries; rush matting lay across the paving stones; candles glowed in brass holders and small, tin pots, full of fragrant herbs, were placed on shelves or in corners.

Moth led them silently into the parlour, which was a comfortable, cosy chamber. Tripham and Lady Mathilda were sitting in box chairs before the fire. Moth, helped by a servant, brought stools for Corbett and his companions. Greetings were stiffly exchanged, the offer of wine and small portions of toasted cheese made and taken. Tripham must have caught Ranulf's sardonic glance at the luxuries round the room: the tapestries, Turkish rugs, pewter and silver pots glistening on shelves; the small, metal coffers and three long chests standing under a table in one corner.

'Sir Hugh,' Tripham apologised, sipping from his wine, 'I appreciate that the hostelry is, perhaps, not the best or most luxurious of quarters.'

Corbett quietly kicked Ranulf before he could reply.

'I've slept in worse,' Corbett retorted. 'Master Norreys does his best!'

'You see,' Lady Mathilda spoke up, 'the statutes of Sparrow Hall make it very clear. My brother, God bless his

67

memory, decreed this was a house of study and, apart from myself, no other visitors can be lodged here.'

'You are not a visitor,' Tripham declared tactfully.

Lady Mathilda just sniffed and looked away.

'How long has the college been founded?' Corbett asked.

'Thirty years,' Lady Mathilda replied. 'The year after King Edward's coronation. My brother –' her eyes brightened '– wanted a place of scholarship, of books and manuscripts. Sparrow Hall has produced clerks, scholars, priests and bishops,' she continued proudly. 'My brother would have been pleased, though,' she added darkly, 'perhaps his contribution to the hall and its founding have not been fully recognised.'

'Lady Mathilda,' Tripham sighed. 'We have been down this path many a time. Our resources are few.'

'I still believe,' Lady Mathilda sniffed, 'that the Hall could find new resources to found a Chair in the University in my brother's name.' She pulled at the skin of her throat. 'Soon all those who knew my brother will be dead and his great achievements forgotten.' She glanced at Corbett. 'The King, too, is ungrateful: a grant of monies . . .'

'His Grace cannot grant,' Corbett replied, 'what he has not got.'

'Ah yes,' Lady Mathilda agreed. 'The war in Scotland. It's a pity.' She picked up her wine cup and stared at the fire. 'It's a pity Edward has forgotten my brother and the day he defended the royal standard at Evesham when de Montfort fell.'

'No one forgets,' Tripham interrupted tactfully.

'No, and neither do I,' Lady Mathilda retorted. 'Perhaps the Hall's accounts should be examined more carefully.'

'What are you implying?' Tripham's scraggy neck tensed, his Adam's apple bobbing like a cork in a pond.

Ranulf and Maltote sat bemused at the rancour between two of their hosts. Corbett, embarrassed, stared at the sparrow carved above the motto on the stone mantelpiece. He translated the Latin, a quotation from the Gospel, 'Are you not worth more than many sparrows?' Lady Mathilda must have noticed Corbett's distraction for she sighed, gesturing at Tripham that these matters would have to wait.

'Sir Hugh, do you make any sense of Passerel's death? Could he have been the Bellman?' Tripham asked. 'I mean, the attack by the students was unforgiveable. But—' He pulled a face. 'Ascham was a well-loved master, child-like in his innocence. He did scrawl most of Passerel's name on a piece of parchment before he died.'

'It would be tempting,' Corbett replied, 'to claim Passerel as the Bellman; to think that he murdered Ascham because the librarian had discovered his secret identity and that Passerel later fled to St Michael's where he was murdered out of revenge.' Corbett put his cup down on the floor. 'If that was the truth, and I could prove it, the King would dismiss Passerel's death as a mere nothing. He'd declare that the Bellman had been silenced, that justice had been done and I could leave Oxford.' Corbett shrugged. 'Who knows, we could even build a case that Passerel may be behind the deaths of these old beggars who have been found in the woods outside the city.'

'But would your logic be so flawed?' a voice called out from behind him.

Corbett turned as Master Leonard Appleston picked up a stool and came across to join them. He introduced himself, giving Corbett and his companions a vigorous shake of the hands.

'You are skilled in logic?' Corbett asked.

Appleston's square, sunburnt face creased into a smile; his eyes took on a rather shy look. He scratched at an angry sore on the corner of his mouth, like some schoolboy wondering whether he should be praised or not.

'Leonard is a master in logic,' Lady Mathilda spoke up. 'His lectures in the schools are most popular.'

'I heard what you said,' Appleston declared. 'It would be neat and tidy if poor Passerel was cast as the assassin, the "*fons et origo*" of all our troubles.'

'Do you believe that?' Corbett asked.

'If a problem exists,' Appleston said, smiling at Ranulf and making more room, 'then a solution must exist.'

'Aye, and that's the problem,' Corbett replied. 'But what happens if the problem is complex but the solution so simple that you wonder if a problem existed in the first place?'

'What do you mean?' Appleston asked, taking a goblet from Master Moth.

Corbett paused to collect his thoughts.

'Master Appleston, you lecture in the schools on the existence of God?'

'Yes, my lectures are based on Aquinas's *Summa Theologica*.'

'And you comment on his proofs of God's existence?'

'Of course.'

'In which case,' Corbett replied, 'wouldn't you agree that, if I could prove God exists, God would cease to exist?'

Appleston narrowed his eyes.

'I mean,' Corbett continued. 'If I, who am finite and mortal, can prove, beyond a doubt, that an infinite and immortal being exists, then either I am also infinite and immortal, or that which I am proving can't exist in the first place. In other words, such slight proof for the existence of God is too simple, and is, therefore, not logical. It's a bit like me saying I can put a gallon of water into a pint tankard: if I could then it is either not a gallon or the tankard can hold more than a pint.'

'*Concedo*,' Appleston said grudgingly. 'Though I would have to think about what you said, Sir Hugh.'

'The same applies to Passerel,' Corbett added quickly. 'If he *is* the Bellman, the assassin of Robert Ascham and John Copsale, not to mention the old beggars, then I would say the solution is simple, too tidy, too neat and, therefore, totally illogical.'

'I agree,' Ranulf declared, pulling a face at Maltote.

'So, who did kill Ascham?' Tripham asked quietly.

'I don't know,' Corbett replied. 'That's why I am here.' He turned to Tripham. 'I would like to visit the library tonight, perhaps after dinner?'

'Of course,' the Vice-Regent replied. 'We can take our sweet wine down there: it's a comfortable chamber.'

Master Moth came over. He tapped Lady Mathilda on the shoulder, making strange signs with his fingers.

'Dinner will be served soon,' she declared, getting to her feet. She grasped her cane which stood in the corner of the fireplace. 'Gentlemen, I shall meet you later.' She hobbled out, one hand resting on the cane, the other on the arm of her silent servant.

The conversation continued in a rather desultory fashion. Appleston and Tripham asked questions about the court and the price of corn at Leighton Manor. They were joined by other Masters: Aylric Churchley, a Master of the Natural Sciences, thin as an ash pole, with a waspish face and grey tufts of hair standing high on a balding head. He spoke in such a high, squeaky voice Corbett silently had to warn Ranulf and Maltote not to laugh. Peter Langton, a small, wrinkled-browed, narrow-faced man with rheumy eyes, who deferred to everyone, especially Churchley, whom he hailed as Oxford's greatest physician. Bernard Barnett was the last to arrive, fat-faced with a high forehead; a tub of a man with his startling eyes and protruding lower lip. He had a pugnacious look as if ready to dispute, at the drop of a coin, how many angels could sit on the edge of a pin.

71

Lady Mathilda returned and Tripham led them out, along the passageway into the dining hall. This was a luxurious, oval-shaped room, cosy and warm. The table down the centre was covered in white samite cloths which shimmered, in the light of the beeswax candles, on the silver and pewter cups, jugs and cutlery. Beautiful hangings and tapestries, depicting scenes from the life of King Arthur, hung above the dark-brown wainscoting. Small rugs covered the floor; sweet-scented braziers stood in each corner while large pots of roses had been placed on the cushioned window seats, their sweet, fragrant smell mingling with the cloying and mouth-watering odours from the buttery at the far end. Tripham sat at the top, Lady Mathilda on his right, Corbett on his left. Ranulf and Maltote were placed at the far end with Richard Norreys who had been supervising the cooks in the kitchen. Tripham said Grace, sketched a hasty blessing and the meal was served: quail soup followed by swan and pheasant in rich wine sauces, and roast beef in mustard. All the time the wine flowed freely, served by silent waiters who stood in the shadows. Corbett tasted every dish and drank sparingly but Ranulf and Maltote fell on the delicious dishes like starving wolves.

Most of the Masters drank deeply and quickly, their faces becoming flushed, their voices rising. Tripham was unusually silent whilst Lady Mathilda, whose rancour against the Vice-Regent was apparent, only nibbled carefully at her food and sipped from her wine cup. Now and again she'd turn and make those strange finger gestures to Master Moth.

Tripham leaned across. 'Sir Hugh, you wish to talk to us about your presence in Oxford?'

'Yes, Master, I do.' Corbett looked down the table. 'Perhaps now is as good a time as any.'

Tripham rapped the table and asked for silence.

'Our guest, Sir Hugh Corbett,' he announced, 'has certain questions to ask us.'

'You all know,' Corbett began brusquely, 'about the Bellman and his treasonable publications.'

All of the Masters refused to meet his eyes but stared at each other or toyed with their cups or knives.

'The Bellman,' Corbett continued, 'proclaims he is from Sparrow Hall. We know the handwriting to be a clerkly hand, albeit anyone's, and the parchment expensive; consequently the writer is a man of some wealth and learning.'

'It's none of us!' Churchley screeched, running his fingers round the collar of his dark-blue robe. 'No man here is a traitor. Satan could claim that he lives in Sparrow Hall but, whether he does or not, is another matter.'

His words were greeted with a murmured assent, even the soft-spoken Langton nodding his head vigorously.

'So, no one here has any knowledge of the Bellman?'

A chorus of denials greeted his question.

'He writes and posts his proclamations at night,' Churchley explained. 'Sir Hugh, we are all eager for our beds. Even if we wanted to wander abroad, Oxford, after dark, is a dangerous place. Moreover, our doors are locked and bolted. Anyone who left at such a late hour would certainly provoke attention.'

'Which is why,' Appleston spoke up hurriedly, 'the writer may well be a student. Some scholars are poor but others are rich. They have a clerkly hand and, amongst the young, de Montfort still has the status of a martyr.'

'Is there a curfew at the hostelry?' Corbett asked Norreys.

'Of course, Sir Hugh, but proclaiming one and enforcing it on hot-blooded youths is another matter – they can come and go as they wish.'

'Let us say,' Corbett said, '*causa disputandi*, that the

Bellman is neither a member of Sparrow Hall nor the hostelry – why then should he say he is?'

'Ah!' Lady Mathilda sniffed, folding back the voluminous cuffs of her robe. 'There's so much nonsense written about de Montfort. When my beloved brother came here and founded the Hall and bought the tenements opposite for the hostelry, a widow woman with a child lived in the wine cellars across the lane. She was quite fair but something of a madcap; apparently her husband had been one of de Montfort's councillors. My brother, God bless him, had to ask her to leave. He offered her alternative dwellings but she refused them.' Lady Mathilda ran her finger round the rim of her cup. 'To cut a long story short, Sir Hugh, the woman took to wandering the streets with her boy, until one winter's night he died. She brought his little corpse down to the lane. She had a hand-bell and began to ring it. A crowd assembled, my brother and myself included. Then she lit a candle, fashioned, so she claimed, from the fat of a hanged man, and she cursed both my brother and Sparrow Hall. She vowed that one day the Bellman would come and wreak revenge, both for her and for the so-called glorious memory of Earl Simon.'

'What happened to her?' Corbett asked.

Lady Mathilda grinned; in the flickering candlelight she reminded Corbett of a cat, with narrowed eyes, the skin of her face drawn tight, one hand curled like a claw on the table.

'Now that's a coincidence, Sir Hugh. She entered the nunnery at Godstowe but, because of her extravagances, left there. She is now an anchorite at St Michael's Church. Oh yes! The same place in which Passerel was poisoned.'

'Why the Bellman?' Maltote, usually quiet but now emboldened by drink, spoke up. 'Why did the anchorite refer to the Bellman?'

'Because,' Tripham intervened quickly, 'in London, the Bellman stands outside the Fleet and Newgate prisons on the night before execution day. He warns the prisoners in the condemned cell that they are about to die.'

'It's not only that,' Langton spoke up shyly. 'Sir Hugh, many years ago when I was a mere stripling, I was an apprentice to a scrivener near St Paul's. When de Montfort raised the banner of rebellion against the King, the trained bands of London were summoned by his herald, who called himself the Bellman.'

Corbett smiled his agreement but secretly wondered how many at Sparrow Hall had fought or supported the dead earl.

'So, you know nothing,' he asked, 'about the present Bellman or these gruesome deaths amongst the beggars?'

'Come, come!' Churchley tapped the table. 'Sir Hugh, Sir Hugh! Why should any man here want to take the heads of such destitute people?'

'Oxford is full of covens and groups,' Appleston spoke up. 'The young dabble in strange rites and practices. We have men from the eastern marches whose Christianity, to put it bluntly, is wafer thin.'

'Let us return to more familiar domestic matters,' Corbett replied. 'Master John Copsale's death?'

'He had a weak heart,' Churchley declared. 'I often made him a concoction of digitalis to temper the heat and make the blood flow more evenly. Sir Hugh, I was Copsale's physician. He could have died at any time: when I dressed his corpse for burial, I noticed nothing amiss!'

'Where was he buried?' Corbett asked.

'In the churchyard of St Mary's. Passerel will also be buried there. The Hall owns a plot of land adjoining the cemetery.'

'Did Passerel say anything?' Ranulf spoke up from the

end of the table. 'Anything at all to explain why Ascham should write his name, or most of it, on a piece of parchment?'

'He hotly denied any blame,' Norreys replied. 'Every time he came over to check on the stores or sign the accounts, the poor fellow would begin a speech in his own defence.'

'We all agreed with him,' Tripham said. 'The day Ascham was killed, Passerel was travelling back from Abingdon.'

'Ascham's corpse must have been cold,' Churchley spoke up, 'when Passerel arrived back about five o'clock. It was he who initiated the search for poor Robert, and when we forced the door Ascham was as cold as ice.'

'What time do you think he died?' Corbett asked.

'We know,' Tripham replied. 'He went into the library – oh, between one and two o'clock in the afternoon. He locked and bolted the library door behind him. He must have been searching for something but exactly what he never mentioned. Now, for some of that afternoon, I was with Lady Mathilda discussing the Hall's revenues.' He glared meaningfully to his right. 'We then went down to the buttery. Passerel burst in, saying the library was locked and he could get no answer from Ascham.'

'And where were the rest of you?'

The mumbled replies told him little. Norreys had been across in the hostelry doing his accounts: the rest had been in their chambers before going down to the buttery.

'I ordered the door to be broken down,' Tripham declared. 'When we went in, Ascham was lying in a pool of blood, the letter beside him; the candle was burnt down and the garden window was shuttered.'

'I examined him,' Churchley spoke up. 'It was just after five o'clock in the evening when we broke in. He must have been dead for about an hour.'

'And what happened on the day Passerel fled to St Michael's?' Corbett asked.

'The scholars,' Tripham replied, 'loved old Ascham. On the day in question, a mob gathered threatening violence.'

'Couldn't you have sent to the Sheriff for help?'

'Aye, and we'd still be waiting,' Appelston replied. 'I told Passerel to flee: it seemed the best course of action.'

'We thought it wise to let hot blood cool,' Tripham added. 'The following morning, I would have petitioned for help.' He tapped the table cloth. 'In the circumstances, it's difficult to blame the students.'

Corbett pushed his wine cup away. At the far end of the table Maltote and Ranulf looked at him expectantly. Maltote was completely bemused. Ranulf was grinning, running his tongue round his lips. As he often whispered to Maltote, 'I love to see old Master Long Face get to the questioning. A true lawyer he is, with those sharp, hooded eyes. He sits and questions and then he'll go away and brood.' Ranulf took great pleasure in what was happening. Apart from Norreys, the rest of the Masters had ignored him as if he did not exist. Suddenly a screech owl called outside and Ranulf shivered. Wasn't Uncle Morgan always saying that a screech owl's call was the harbinger of death?

Chapter 5

Corbett sat in silence. He studied his wine cup, a trick he often used to force others to speak. This time he was disappointed. Lady Mathilda and the rest just stared back expectantly.

Corbett began his questioning again. 'Did Ascham ever say anything untoward? If the Bellman killed him there can only be one reason for that: Ascham must have begun to suspect his identity.' He clasped his hands together on the table. 'Now students are not allowed to come into the Hall, are they?'

'No,' Tripham retorted. 'They are not.'

'Or walk in the garden?'

'No.'

'Therefore Ascham's killer must have been in the Hall itself, either one of you or one of the servants. So, I ask you again, did Ascham ever say anything about the Bellman or his possible identity?'

'He did to me,' Langton declared, rather embarrassed by his own outspokenness. 'I asked who he thought the Bellman could be.' He continued in a rush, 'But Ascham only replied with that quotation from St Paul: "We see through a glass darkly".'

'He said as much to me,' Churchley spoke up. 'Once I met him in the buttery. He looked worried, so I asked him what was the matter? He replied that appearances were deceptive: there was something not right at Sparrow Hall. I asked him what he meant but he refused to answer.'

'Why did your brother,' Corbett asked, changing tack abruptly, 'call his foundation Sparrow Hall?'

'It was my brother's favourite quotation from the Gospels,' Lady Mathilda explained. 'Christ's words about the Father knowing even when a sparrow fell to the earth, yet that each of us was worth more than many sparrows.'

'He was also a student of the Venerable Bede,' Appleston explained. 'Particularly his *Ecclesiastical History of the English People*. Henry loved Bede's story about the thane who compared a man's life to a sparrow which flies into a hall, where there's light and warmth, before continuing his flight out into the cold darkness.' Appleston smiled. 'I only met Sir Henry a few months before he died: he often took comfort from that story.'

'Did Ascham spend a great deal of time in the library in the days before his death?' Corbett asked.

'Yes, yes he did,' Tripham replied. 'But what book he was looking for or reading none of us knew.'

'I'd like to go down there,' Corbett declared. 'Is that possible?'

Tripham agreed and servants were sent to light candles. When they returned, the Vice-Regent ordered them to bring wine to the library. He rose, with Corbett and the rest following him out into the passageway. The library was across the garden, at the far side of the Hall. It was a long, spacious room with wooden wainscoting, and gold and silver stars delicately painted on the white plaster above. Shelves, at right angles to the wall, were ranged on either side, with tables and stools between and a long writing table down the centre. The air was sweet and smelt of pure beeswax, parchment and leather. Corbett sniffed appreciatively and exclaimed in surprise at how many books, manuscripts and folios the library held.

'Oh, we have most of the great works here,' Lady Mathilda declared proudly. 'My brother, God rest him, was a bibliophile: his books, as well as his private papers, are kept here. He also bought extensively both at home and abroad.'

Corbett was about to question the source of such wealth but remembered just in time: Sir Henry Braose, like many who had supported the King against de Montfort, had received lavish rewards from the Crown, including the revenues and lands of de Montfort's adherents. No wonder the Braoses had been cursed here in Oxford, where there had been much support for the dead earl.

The rest of the Masters, rather unsteady on their feet, leaned against the tables or sat on stools as Corbett walked the full length of the library. He admired its books, shelves and coffers, its two ornately carved lecterns, as well as the fresco on the far wall, which depicted a scene from the Apocalypse where the Angel opened the Great Book for St John to read. Corbett came back into the centre of the room and studied the faint, dark stains on the floor.

'This is where Ascham was found?'

'No, as soon as we opened the door, we could see him lying just before the table there.'

'And where was the parchment?'

Tripham pointed to a place near the table. 'It was lying there as if Ascham had pushed it away from him.'

'We tried to clean the blood away,' Appleston explained. 'Passerel was to hire special polishers.'

Corbett studied the blood stains in the centre of the room and beside the table.

'So,' Corbett said, 'it looks as if Ascham crawled along the floor to get to something at the table?'

'There were also blood stains on the table,' Tripham explained. 'As if Ascham had dragged himself up. Why, Sir Hugh?'

Corbett walked on down the library, past the table to the shuttered window at the far end.

'And this was locked and barred?'

'Yes,' Churchley agreed. 'I remember it was.'

'And the window behind it was locked?'

'I think so,' Tripham replied. 'Why, Sir Hugh?'

Corbett lifted the bar across the shutters. It swung down easily and he noticed how well oiled it was. He pulled back the shutters; the lattice window behind was large. Corbett lifted the catch, opened it and stared out on to the moon-washed garden: the air was thick with the sweet smell of roses. He peered around: the window was low, anyone who stood in the garden bed beneath could look in and be hidden by the hedgerow which stood about a yard away. Corbett closed the window: he brought the shutters back with a bang, and the bar immediately fell into place.

'Should the window have been closed and the shutters barred?' he asked. 'I mean, it was a summer's evening. Wouldn't Ascham need both light and air?'

'I was in the garden,' Churchley spoke up. 'Early in the afternoon. The window was shuttered then. I don't think,' he added, 'that Ascham wanted anyone to see what he was doing.'

'Of course,' Corbett murmured. 'That is why the door was bolted and locked.' He glanced at Tripham. 'There was no mistaking that, was there?'

'No,' Tripham replied. 'You can inspect it yourself. We had to fashion new bolts and a lock as well as re-hang the leather hinges.'

Corbett walked back to the door. Tripham had told him the truth: the bolts, hinges and lock were all new. He returned to the blood stains, studied them carefully and edged his way along the table back to the window. Now and again, he could see faint flecks.

'What are you looking for, Sir Hugh?'

'I am trying to imagine how Ascham died. How he could be struck by a quarrel when both the door and the windows of the library were sealed and where he stood when it happened.'

'And?'

'Well, there are two logical conclusions. First, someone was in the library with him who managed to conceal himself here and leave afterwards.'

'Nonsense!' Tripham declared. 'The chamber was searched. Not even a mouse could get in or out.'

'Well then—' Corbett was about to continue but paused as a servant entered carrying a tray of wine cups. These were distributed, and Corbett took a sip from his. Once the servants had left, Corbett pointed to the window.

'In which case, if only one conclusion remains, that, logically, must be the correct one.'

'But the window was closed,' Lady Mathilda spoke up. 'Ascham was secretive. He'd locked and bolted the door. He wouldn't leave the window open!'

'Ascham was searching for something,' Corbett replied, 'that would unmask the Bellman. He came in and locked and bolted both door and window. However,' Corbett continued, 'what he didn't know was that his murderer was hunting him. Late that summer afternoon –' Corbett pointed to the table '– Ascham was probably seated here studying some manuscript or book, a matter I'll return to. He hears a rap on the window. Deep in his studies, Ascham probably thinks it's someone trying to get his attention. He pulls back the shutters and opens the window. The person he has been hunting is standing there, a small arbalest in his hand. The quarrel is loosed. Ascham staggers back, naturally he wanted to reach the door. He collapses and the assassin throws in his contemptuous note.'

'But who closed the window and shutters?' Tripham exclaimed. 'And how could the assassin have counted on not being seen?'

'Outside that window,' Corbett replied, 'there's a small garden bed, screened off from the rest of the garden by a hedgerow?'

'Of course,' Norreys spoke up excitedly from where he sat on a stool leaning against the shelves. 'The assassin would simply have to come out into the garden, walk at a crouch between the wall and bushes, then tap on the window.'

'But how were the window shutters closed afterwards?' Tripham insisted.

'Ascham himself might have done that,' Corbett replied. 'To protect himself further from the assassin. However, I have examined the shutter and noted that the bar has been freshly oiled. What the assassin probably did was pull the shutters closed from the outside, with such force the bar simply slid back into place. Consequently, when you came into the library, you'd see the bar down and conclude the window behind also had its catch in place.'

Churchley nodded; his eyes narrowed as he studied Corbett afresh. 'No one ever thought of examining that!' he exclaimed.

'I also suspect,' Corbett added, 'that the assassin later locked the window; just in case anyone did come back to search – it would be a small matter.'

'So, you are implying,' Churchley asked, 'that the assassin deliberately greased the shutter bar?'

'Of course. So that, when he pulled it from outside, the bar would drop down again. Watch.'

Corbett went and opened the shutters, tilting the bar back. He then closed one side and slammed the other: as soon as the shutters met, the raised bar fell into place.

'As pure as logic,' Appleston breathed.

'Did any of you think of looking for what Ascham was studying?' Corbett asked.

'I did,' Lady Mathilda stepped forward, resting on her cane. 'I did, master clerk. There was a book, a folio or manuscript on the table but, when I returned the following morning, it was gone.' She gestured round the library. 'And God knows where or what it could have been.'

Corbett studied each of the Masters: which one of them was the royal spy? Surely, a man of learning and sharp intelligence would have noticed something amiss?

'How do you know?' Churchley paused and looked at Langton who abruptly belched and patted his stomach. 'How do you know,' he continued, 'that Ascham went to the window?'

'Because there are faint flecks of blood on the floor.' Corbett replied. 'Only small drops from when the crossbow bolt took him in the chest. Ascham would turn and hurry away from the window, but then he'd collapse. As he did so, Ascham must have noticed the small scroll the assassin had tossed through the window before closing it. He dragged himself to the table, grasped the piece of manuscript and began to write out his dying message which,' Corbett sighed, 'does seem to point the finger of accusation at poor Passerel.'

'And you have no explanation of that, have you?' Tripham accused.

'No, I—'

Corbett's reply was broken off as Langton rose to his feet, his face taut and pale. He dropped the cup, clutching his stomach. He staggered towards Corbett, his mouth opening and shutting.

'Oh, sweet Jesu!' he gasped. 'Oh, Christ have mercy!'

He crashed into the table and then fell to his knees, both hands still clutching his belly. Corbett hurried towards him.

Langton convulsed on the floor, his face purple as he gasped for air. Corbett tried to turn him over. All around was confusion, the others pushing and shoving. Langton gave one final convulsion, a deep shudder. He sighed, and his head fell sideways, eyes open, a dribble of spittle running out of the corner of his mouth. Corbett placed the man's head gently on the floor. He tried to close the eyes but this was impossible. He stared up at the ring of faces, searching vainly for any clue or glimpse of satisfaction on the part of the unknown assassin. Churchley elbowed his way through. He knelt down beside the corpse, looking for the blood beat in Langton's neck and wrist.

'Lord have mercy!' he whispered. 'He's dead! Langton is dead!'

The rest drew away. Corbett saw Lady Mathilda raise her cup to her lips.

'Don't drink!' he shouted. 'All of you, put your cups down!' He tapped Churchley on the shoulder. 'Was Langton an ill man?'

'He suffered from stomach trouble,' the fellow replied. 'But nothing serious. I gave him some medicine. I don't know if he—'

Corbett undid the pouch on the dead man's belt. He drew out a square piece of parchment and handed this to Churchley. He searched again but, apart from some coins and a broken quill, found nothing.

'This is yours.' Churchley handed the parchment back. 'It bears your name.'

Corbett took the piece of vellum, a neat square about four inches long, the corners expertly gathered and sealed with a blob of red wax. It bore his name, 'Sir Hugh Corbett', but he recognised the same clerkly hand that was behind the Bellman's proclamations. He stood up, leaving the rest to gather round Langton's corpse. Corbett broke the seal. The words written inside seemed to leap up in their cry of defiance.

> 'The Bellman greets Corbett the King's crow: the royal lap dog. The Bellman asks what the crow does in Oxford? The crow should be careful where he pecks and where he flies. This follower of carrion, this hunter of bloody morsels has been warned. Do not tarry long in the fields of Oxford or your beak may be bent, your claws broken, your wings pinioned, to be despatched back dead to your royal master. Signed 'the Bellman'.

Corbett hid his fear and passed the proclamation around. Ranulf swore. Maltote, who could barely read, asked what it was? Lady Mathilda's fingers went to her lips, and the rest of the Masters seemed to sober up.

'This is treason,' Ranulf hissed. 'This is treason against the King's clerk and against the Crown itself!'

'It's murder,' Corbett retorted. 'Horrible murder. Bring the cups here, all of you!'

They scurried about until all the cups were on the table in front of him: it was difficult to tell which had been Langton's. Corbett and Ranulf, assisted by Churchley, sniffed tentatively at each. All bore the juicy fragrance of sweet wine except one: Corbett held it up to his nose and caught a sharp, acrid smell.

'What is it?' He passed the cup to Churchley who sniffed it, swilling it around.

'White arsenic,' he finally declared. 'Only arsenic has that tang, particularly white arsenic: it is deadly in its effect.'

'Wouldn't Langton have tasted it?'

'Perhaps,' Churchley replied. 'But, there again, if his palate was sweetened by what we have eaten and drunk, he might dismiss it.'

'But how did it get there?' Barnett bellowed. 'Master Alfred.' He grasped Tripham's arm. 'Are we to be poisoned in our beds?'

Lady Mathilda snapped her fingers and gestured to Master Moth who, throughout it all, had stood silently near the door. She made those strange, bird-like gestures and Moth hurried off. He returned accompanied by two sleepy-eyed servitors who had arranged the library and brought the wine down. Somehow the news of Langton's death had already begun to spread and the servitors crept like mice into the library. Tripham interrogated them but their mumbled replies shed no light on what had happened.

'Master Tripham,' one of them wailed, 'we filled the wine and put the goblets on a tray.'

Corbett dismissed them. 'Did any of you see someone playing with the cups, moving them about?' he asked the rest.

'No,' Barnett replied on behalf of them all. 'I was next to Langton all the time.' His voice faltered as he realised the implications of what he had said. 'I did nothing!' he gasped. 'I would not do such a thing!'

'Was Langton holding his cup all the time?' Corbett asked.

Churchley flailed his hands. 'Like the rest,' he whispered, 'he probably put it down on the table and then picked it up.'

'But what I can't understand,' Barnett declared, 'is why Langton should be carrying a message to you, Sir Hugh, from the Bellman?'

'I know.' Corbett sat on a stool. 'Master Alfred Tripham. Bring the servants back, and have the corpse removed! The rest of you stay!'

The Vice-Regent hurried off. He returned with four servants carrying a sheet and Langton's corpse was placed in it. Tripham told them to take it to the corpse house at the far side of the garden.

Corbett sat, head bowed. How could this have happened? He closed his eyes. Think! Think! Why did Langton have a letter addressed to me in his wallet? If Langton hadn't died, would he have handed it over, and would he have been able to tell me who the writer was. The Bellman must have been taking a huge risk. What would have happened if Langton had suddenly handed it across during the meal or afterwards? And how did the poisoner know which cup to taint? He opened his eyes. Langton's corpse had now been removed. The rest were looking at him strangely.

'Sir Hugh,' Lady Mathilda spoke up. 'The night is drawing on, we are all tired.'

Corbett got up, trying to hide his confusion and fear at the menacing threats of the Bellman.

'Little can be done now,' he said. 'Sufficient unto the day is the evil thereof.'

'I would like to have words with you before you go,' Lady Mathilda said. 'Sir Hugh, I am, with my brother of blessed memory, the founder of this Hall.' She stared defiantly at Tripham. 'I demand to have words with you!'

The Vice-Regent looked as if he was going to protest but instead, gesturing in exasperation, left the chamber. The others followed. Lady Mathilda asked Ranulf and Maltote to stand outside with Master Moth. She locked and bolted the library door behind them and then returned. She sat down at the table and flicked her fingers for Corbett to sit opposite her.

'We can't be heard here,' she whispered, leaning across. 'Sir Hugh, you must have been told that the King had a spy at Sparrow Hall?'

Corbett just stared back.

'Someone who tells the King what happens here.' Lady Mathilda pushed back the sleeves of her dress. 'I am that spy, Sir Hugh. My brother was the King's man in peace and war. This Hall, this college –' her voice rose slightly, and spots of anger appeared high in her cheeks '– this place was founded for learning and now it has become a mockery!'

'Did the King ask you to spy?' Corbett asked.

Lady Mathilda's sallow face relaxed, her eyes still glittered with anger.

'No, I offered my services, Sir Hugh. Don't you know my history? As a damsel, I played cat's cradle with de Montfort's knights.' Her face softened. 'In my day, Corbett, I was beautiful. Men begged to kiss this bony, vein-streaked hand. The King's knights often wore my colours in the lists and tournaments.' She grinned, her face becoming impish. 'Even Edward Longshanks tried to enter my bed. I suppose I was the King's in war and peace,' she added wryly. She clasped her bejewelled fingers together. 'Those were great days, Corbett. Days of war; of armies marching and banners flying, of spying and treachery. If de Montfort had won, a new king would have sat on the throne at Westminster and the likes of me and my brother would have gone into the darkness. You have heard the story?'

Corbett shook his head, fascinated by the intensity of this old but vibrant woman.

'At Evesham, at the height of the battle, five of de Montfort's knights tried to break through to kill the King. They hacked down his bodyguard and burst into the royal circle – but my brother Henry was there.' She lifted her face, her eyes brimming with tears. 'Like a rock he was, so the King said; feet planted like oaks in the ground, his great two-handed war sword whirling like the wind: those knights never reached the King. My brother killed them all. Afterwards, that night in his tent, Edward swore a great oath.' She closed her eyes, her voice thrilling, '"I have sworn a great oath and I will never repent of it", the King declared, his hand over a relic of Edward the Confessor. "Whenever Henry Braose, or any of his family, seek my help I shall not forget".' Lady Mathilda opened her eyes. 'My brother did not kill de Montfort,' she continued, 'to see his great enterprise here overturned by pompous scholars. So yes, Corbett, I volunteered my services to the King.'

'And what have you found?'

'It's not a question of finding,' she retorted. 'Sir Hugh, I have lived here for years, and I have seen Masters come and go but . . . this group!' She sighed. 'Old Copsale was a true scholar but as for the rest! Passerel was fat, living only for his belly. Langton was a mere ghost of a man, who won't be missed in death just as he wasn't noticed in life. Barnett's a drunkard who likes pretty whores. Churchley's so narrow-minded I don't think he even knows there's a world outside Oxford.'

'And Tripham, your Vice-Regent?'

'Oh, Master Tripham is a viper,' she replied. 'A cosy snake who's coiled himself round Sparrow Hall and wishes to make it his. He wants to become Regent. He'll not weep at Passerel's or Langton's death. He'll slither about ensuring that his cronies are appointed to the vacant positions. He's a parvenu!' she spat out. 'A thief and a blackmailer who tramples over my brother's memory . . .!'

'Why a thief?' Corbett interrupted.

'He's also the treasurer,' Lady Mathilda explained. 'And the Hall receives revenues from many quarters: a field here, a barn there; manors in Essex; fishing rights at Harwich and Walton-on-Naze. The money comes in piecemeal. I am sure some sticks to Master Tripham's fingers.'

'And a blackmailer?' Corbett asked.

'He knows all the little sins of his fellows,' Lady Mathilda replied. 'Barnett is well known to the whores. Churchley likes boys, particularly young men from Wales. You've met the loud-mouthed David Ap Thomas? I've seen Churchley pat his bottom. A bum squire, born and bred.'

'And Appleston?'

Lady Mathilda's eyes softened.

'Leonard Appleston's a good Master: a fine scholar, skilled in logic and debate. The scholars flock to his lectures in the schools.'

'But?'

'He has secrets from his past. Master Tripham tries to ingratiate himself with me.' She sniffed. 'Anyway, Appleston is not his real name.' She pulled at the corner of her mouth. 'His name is de Montfort. Oh, no, no.' She waved a hand at the surprise in Corbett's face. 'Born the wrong side of the blanket he was: a bastard child.'

'Does the King know this?'

'Yes.'

'And what happened?'

She shrugged. 'Appleston cannot be arrested simply because he was the by-blow of a traitorous earl.'

'And his sympathies?'

'He keeps himself to himself. Once I caught him in the library amongst my brother's papers where there are some of de Montfort's proclamations. I passed him before he turned the book over, and I saw the title. When Appleston looked up, he had tears in his eyes.'

'So he could be the Bellman?'

'Anyone could be the Bellman,' Lady Mathilda retorted. 'Except Master Moth.'

'He slides like a ghost round the hall.'

Lady Mathilda tapped her head. 'Master Moth is not a madman, Sir Hugh, but he finds it difficult to concentrate or remember anything. Remember, he can neither hear, nor speak or read and write.' Lady Mathilda rose to her feet, cocking her head to one side, as if listening to something. 'I don't know who the Bellman is, Corbett. You've met Bullock the Sheriff?'

Corbett nodded.

'Now,' she said, 'there's a man who hates us! And, of course, there are the students – you must not think they are as poor as they look. Many of them come from very wealthy families, particularly the Welsh. Their grandfathers fought for de Montfort and later their fathers and elder brothers fought the King in Wales.' She came over and touched the greying locks on Corbett's head. 'Like the lovely Maeve, your good wife!'

'Aye, God bless her!' Corbett rose. 'She's in bed and so should I be, Lady Mathilda.'

He grasped her cold, thin hand and kissed it.

'Are you frightened, Corbett?' she asked. 'Will the Bellman's threats keep you awake at night?'

'*In media vitae*,' he replied, '*sumus in morte*! In the midst of life, Lady Mathilda, we are in death.' He walked to the door then turned. 'What concerns me is what the others will say about you?'

Lady Mathilda laughed, the age and pain disappearing from her face. Corbett glimpsed the beautiful young woman she once had been.

'They'll call me an interfering, sinister, old witch,' she replied. 'Do you know what I think, Corbett?' She paused, fingering the tassel of the cord round her waist. 'I think the Bellman's coming. He might come after you, Sir Hugh, but, remember, I am Sir Henry Braose's sister.' She drew herself up. 'I know he will not let me live!'

Chapter 6

Corbett left the library, Master Moth pushing by him in his haste to return to his mistress. Ranulf tapped the side of his head.

'Take no offence, Master. Moth is only a child. Lady Mathilda is both his mother and his God. He was fair scratching at the door to get in.'

'I know,' Corbett replied. 'She's frightened. She believes the Bellman has a list and that her name is on it.'

A servitor was waiting to escort them out. Corbett excused himself and went out through a small postern door which led into the garden. A full moon bathed the lawns, flower beds and raised herb patches in its silvery light. On the left and far side was a curtain wall, to the right a line of buildings. Corbett glanced towards the library window.

'Yes, it's possible,' he murmured. 'Look, Ranulf. There are two small buttresses on either side, not to mention the hedge in front: these would conceal the assassin.' Corbett indicated the small path which ran between the hedge and the wall of the building. 'Provided no one saw him come out, he'd be almost invisible.'

Corbett walked down gingerly; the hedge was prickly and sharp and the soil underneath wet and slippery after the recent rain. He stopped outside the library window: it was fastened shut, the shutters behind betraying faint chinks of light. He walked back to his companions. Maltote was leaning against the door, falling asleep.

'So the assassin could have shot from there?' Ranulf asked. 'Pulled back the shutters then closed the window over?'

'I think so,' Corbett replied slowly. 'But I'm not as clever as I think. We know the window was closed and shuttered. We also know Ascham was in the library looking for something which would unmask the Bellman, or at least we think he was. Imagine him sitting at the table. He hears a tap on the window so he goes and opens the shutters.'

'And then the window?' Ranulf added helpfully.

'No,' Corbett replied. 'That's where my clever theory fails. Tell me, Ranulf – if you had an inkling of who the Bellman was and you'd sealed yourself in the library to hunt for the necessary evidence. You hear a tap on the window, open the shutters and, through the window, see the face of the very person you suspect – would you open the window? Bearing in mind this Bellman may have also murdered the Regent, John Copsale?'

'No,' Ranulf replied. 'I wouldn't. But maybe Ascham was not sure and had more than one suspect?'

'Perhaps . . . ah well!' Corbett shook Maltote's arm. 'It's well after midnight and time we were in our beds.'

They walked back into the hall and out, through the main door, into the lane. Only the faint glow of candles from windows high in the hostelry provided any light. A beggar, his legs shorn off at the knees, came out from an alleyway, pushing himself on a small barrow, waving his clacking dish.

'A penny!' he whined. 'For an old soldier!'

Corbett crouched down and stared at the man's rotting face: one eye was half-closed, and there were large festering sores around his mouth. Corbett put two pennies in the earthenware bowl.

'What do you see, old man?' he asked. 'What do you see at night? Who leaves the hall or hostelry?'

The beggar opened his mouth, in which only one tooth hung down, sharp and pointed like a hook.

'No one bothers poor Albric,' he replied. 'And I sees no one. But there again, sirs, rats have always got more than one hole.'

'So, you have seen people sneak out at night?'

'I see shadows,' Albric replied. 'Shadows, cowled and muffled, slip by poor Albric, not a penny offered, not a penny given.'

'Where do they go?' Corbett asked.

'Into the night like bats.' The beggar pushed his face closer. 'A coven they are.' Albric fluttered his fingers before Corbett's eyes. 'Albric can count; I went to the abbey school I did, as a child. Thirteen go by, thirteen come back: a warlocks' coven! That's all I know.'

Corbett pushed another penny into the dish: he glanced over his shoulder at Ranulf who was now supporting Maltote. They continued across the lane. After a great deal of knocking the ostarius or porter pulled back the bolts, locks screeching as the keys were turned. They entered the gloomy passageway. Corbett made towards the stairs but Ranulf, having shaken Maltote awake, pulled at his sleeve and pointed at a door under which candlelight seeped out. Corbett paused and heard the faint murmur of conversation and laughter: he opened the door and went into the refectory. David Ap Thomas, his hair even more tousled than ever, was holding court round one of the tables, surrounded by other scholars. Corbett smiled a greeting. Ap Thomas put down his dice and scowled back. Corbett shrugged and started to leave.

'No, no, Master,' Ranulf whispered. 'You take Maltote up to our chamber. I wish to have words with our Welshman.'

'No trouble!' Corbett warned.

Ranulf smiled, pushed by and sauntered down the refectory. He threw his cloak over his shoulder so the long stabbing dagger sheathed in his belt could be clearly seen. As he approached, one of the group began to caw like a crow, making fun of La Corbière, the crow, the Norman origin of Corbett's name. Ranulf grinned. He pushed his way through, taking his own loaded dice out. He kept his eyes on Ap Thomas and threw, the dice rattling on the table.

'Two sixes!'

Ap Thomas shook his dice but only managed to raise a four and a three. Ranulf, whose dice had been fashioned by the best trickster in London, threw again. Ap Thomas had no choice but to follow but, each time, his throw was less than that of Ranulf's. Ranulf sighed, picked up his dice and slipped them into his purse.

'You've lost, Welshman,' he said. 'But, there again, could you ever win?'

Ap Thomas pushed back his stool and stood up, his hand going to his knife. Ranulf moved sideways and, suddenly, the point of his dagger was pressing at the softness of the Welshman's throat.

'I am sure,' the clerk declared, 'that none of your friends will move or my hand might slip. But you, sir, if you wish, can pull your dagger.'

'It was only a game,' Ap Thomas said tightly, chin up. 'I thought you were cheating.'

'But, now you realise I was not.'

'Of course,' Ap Thomas grated.

'Good!' Ranulf smiled. 'So, next time when you meet my master, smile when he smiles. And no more cawing noises. Agreed?' He glanced around and there was a quick murmur of assent. 'Good!' Ranulf re-sheathed his dagger, sauntered out of the refectory and up the stairs.

Maltote was already on the bed, snoring like a little pig.

Next door Corbett was kneeling on the floor, his rosary beads tight round his fingers, his eyes shut, his lips moving wordlessly.

'Good night, Master.'

Corbett opened his eyes and smiled. 'Good night, Ranulf. We will not talk here,' he added, 'God knows that the walls have ears. But, tomorrow yes, after Mass?'

Ranulf returned to his own chamber. He made sure Maltote was comfortable and went to the window, pulling back the shutters. He stared through the narrow arrow slit up at the starlit sky. He was pleased to be back on the King's business, away from Leighton and its lonely fields and woods. More importantly, doors would be opened, and Ranulf's ambition to climb the steep, slippery ladder of advancement burned as fiercely as ever. He was too proud to whine to Corbett, too grateful to leave his master and the Lady Maeve to make his own fortune. The King's arrival at Leighton had changed all that. Just before the King had left, when Corbett had been elsewhere, Edward had plucked at Ranulf's sleeve. He had taken him away to a far corner, loudly proclaiming he had a story about a certain bishop they both knew. Once they were out of sight, in a quiet, narrow passageway, the King's mood had changed.

'Sir Hugh is well, Ranulf?'

'Aye, your Grace, and as loyal as ever but he worries about the Lady Maeve and, perhaps, does not have other men's stomach for bloodshed and war.'

The King had grasped Ranulf's shoulder, his fingers digging into his skin.

'But you, Ranulf, you are different, aren't you, my clerk of the Green Wax?'

'Each man walks his own path, your Grace!'

'Aye, they do, Ranulf, and sometimes they walk alone. If Corbett will not return permanently to my services,' the

King added, 'then you must.' The King smiled. 'I see ambition in your eyes, Ranulf-atte-Newgate; it burns like a flame. Skilled in French and Latin, are you now? Expert in drafting a letter and attaching the Seals? A man quick on his feet, sharp of eye, keen of wit and not averse to trapping and killing the King's enemies?'

'What Your Grace thinks, Your Grace must believe.'

The King's finger relaxed. He slipped an arm round Ranulf's shoulders, pulling him closer.

'Corbett is a good man,' Edward whispered. 'Loyal and honest, with a passion for the law. He will go to Oxford, Ranulf, and he will trap the Bellman. I know that: you, however, have a special task.'

'Your Grace?'

'I don't want the Bellman brought south for trial before the King's Bench at Westminster. I don't want to provide him with a pulpit to lecture me and the people about the blessed de Montfort!' The words were spat out. The King paused, his eyes never leaving those of Ranulf.

'Your Grace?'

'Your Grace!' Edward mimicked back. 'What Your Grace wants, Ranulf-atte-Newgate, is that when Corbett traps the Bellman, you kill him! Do you understand! Carry out that lawful execution on behalf of your King!'

Edward then pushed him away gently and walked back to rejoin his companions. The meeting had only stoked Ranulf's ambitions, yet he was worried: there was something the King had not mentioned. Ranulf tapped the hilt of his dagger: the Bellman seemed to be intent on bringing both the Crown and Sparrow Hall into disrepute. And what better way than to murder the King's principal clerk? Ranulf closed the shutters. He took off his boots and lay down on the bed. He lay for a while quietly thinking before turning to douse the candle, his mind going back to Ap Thomas and those scholars in the refectory. One night, soon, he thought, he must find out why Ap Thomas and his cronies had blades of rain-soaked grass on their boots and leggings. There was no garden here in the hostelry and the streets of Oxford were muddy trackways. Had Ap Thomas been elsewhere, out in the countryside where those grisly corpses had been discovered? And those amulets he'd glimpsed round the scholars' necks . . .?

Corbett knelt in a side chapel, consecrated to the Guardian Angels, in the church of St Michael. At the high altar the priest was celebrating a lonely, dawn Mass. Corbett looked over his shoulder and grinned. Maltote was leaning against a pillar, eyes closed, mouth drooling; he'd still not recovered from the feasting of the night before. Ranulf sat back on his heels, eyes closed; Corbett wondered to what God his manservant prayed. Ranulf never mentioned religion but dutifully went to Mass and the sacraments without making any comment. Corbett's gaze moved to the walls of the chapel. He was intrigued by the hunting scenes painted there: to the left, devils with huge nets hunted souls in some mythical forest, whilst above them angels, swords drawn, tried to rescue the virtuous from their snares. On the other wall, the artist, in garish vigorous strokes, had depicted a world turned upside down with the rabbit as the hunter and man as the quarry. Corbett was particularly fascinated by a huge hare, russet brown, its belly white as snow, who walked upright on its hind legs with a net slung over its shoulder, containing some hapless souls.

Once Mass was finished, Corbett questioned Father Vincent.

'Oh!' The priest smiled. 'So you like our paintings?' He took off his chasuble, folding it neatly before putting it on the altar steps.

'Yes, they are original,' Corbett replied.

'I did them myself,' Father Vincent replied grandly. 'I am afraid I am not a very good painter but, in my youth, I was a huntsman, a verderer in the King's service at Woodstock.' The priest finished divesting and blew the candles out on the side altar. 'So, you are the King's clerk, are you?' he asked. 'So many visitors here! But you haven't come to admire my handiwork, you've come about poor Passerel, haven't you?'

The priest took them down the steps and pointed to the entrance to the rood screen.

'That's where the poor man fell, dead as a worm he was! His face all swollen, his body twisted in agony.' He tapped Corbett on the shoulder and pointed to Maltote. 'He can sit on one of the stools if he wants. He looks as if he's not awake yet.'

Maltote happily complied as Father Vincent took Ranulf and Corbett out of the main sanctuary. He led them behind the high altar.

'That's where I left Passerel. I gave him a jug of wine and a platter of food, after he'd sought sanctuary. He didn't say much to me so I left him. I told the crowd of scholars who pursued him here that, if they didn't leave God's Acre, I'd excommunicate them on the spot. I left the side door open and went to bed.'

'Stay awake!' a voice shouted. 'Stay awake and be ready! Satan is like a roaring lion who wanders about seeking whom he may devour!'

Ranulf whirled round, hand on his dagger, at the sound of the voice which boomed like a bell round the church.

'That's only Magdalena our anchorite,' Father Vincent apologised.

Corbett stared at the strange box-like structure built over the main door. It reminded him of a nest Maeve had built

102

and placed in the trees during wintertime so the birds could come and feast.

'You know nothing of Passerel's murder?' he asked.

'Nothing whatsoever.'

'Wouldn't Magdalena have alerted you?'

'Oh, she's half-mad,' Father Vincent whispered. 'As I said, I gave Passerel his food and retired for the night. The side door was left open so, if he wished, he could go out to relieve himself.'

'And he said nothing,' Corbett persisted. 'Nothing to explain his sudden flight from Sparrow Hall?'

'No, he was just a frightened, little man,' Father Vincent replied, 'who bleated about his innocence.'

Corbett looked over his shoulder to where Ranulf was trying to shake Maltote awake.

'Maltote!' he ordered. 'Go back to Sparrow Hall and wait for us there!'

Maltote needed no second bidding but lumbered down the church and out through the main door.

'I'd like to meet the anchorite,' Corbett said. 'I understand she not only saw Passerel's murderer but, many years ago, cursed the founder of Sparrow Hall, Sir Henry Braose?'

'Ah, so you have heard the legends?'

Father Vincent led them down the church and stopped before the anchorite's makeshift cell.

'Magdalena!' the priest called up. 'Magdalena, we have visitors from the King! They wish to speak to you.'

'I'm here,' the voice replied. 'In the service of the King of Kings!'

'Magdalena!' Corbett called out. 'I am Sir Hugh Corbett, king's clerk. I wish you no ill. I must ask you questions, but I do not wish to shatter your privacy by entering your cell. Before I leave, I would like to make an offering, so you can light candles and pray for my soul.'

103

Corbett saw the leather covering over the small window pulled slightly aside. He glimpsed a grey-haired, shabby figure shuffling along the narrow gallery, followed by the slap of sandals on stone steps. Magdalena crawled into the church. She was almost bent double, her dirty-white hair fell down to her waist. Her eyes were bright but Corbett was struck by the lurid manner in which she'd painted her face: the right cheek black, the left white. In her hands she carried a small, cracked hand mirror. She shuffled and sat down at the base of a pillar. Magdalena stared into the mirror, even as her thin, bony fingers clawed at the crude rosary wrapped round her right wrist, her lips moving soundlessly in prayer. She glanced up, her bright piercing eyes studying Corbett.

'Well, dark-faced clerk? What do you want with poor Magdalena?' Her gaze shifted to Ranulf. 'You and your man of war. Why do you shatter my stillness?'

'Because you see things.' Corbett crouched beside her, taking a silver coin out of his purse.

'Magdalena sees many things in the darkness of the night,' she replied. 'I have seen demons spat out from hell and the glory of God light up the sanctuary. I am the Lord's poor sinner.' She tapped the mirror against her face. 'Once I was fair. Now I daub my face black and white and keep the mirror close at hand. Black is the badge of death. White the colour of my winding sheet.'

'And what other things do you see?' Corbett asked. He pointed up to her cell. 'You kneel above the church door. Have you seen the Bellman?'

'I heard him,' she replied. 'The night he pinned one of his proclamations on the door, breathing heavily, gasping for air. Now, says I, there's a man pursued by demons! But it's only right,' she continued, her voice becoming sing-song. 'Sparrow Hall is cursed. Built on sand.' Her voice rose. 'The

104

rains will fall, the winds will blow! That house will fall and great will be the fall thereof!'

'What curse?' Corbett asked.

'Years ago, Dark Face.' She touched Corbett on the side of his mouth. 'Your eyes are hooded but gentle. You should not be with me but with your wife and child.' She glimpsed the surprise in Corbett's eyes. 'I can see you are a lady's man,' she continued. 'My husband had your looks. A keen man, he went and fought for the great de Montfort. He never came home – hacked and cut his body was, like collops of meat on a butcher's slab. I and my boy were left in the house. We lived in the cellar and passageways, dark but safe.' She blew the spittle from her lips, her rosary cracking against the mirror. 'But then the Braose came; arrogant he was, carrying his head as if it was something sacred. Him and that beautiful bitch of a sister! Threw me out! My child died and I cursed them!' Magdalena rattled the rosary beads. 'Now the Bellman comes, warning of impending death and destruction.'

'But you don't know who the Bellman is?' Corbett asked.

'A demon sent from Hell! A goblin who has not done yet!'

'And you saw poor Passerel die?'

Magdalena's head came up, a cunning look in her eyes.

'I was kneeling before my window,' she replied. 'Eyes on God's holy light.' She pointed down to the sanctuary. 'I hear the door open and a dark shape creeps in like a thief in the night. Aye, that's how it happened. Sprung like a trap! Passerel, the stupid man, drinks the wine and dies in his sin before the All Mighty. Oh!' She closed her eyes. 'What a terrible thing it is for a sinful soul to fall into the hands of the living God!'

'What was the shape like?' Corbett asked.

Magdalena was now studying the silver piece Corbett held.

'I couldn't see,' she replied wearily. 'Hooded and cowled, no more than a shadow.' She scrambled to her feet. 'I have spoken enough.'

Corbett handed over the silver piece, and the anchorite scuttled back up the staircase. Father Vincent led them out of the church.

'What happened to the jug and cup?' Corbett asked.

'I threw them away,' the priest replied. 'They were nothing much: the like you'll see in any tavern.'

Corbett thanked him. They walked down the cemetery path and out under the lych-gate.

'Shall we have something to eat?' Ranulf asked hopefully.

Corbett shook his head. 'No, first let's visit St Osyth's.'

'We learnt nothing back there,' Ranulf declared.

'Oh, perhaps we did.' Corbett smiled back.

They took directions from a pedlar and went down an alleyway and into Broad Street. The day was proving a fine one. The thoroughfares were packed: carts full of produce, barrels and casks jammed the street and strident noise dinned the air as shops and stalls opened for another day's business. Hammers beat in one place, tubs and vats were being hooped in another, the clinking of pots and platters came from the cook shops. Men, women and children moved down the streets, in shoals, pushing and jostling. The houses on either side leaned out, their buckling walls held up by posts which impeded progress even further. Carters and barrow boys fought and cursed with each other. Porters, drenched with sweat under the burdens they carried, tried to force their way through by lashing out with white willow wands. Fat merchants, grasping money bags, moved from shop to stall. Chapmen, their trays slung round their necks by cords, tried to inveigle everyone, including Corbett and Ranulf, to buy the geegaws piled there. At one point Corbett had to stop, pulling Ranulf into the doorway of a shop. However, an apprentice, thinking they wished to buy, plucked at their sleeves until they were forced to continue on their way.

'Is it always like this?' Ranulf whispered.

Any reply Corbett made was drowned by the strident street cries which cut the air.

'Hot peas!' 'Small coals!' 'New brooms!' 'Green brooms!' 'Bread and meat for the Lord's sake for the poor prisoners of the Bocardo!'

Beggars grasping their flat dishes swarmed like fleas. Costermongers sold bright apples from the city orchards and, on the market cross, chanteurs were locked in bitter rivalry over giving news or singing songs. Even the whores and their pimps, the cross-biters, were out looking for business. Everywhere students, some dressed in samite, others in rags, swaggered in groups, narrow-eyed, their hands never far from the hilts of their daggers.

Corbett stopped at the Merry Maidens tavern and told Ranulf to go in and hire a room which they might use later on. Once this was done, they continued to push across Carfax and down a narrow, foul lane to St Osyth's Hospital, a shabby, three-storeyed tenement which stood behind its own curtain wall. The gateway was packed with beggars. In the cobbled yard a weary-looking lay brother, dressed in a brown robe with a dirty cord round the middle, was distributing hard rye bread to a group of beggars. They lined up before a wooden table where two other brothers were serving steaming bowls of meat and vegetables. Corbett and Ranulf made their way through.

'I have never seen a place like this,' Ranulf whispered. 'Not even in London.'

Corbett could only agree. There must have been at least a hundred beggars there, some of them young and sprightly, most old and bent and clothed in rags. In the main they were former soldiers, still suffering the horrible wounds of war: a face scalded by boiling oil; an eye missing with the socket closed up; legs twisted and bent; a myriad of men on makeshift crutches. Corbett was struck by something he had seen in other hospitals: despite their age, wounds and poverty, these men were determined to live, to snatch whatever remained from life. In a way, he concluded, the murder of such men was much more cruel than the assassin's work at Sparrow Hall. These were innocents: men who, despite the overwhelming odds, still fought on.

'Can I help you?'

Corbett turned round. The voice was soft and gentle but the man who had spoken was tall and squat. He was dressed in a brown Franciscan robe, his head neatly tonsured but his face looked like that of a friendly toad, with constantly blinking eyes and fat lips gaped into a smile.

'I am sorry I'm ugly,' the Franciscan declared. He patted Corbett on the shoulder, his hand like that of a bear's paw. 'I can see the thought in your eyes, sir. I am ugly to man but, perhaps, God thinks otherwise.'

'I am looking for Father Guardian,' Corbett said. 'And no man who works amongst the poor can be ugly.'

The friar grasped Corbett's hand and shook it vigorously.

'You should be a bloody Franciscan,' he growled. 'Who the hell are you anyway?'

Corbett explained.

'Well, I'm Brother Angelo,' the friar replied. 'I'm also Father Guardian. This is my manor, my palace.' He looked up, narrowing his eyes against the sun. 'We feed two hundred beggars a day,' he continued. 'But you are not here to help us, are you, Corbett? And you certainly haven't brought gold from the King?'

He waved Corbett up the steps into the hospital and led him into his cell, a narrow, white-washed chamber. Corbett and Ranulf sat on the bed whilst Father Angelo squatted on a stool beside them.

'You're here about the Bellman, aren't you? We've all heard about that mad bastard and the deaths at Sparrow Hall.'

'The King has also heard about the deaths here at St Osyth's, or rather –' Corbett added hastily as the smile faded from the Franciscan's face '– the corpses found in the woods outside the city.'

'We know little of that,' Brother Angelo confessed. 'Look around, master clerk; these are poor men, decrepit, old beggars. Who, on God's earth, could be so cruel to them? There's neither rhyme nor reason to it,' he added. 'I cannot help you.'

'You've heard no rumours?' Corbett asked.

Brother Angelo shook his head. 'Nothing except Godric's wild rantings,' he murmured. 'But you see, Corbett, men come and go here as they please. They beg in the city streets. They are helpless, easy prey for anyone's malice or hatred.'

'Do you remember Brakespeare?' Corbett asked. 'A soldier, a former officer in the King's army?'

'There are so many,' Brother Angelo apologised, shaking his head. He glanced at Ranulf. 'You have the look of a fighting man.' He pointed to Ranulf's sword, dagger and leather boots. 'You walk with a swagger.' He leaned across and nipped the skin of Ranulf's knuckle. 'Go outside, young man, and see your future. Once they too swaggered under the sun. But come on. I'll find old Godric for you.'

He led them out, down a white-washed passageway, up some stairs and into a long dormitory. The room was austere, yet the walls and floor had been well scrubbed and smelt of soap and sweet herbs. A row of beds stood on either wall with a stool on one side and a small, rough-hewn table on the other. Most of the occupants were asleep or dozing fitfully. Lay brothers moved from bed to bed, wiping hands and faces in preparation for the early morning meal.

Ranulf hung back. 'I'll not be a beggar,' he whispered. 'Master, I'll either hang or be rich.'

'Just be careful,' Corbett quipped back, 'that you are not both rich and hanged!'

'Come on!' Brother Angelo waved them over to a bed where a man was propped up against the bolsters: he was balding, his face lined and grey with exhaustion though his eyes were lively.

'This is Godric,' Brother Angelo explained, 'a long-time member of my parish. A man who has begged in London, Canterbury, Dover and even at Berwick on the Scottish march. Very well, Godric.' Brother Angelo tapped him on his bald pate. 'Tell our visitors what you have seen.'

Godric turned his head. 'I've been out in the woods,' he whispered.

'Which woods?' Corbett asked.

'Oh, to the north, to the south, to the east of the city,' Godric replied.

'And what have you seen, old man?'

'God be my witness,' the beggar replied. 'But I've seen hellfire and the devil and all his troupe dancing in the bright moonlight. Listen to what I say –' he grasped Corbett's hand '– the Lord Satan has come to Oxford!'

Chapter 7

Corbett laid his hand over that of the beggar.

'What devils?' he asked.

'Out in the woods,' Godric replied. 'Dancing round Beltane's fires! Wearing goat skins, they were!'

'And did you see any blood?' Corbett asked.

'On their hands and faces. Oh yes,' Godric continued. 'You see, sir, when I was greener, I was a poacher. I can go out and hunt the rabbit and take a plump cock pheasant without blinking. Since early spring this year I've tried my luck again and twice I saw the devils dance.'

'How many devils?' Corbett asked.

'At least thirteen. The cursed number,' Godric replied defiantly.

'And have you told anyone else?' Corbett asked.

'I told Brother Angelo but he just laughed.' Godric laid his head back on the bolsters. 'That's all I know and now old Godric has got to sleep.' The beggar turned his face away.

Corbett and Ranulf left the infirmary. They followed Brother Angelo out, down the stairs and into the still busy yard.

'Have you heard such stories before?' Corbett asked.

'Only Godric's babble,' the friar replied. 'But, Sir Hugh –' Brother Angelo's lugubrious fat face became solemn '– God knows if he's roaming in his wits or what?' He lifted one great paw in benediction. 'I bid you adieu!'

111

Corbett and Ranulf left the hospital and entered Broad Street. The crowd had thinned because the schools were open, and the students had flocked there for the early morning lectures. Corbett led Ranulf across the street, stepping gingerly along the wooden board placed across the great, stinking sewer which cut down the centre of the street.

Outside the Merry Maidens tavern, a butcher, his stall next to that of a barber surgeon, was throwing guts and entrails into the street. Beside the stall, a hooded rat-catcher, his ferocious-looking dog squatting next to him, was touting for business.

'Rats or mice!' he chanted above the din,
'Have you any rats, mice, stoats or weasels?
Or have you any old sows sick of the measles?
I can kill them and I can kill moles!
And I can kill vermin that creep in and out of holes!'

The man hawked and spat; he was about to begin again but stood aside as Corbett and Ranulf kicked their way through the mess.

'Do you have any rats, sir?' the fellow asked.

'Aye, we have,' Ranulf replied. 'But we don't know where they are and they walk on two legs!'

Before the startled man could reply, Ranulf followed Corbett into the tavern. The greasy-aproned landlord, bobbing like a branch in the breeze, showed them to the garret Ranulf had rented: a stale-smelling chamber with a straw bed, a table, a bench and two stools. Ranulf stretched out on the bed only to leap up, cursing at the fleas gathering on his hose. He sat on a stool under the open window and watched as Corbett opened his chancery bag and laid out his writing implements: quill, pumice stone and ink horn.

'What do we do now, Master?' Ranulf asked sharply.

Corbett grinned. 'We are in Oxford, Master Ranulf, so let's follow the Socratic method. We state a hypothesis and question it thoroughly.'

He paused at a knock on the door and a slattern asked if they wished anything to eat or drink. Corbett thanked her but refused.

'Now,' he began. 'The Bellman. Here is a traitor who writes proclamations espousing the cause of the long-dead de Montfort. He pins them up on church or college doors throughout the city. This, apparently, is always done at night. The Bellman claims also to live in Sparrow Hill. So, what questions do we ask?'

'I cannot understand,' Ranulf broke in, 'why we can't discover the identity of the Bellman by his writing and style of letters?'

Corbett dipped his quill into the open ink-horn and carefully wrote on the parchment. He handed this to Ranulf who pulled a face and passed it back.

'The Bellman,' he declared. 'It's the same letters, you'd think it was the same hand.'

'Precisely,' Corbett replied. 'A clerkly hand, Ranulf, as you know, is anonymous. All the clerks of the Chancery or Exchequer are taught what quills to use, what ink, and how to form their letters and the Bellman hides behind these. Even if we did find the scribe, it does not necessarily mean he is the Bellman.'

'But why does he claim to live at Sparrow Hall?' Ranulf asked.

Corbett rocked backwards and forwards on his stool.

'Yes, that does puzzle me. Why mention Sparrow Hall at all? Why not the church of St Michael's, or St Mary's or even the Bocardo gaol?'

'There's the curse?' Ranulf offered. 'Maybe the Bellman

knows of this? He not only wishes to taunt the King but also the memory of Sir Henry Braose who founded Sparrow Hall.'

'I would accept that,' Corbett replied. 'There is a bravado behind these proclamations, as well as a subtle wit. The Bellman might truly be from elsewhere but he hopes the King will lash out and punish Sparrow Hall. Yet –' he scratched his head '– we do suspect the Bellman is at Sparrow Hall, what with Copsale dying mysteriously in his bed; Ascham in his library; Passerel poisoned in St Michael's church and Langton's death last night.'

'Yes,' Ranulf added. 'Langton's murder seems to prove the assassin lurks in Sparrow Hall.'

'Let's move on,' Corbett replied. 'We have the Bellman posting his proclamations. He does so in the dead of night. Now, who could flit like a bat through the streets?'

'At Sparrow Hall?' Ranulf replied. 'All the Masters, including Norreys, are strong-bodied men. Lady Mathilda, however, has no reason to hate the Hall her brother founded. I can't see her hobbling through the streets of Oxford at night, her arms full of proclamations.'

'There's Master Moth!' Corbett replied.

'He's witless,' Ranulf replied. 'A deaf mute, who can neither read nor write. I noticed that in the library last night. He picked up a book and was looking at it upside down.' He grinned. 'Can you imagine him, Master, going through the streets of Oxford in the pitch dark, posting the Bellman's proclamations upside down?'

'Of course,' Corbett added, 'there's also our scholars, led by the redoubtable David Ap Thomas. You challenged him last night?'

'No, Master, I frightened him. But I did notice something: Ap Thomas was wearing his boots, as were his companions, and all had wet streaks of grass clinging to their footwear and clothing. Moreover, Ap Thomas wore a charm

114

or amulet round his neck, as did some of his companions: circles of metal with a cross in the centre, surmounted by a cheap piece of glass in the shape of an eye.'

'A wheel cross,' Corbett explained. 'I saw them in Wales. They are worn by those who believe in the old religion, who hark back to the glorious days of the Druids.'

'Who?' Ranulf asked.

'Pagan priests,' Corbett explained. 'The Roman historian, Tacitus, mentions them when writing of Anglesey: they worshipped gods who lived in oak trees by hanging sacrificial victims from the branches.'

'Like the heads of our beggars?'

'Possibly,' Corbett replied. 'There's Godric's wild ravings about fires and garishly dressed people practising rites in the woods. But is that our Bellman?' Corbett shrugged. 'Let us keep to our hypothesis. Who is the Bellman and how does he act?' He drew a deep breath. 'We know Ascham was close to the truth. He was searching for something in that library but he betrayed himself to the Bellman. *Ergo*—' Corbett tapped the quill against his cheek. 'Ascham was an old and venerable man. He was not used to going to the schools or wandering around Oxford so he must have voiced his suspicions to someone at Sparrow Hall.' Corbett rose, walked over and looked out of the window. 'I think we can rest assured,' he declared, 'that the Bellman lives in Sparrow Hall or the hostelry across the lane.'

'But what was Ascham looking for?' Ranulf asked.

'Again that proves the conclusion we have reached,' Corbett replied. 'Apparently Ascham had a book out on the table but this was later returned to the shelves: an easy enough task for someone at the Hall. However, let's move on. Ascham was shot by a crossbow bolt, fired by an assassin who persuaded him to open the library window. The Bellman then tossed in his contemptuous note. Ascham, knowing he was dying, grasps it and begins to write what appears to be Passerel's name in his own blood. Now, why should he do that?'

'I know.' Ranulf sprang to his feet, clapping his hands with excitement. 'Master, how do we know Ascham wrote those letters? How do we know that the assassin didn't climb through the window, take Ascham's finger, dip it into his own blood and scrawl those letters to incriminate Passerel?'

Corbett returned to sit at the table. He wafted at the flies which were hovering above the stains in the wood grain.

'I hadn't thought of that, Ranulf,' he declared. 'It's possible; but let's continue. Passerel is depicted as Ascham's murderer and he, in turn, flees the college only to be later murdered at St Michael's. But why was Passerel killed?' he asked. 'Why not leave him as he was depicted, the possible murderer? Unless, of course,' Corbett concluded, 'Passerel might reflect on what his good friend Ascham had told him.' He paused and glanced up. 'Do you know something, Ranulf? When we return to Sparrow Hall I must do two things. Firstly, I want to look through Passerel's and Ascham's possessions, particularly their papers.' Corbett began to write.

'And secondly?' Ranulf asked hopefully.

'I want to ask our good physician, Master Aylric Churchley, if he keeps poisons? Copsale was probably poisoned and we know Passerel and Langton certainly were. Now such potions are expensive to buy; moreover, some apothecary or leech would certainly recall anyone asking to buy them...'

'But would Churchley have some?' Ranulf asked.

'Yes, and I suspect the poisons used were from his stock. Anyway, to conclude—' Corbett sighed. 'We know the Bellman is at Sparrow Hall or the hostelry. We are not too sure about his motives, except for his deep hatred for the

King and the Hall itself. We know the Bellman is a skilled clerk, able to move round Oxford in the dead of night. A ruthless murderer who has already killed four men in order to conceal his identity . . .'

'Master?'

Corbett glanced at Ranulf.

'If, as you say, the Bellman hates the King and Sparrow Hall, then that places me, and certainly you, in grave danger. Can you imagine what would happen if Sir Hugh Corbett, the King's principal clerk, friend and companion, was found poisoned or with his throat cut in some Oxford alleyway, with a proclamation from the Bellman pinned to his corpse?'

Corbett didn't flinch but Ranulf saw the colour fade from his face.

'I am sorry, Master, but if we are going to put up hypotheses then I am going to study mine very carefully. If Sir Hugh Corbett is hurt or killed, the King's wrath would know no bounds. That sullen bastard at the castle would soon find the King shaking him by the collar whilst the Royal Justices would be in Sparrow Hall as quick as an arrow, expelling the community, sealing its rooms and confiscating possessions.'

Corbett smiled thinly. 'You put a very high price on my head, Ranulf.'

'No, Master. I am a rogue, a street fighter, and, whoever he is, the Bellman is no different: he will reach the same conclusion as I have, if he hasn't already.'

'Then we should be careful.'

'Aye, Master, we should. No more food or wine in Sparrow Hall. No wandering the streets of Oxford at night.'

'That is going to be hard!'

Corbett returned to his writing, listing quickly the conclusions he had reached, his pen skimming over the smooth vellum he had taken from his chancery bag. He put the quill down.

'And now to our final problem,' he declared. 'Every so often, the headless corpse of a beggar is found in the fields outside Oxford, the head tied by its hair to the branches of some nearby tree. We know that beggars are chosen as victims because they are lonely and vulnerable. In a sense, no one will miss them. However—' Corbett ticked the points off on his finger. 'Firstly, why aren't the corpses found within the city walls? Secondly, according to Bullock there's been very little sign of violence around where the severed corpses were found. Thirdly, why are they always found near some trackway? And finally, why are they never found along the same road but at different places around the outskirts of the city?'

Corbett dropped his hand. 'Which means, my dear Ranulf, that they must have been killed inside Oxford and then transported out by different routes to be later disposed of. However, if the murders occur within the city, surely someone would notice? The only conclusion we can draw is that, perhaps, they are killed outside the city at one particular spot but the remains deliberately displayed elsewhere. What else?'

'I am just thinking about Maltote. We shouldn't leave him alone too long.'

Corbett shook his head. 'No, if you are correct, the Bellman will hunt the King's dog or crow. Maltote is safe – except, perhaps, from the teasing of Ap Thomas and others.' He picked up his quill. 'Concentrate on the problem. What other questions can we ask about the murders of these poor beggars?'

'Why?' Ranulf asked. 'Why are they killed in such a barbaric way?'

Corbett stared at a wine stain on the far wall. 'Godric may

indeed have seen something in the woods around Oxford: the activities of a coven or a group of warlocks, and this group must be based here in Oxford. We know there's some connection with Sparrow Hall, because of the button we took from the last corpse. Now, I can't see any of the Masters engaged in some devilish activity. However, our scholars, under David Ap Thomas, might have something to answer.'

'Do you think Ap Thomas could be the Bellman?' Ranulf asked. 'After all, scholars can move round Oxford at night? David Ap Thomas is a rebel by nature: he might enjoy baiting the King.' He paused. 'Have you forgotten Alice atte-Bowe and her coven?'

Corbett closed his eyes. So many years ago, he thought. It had been the first task entrusted to him by Chancellor Burnell, the rooting out of a coven of witches and traitors around the church of St Mary Le Bow in London. Corbett recalled Alice's dark, beautiful face. He opened his eyes.

'I shall never forget,' he replied. 'I think I have but then – a sound, a smell and the memories come tumbling back.' He packed away his writing equipment. 'There's always the library,' he added. 'We have yet to search for what Ascham was studying, although that might be an impossible task: there are so many books and manuscripts! We don't even know if the book is still there. We could waste days, even weeks, playing a game of Blind Man's Buff!' Corbett rose. 'It's time we left for Sparrow Hall.'

They left the chamber and went downstairs. The landlord was waiting for them, a battered leather bundle in his hands.

'Sir Hugh Corbett?' he asked.

'Yes.'

The landlord thrust the small bundle into Corbett's hands.

'A beggar child came in.' He pointed to the doorway. 'A man, cowled and hooded, was standing behind. The child gave me this for you.'

Corbett wrinkled his nose at the foul smell and the greasy scrap of parchment, with his name scrawled on it, tied on a string round the leather bundle. He walked out into the street, stood in the mouth of an alleyway and cut the cord. He crouched down and gingerly tipped the contents into the muddy street. His stomach clenched and he gagged at the sight of the tattered, foul remains of a crow, its body slit from throat to crotch, the innards spilling out. Corbett swore, kicked the dead bird away and went back into the street.

Ranulf stayed behind. He examined the bird carefully and then the tattered, leather bag.

'Leave it, Ranulf!' Corbett called.

'A warning, Master?'

'Aye,' Corbett breathed. 'A warning.'

He stared across Broad Street. The crowd had thinned: it was well past noon: the Angelus bell had tolled and the cookshops and taverns were now full, the traders enjoying a slight lull in the day's frenetic activities. Corbett and Ranulf walked back towards Sparrow Hall. Now and again Ranulf would turn, staring up a narrow alleyway or glancing at the windows on either side, but he could detect no sign of pursuit. They entered the lane; the door to Sparrow Hall was closed so they crossed the street, went down an alleyway and into the yard of the hostelry. Norreys, assisted by some porters, was rolling great barrels out of a cart to be lowered through an open trap door into the cellar below.

'Provisions,' Norreys called out as they walked across. 'Never buy in an Oxford market, it's cheaper and fresher from outside.'

'Have you just returned?' Corbett asked.

'Oh yes, I left well before dawn,' Norreys replied, his face flushed and covered in a sheen of sweat. 'I've made a handsome profit.'

Corbett was about to continue when a group of students burst into the yard, led by David Ap Thomas. The Welshman, stripped to his waist, flexed his muscles and swung a thick quarterstaff in his hand, much to the admiration of his henchmen. Ap Thomas was well built, his chest and arms firm and muscular; he played with the staff as a child would a stick, skilfully and effortlessly turning it in his hands.

'An accomplished street brawler,' Corbett murmured.

'I'd ignore them and go in,' Norreys warned.

Corbett, however, just shook his head. The Welshman was now staring across at them. Corbett glimpsed the amulet round his neck.

'I think this is meant for our entertainment and amusement,' Ranulf muttered. 'As well as a warning.'

Suddenly the door was flung open and a garishly dressed figure came bounding out. One of Ap Thomas's henchman, clothed in black tattered rags, a yellow beak stuck to his face, with boots of the same colour on his bare legs. He, too, held a staff and, for a while, jumped about flailing his arms, cawing like the crow he was so aptly imitating.

'I'll cut the bastards' throats!' Ranulf said hoarsely.

'No, no,' Corbett warned. 'Let them have their laugh.'

The 'crow' stopped its antics and squared up to Ap Thomas, and both scholars began a quarterstaff fight. Corbett decided to ignore the insult. He stood, admiring the consummate skill of both men, Ap Thomas particularly. The quarterstaffs were thick ash-poles wielded with great force, and a blow to the head would send any man unconscious. Nevertheless, both Ap Thomas and his opponent were skilled fighters. The staffs whirled through the air, as both men ducked and leapt. Now and again the sticks would clash as a blow to the head or stomach was neatly blocked or there would be a jab at the legs in an attempt to tip the opposing fighters over by a vicious tap to the ankles. Ap Thomas fought quietly with only the occasional grunt as he stepped back, chest heaving, face and arms coated in sweat, waiting for his opponent to close in once again.

The fight lasted for at least ten minutes until Ap Thomas, swiftly moving his pole from hand to hand, stepped back and, with a resounding thwack to the shoulder, sent his opponent crashing to his knees.

Corbett and Ranulf walked across the yard, ignoring the raucous crowing. Ranulf would have gone back but Corbett plucked at his sleeve.

'As the good book says, Ranulf, "there's a time and place under heaven for everything: a time for planting and a time for plucking up, a time for war and a time for peace." – Now it's time to rouse Maltote, he's slept long enough!'

Ranulf shrugged and followed. He also recalled a phrase from the Old Testament: 'Eye for eye, tooth for tooth, life for life', but he decided to keep his own counsel.

They found Maltote had just woken up. He was sitting, scratching his blond, tousled hair. He blinked owlishly at them, then winced as he stretched out his leg.

'I came back here half asleep,' he explained, 'and caught my shin on a bucket Norreys had left out after he'd been cleaning the cellars.' Maltote limped to his feet. 'I heard the noise from below,' he said. 'What was happening?'

'Just fools playing,' Corbett retorted. 'They were born foolish and they'll die foolish!'

'Are we to eat?' Maltote asked.

'Not here,' Corbett said. 'Ranulf, take Maltote, explain what has happened and how careful he has to be. Go to Turl Lane, where there's a tavern, the Grey Goose. I might meet you there after I've visited the Hall.'

They went downstairs into the lane. A whore, her face painted so white the plaster was cracking, flounced by, shaking her dirty, tattered skirts at them. In one hand she held her red wig, in the other a pet weasel tied by a piece of string wrapped round her wrist. She grinned at them in a display of yellow, cracked teeth but then turned, cursing in a string of filthy oaths, as a dog came out of an alleyway snapping and snarling at her pet. Whilst Ranulf and Maltote helped to drive it away, Corbett crossed and knocked at the door of Sparrow Hall. A servitor let him in. Corbett explained why he was there and the man took him upstairs to Churchley's chamber. Master Aylric was sitting at his desk beneath an open window, watching the flame of a candle burn lower. He rose as Corbett entered, hiding his irritation beneath a false smile.

'How does fire burn?' he asked, grasping Corbett's hand. 'Why does wax burn quicker? Why is it more amenable to fire than wood or iron?'

'It depends on its properties,' Corbett replied, quoting from Aristotle.

'Yes, but why?' Churchley asked, waving him to a stool.

'It's about natural properties I have come.' Corbett abruptly changed the conversation. 'Master Aylric,' he continued. 'You are a physician?'

'Yes, but I'm more of a student of the natural world,' Churchley teased back, his narrow face becoming suspicious.

'But you dispense physic here?'

'Oh yes.'

'And you have a dispensary? A store of herbs and potions?'

'Of course,' came the guarded reply. 'It's further down the passageway, but it's under lock and key.'

'I'll come to the point,' Corbett said briskly. 'If you wished to poison someone, Master Aylric – it's a question, not an accusation – you wouldn't, surely, buy it from an apothecary in the city?'

Churchley shook his head. 'That could be traced,' he replied. 'One would be remembered. I buy from an apothecary in Hog Lane,' he explained, 'and all my purchases are carefully noted.'

'You never gather the herbs yourself?'

'In Oxford?' Churchley scoffed. 'Oh, you might find some camomile out in Christchurch Meadows but, Sir Hugh, I am a busy Master. I am not some old woman who spends her days browsing in the woods like a cow.'

'Exactly,' Corbett replied. 'And the same goes for the assassin who killed Passerel and Langton.'

Churchley sat back in his chair. 'I follow your drift, Sir Hugh. You think the poisons were taken from the dispensary here, yet that would be noticed. The poisons are all held in jars carefully measured. It's not that we expect to be poisoned in our beds,' he continued, 'but a substance like white arsenic is costly. Come, I'll show you.'

He took a bunch of keys from a hook on the wall and led Corbett to a door further down the gallery. He unlocked it and they went in. The room was dark. Churchley struck a tinder and lit the six-branched candelabra on the small table. The air was thick with different smells, some fragrant, others acrid. Three walls of the chamber were covered in shelves. Each bore different pots, cups or jars with its own contents carefully marked. On the left were herbs: spongecap, sweet violet, thyme, hazelwitch, water grass, even some basil, but others, on the right, Corbett recognised as more deadly potions such as henbane and belladonna. Churchley took down a jar, an earthenware pot with a lid. The tag pasted to its side showed it to be white arsenic. Churchley put on a pair of soft kid gloves lying on the table. He took off the stopper and held the pot up against the candlelight. Corbett noted how the jar was measured in half ounces.

'You see,' Churchley explained. 'There are eight and a half ounces here.' He opened a calf-skin tome lying on the table. 'Sometimes it is dispensed,' he continued, 'in very small doses for stomach complaints and I have given some to Norreys as it can be used as a powerful astringent for cleansing. But as you see, eight and a half ounces still remain.'

Corbett picked up the pot and sniffed.

'Be careful,' Churchley warned. 'Those skilled in herbal lore say it should be handled wisely.'

Corbett sifted through the pot, noticing how the powder at the top seemed finer than that lying underneath. Churchley handed him a horn spoon and Corbett shook some of the fine chalk-like substance into it. Churchley stopped his protests and watched quietly, his face rather worried.

'You are thinking the same as I,' Corbett murmured. He scooped some of the powder on to the spoon. 'Master Churchley, I assure you, I am not skilled in physic.' Corbett held the powder up to his nose. 'But I think this is finely ground chalk or flour and no more deadly.'

Churchley almost snatched the spoon out of his hand and, plucking up courage, he dabbed at the powder and put some on the tip of his tongue. He then took a rag and wiped his mouth.

'It's finely ground flour!' he exclaimed.

'Who keeps the keys?' Corbett asked.

'Well, I do,' Churchley replied in a fluster. 'But, Sir Hugh, surely you do not suspect me?' He stepped out of the pool of light, as if he wished to hide in the shadows. 'There could be other keys,' he explained. 'And this is Sparrow Hall, we don't bolt and lock all our chambers. Ascham was an exception in that. Anyone could come into my chamber and take the keys. The Hall is often deserted.' His words came out in a rush.

'Someone came here,' Corbett replied, putting the spoon back on the table, 'and removed enough white arsenic to kill poor Langton. Someone who knew your system, Master Churchley.'

'Well, everybody does,' the man gabbled.

'He filled the jar with powder,' Corbett explained.

'But who?'

Corbett wiped his fingers on his cloak.

'I don't know, Master Churchley.' He waved round the room. 'But God knows what else is missing.' He stepped up close and saw the fear in Churchley's eyes. 'But I ask myself what else, Master Aylric, has been taken?' Corbett turned and walked to the door. 'If I was a Master of Sparrow Hall,' he called over his shoulder, 'I would be very careful what I ate and drank.'

Chapter 8

A worried Churchley locked the door of the store room and followed Corbett down the gallery.

'Sir Hugh,' he wailed. 'Are you saying we are all in danger?'

'Yes, yes, I am. I would strongly advise that you scrupulously search to see if any more powders are missing.'

Corbett paused at the top of the stairs. 'Who is acting as bursar after Passerel's death?'

'Well, I am.'

'Is it possible to sift through Ascham's and Passerel's belongings?'

Churchley pulled a face.

'I need to,' Corbett persisted. 'God knows, man, all our lives are at risk. I might find something there.'

Churchley, grumbling under his breath and anxious to get back to his herbs, led Corbett downstairs. They passed the small dining hall to the rear of the building. Churchley unlocked the door and led Corbett into a store room, a large vaulted chamber full of barrels with sheaves of parchment, ink, and vellum ranged along the shelves; further back stood buckets of sea coal and tuns of malmsey, wine and ale.

Churchley took Corbett over to a far corner. He unclasped two great chests.

'Passerel's and Ascham's possessions are here,' he declared. 'They had no relatives – or none to speak of. Once their wills have been approved by Chancery, I suppose all these items will be inherited by the college.'

Corbett nodded and knelt down beside the chests. He smiled as he recalled his own experience as a clerk of the Chancery court, having to travel to some manor house or abbey to approve a will or order the release of monies and goods. He began to sift through the belongings. Churchley mumbled something about other duties and left Corbett to his own devices. Once Churchley's footsteps faded away, Corbett realised how quiet the Hall had become. He controlled a shiver of unease and went across to close and bolt the door before returning to his task. He then searched both chests, sifting through clothes, belts, baldrics, a small calf-skin-covered Books of Hours, cups, mazers, pewter dishes and gilt-edged goblets that each man had collected over the years. Corbett was experienced enough to realise that what was not actually listed in Ascham's or Passerel's will would have already been removed. He was also sure the Bellman would have also scrutinised the dead men's possessions to confirm that nothing suspicious remained. Ascham's belongings provided little of interest and Corbett was about to give up on Passerel's when he found a small writing bag. He opened this and tossed the fragments and scraps of parchment it contained on to the floor. Some were blank, others scrawled with different lists of provisions or items of business. There was a roll listing the expenses Passerel had incurred in travelling to Dover. Another listed the salaries of servants in both the hostelry and Hall. A few were covered with graffiti: one in particular caught Corbett's attention. Passerel had scrawled the word '*Passera*', '*Passera*', many times.

'What is this?' Corbett murmured, recalling the message left by the dying Ascham. Was Passerel playing some pun on his name? Did '*Passera*' mean something? Corbett put the pieces of parchment back, tidied up both chests and pushed down the clasps. He went back into the hall and along the passageway to the library. The door was half open. Corbett pushed it aside and walked quietly in. The man seated at the table with his back to him was so engrossed in what he was reading that Corbett was beside him before he turned, the cowl falling back from his head, his hands moving quickly to cover what he was reading.

'Why, Master Appleston,' Corbett smiled his apologies. 'I did not mean to alarm you.'

Appleston closed the book quickly, turning on his stool to face Corbett.

'Sir Hugh, I was . . . er . . . well, you remember what Abelard said?'

'No, I am afraid I do not.'

'He said there was no better place to lose one's soul than in a book.'

Corbett held his hand up. 'In which case, Master Appleston, may I see the one you are so engrossed in?'

Appleston sighed and handed the book over. Corbett opened it, the stiff, parchment pages crackling as he turned them over.

'There's no need to act the inquisitor,' Appleston declared.

Corbett continued to turn the pages.

'I have always had an interest in the theories of de Montfort: "*Quod omnes tangent ab omnibus approbetur*".'

'What touches all should be approved by all,' Corbett translated. 'And why the interest?'

'Oh, I could lie,' Appleston replied, 'and say I am interested in political theory, but I am sure the court spies or city gossips have told you the truth already.' He stood up, pulling back his shoulders. 'My name is Appleston, which was my mother's name. She was a bailiff's daughter from one of de Montfort's manors. The great Earl, or so she told me, fell in love with her. I am their child.'

'And are you proud of that?' Corbett asked. He studied the square, sunburnt face, the laughter lines around the eyes and wondered if this man, in some way, was a fair reflection of his father. 'I asked a question.'

'Of course I am,' Appleston retorted, touching the sore on the corner of his mouth. 'Not a day goes by that I don't pray for the repose of my father's soul.'

'*Concedo*,' Corbett replied. 'He was a great man but he was also a traitor to his King.'

'*Voluntas Principis habet vigorem legis*,' Appleston quipped.

'No, I don't believe that,' Corbett retorted. 'Just because the King wants something does not mean it's law. I am not a theorist, Master Appleston, but I know the gospels: a man cannot have two masters – a realm cannot have two kings.'

'And if de Montfort had won?' Appleston asked.

'If de Montfort had won,' Corbett replied, 'and the Commons, together with the Lords Spiritual and Temporal, had offered him the crown, then I and thousands of others would have bent the knee. What concerns me, Master Appleston, is not de Montfort but the Bellman.'

'I am no traitor,' the Master replied. 'Although I have studied my father's writings since I was a boy.'

'How is it –' Corbett asked '– that a member of the de Montfort family is given a benefice here at Sparrow Hall? A college founded by de Montfort's enemy?'

'Because we all feel guilty.'

Master Alfred Tripham entered the library, a small folio under his arm.

'I have just returned from the schools,' Tripham explained. 'Master Churchley told me you might be here.'

Corbett bowed. 'You walk as quietly as a cat, Master Alfred.'

Tripham shrugged. 'Curiosity, Sir Hugh, always has a soft footfall.'

'You spoke of guilt?' Corbett asked.

'Ah, yes.' Tripham put the folio down on the table. 'That prick to the conscience, eh, Sir Hugh?' He looked round the library. 'Somewhere here, amongst these papers, there's a copy of Sir Henry Braose's will but I am too busy to search for it.' Tripham went and sat on a stool opposite Appleston. 'However, in his last years, Braose became melancholic. He often had dreams about that last dreadful fight at Evesham and how the King's knights desecrated de Montfort's body. Braose believed he should make reparation. He paid for hundreds of chantry Masses for the dead Earl's soul. When Leonard here applied for the post . . .'

'He knew immediately,' Appleston broke in. 'He took one look at my face, paled and sat down. He claimed he was seeing a ghost. I told him the truth,' Appleston continued. 'What was the use in denying it? If I had not told him, someone else would have.'

'And the post was offered to you?' Corbett asked.

'Yes, yes, it was, on one condition: I was to retain my mother's name.'

'We all have secrets.' Tripham laced his fingers together. 'I understand, Sir Hugh, that you have been through Ascham's possessions.' He smiled thinly. 'You are no fool, Corbett. I am sure you know that items have already been removed?'

Corbett stared back.

'You might wonder,' Tripham continued, 'why Ascham was so beloved of scholars like Ap Thomas and his cronies. What would an old man, an archivist and librarian, have in common with a group of rebellious hotheads?'

'Nothing seems what it should be here,' Corbett replied.

'And the same applies to Ascham!' Tripham snapped. 'Oh, he was venerable, amusing, a scholar but – like many of us –' he let his gaze fall away '– he had a weakness for handsome youths, for a narrow waist and firm thighs, rather than a lady's eyes or swelling bosom.'

'That is not uncommon,' Corbett declared.

'In Oxford it certainly isn't.' Tripham rubbed the side of his face. 'Ascham also hailed from the Welsh march – or rather Oswestry in Shropshire. He was skilled in pagan lore as well as knowledgeable about the traditions of the Welsh. He used all this knowledge to establish a close friendship with many of our young scholars.'

'So, naturally, his murder was ill received by many in the hostelry?'

'That's why they turned their anger against poor Passerel,' Churchley replied. 'He was their scapegoat.'

'Scapegoat?'

Tripham put his hands up his sleeves and leaned on the table.

'We know Passerel was innocent,' he replied. 'Ascham must have been killed when Passerel was miles away from Sparrow Hall. Ah, well!' Tripham got to his feet. 'And as for poor Appleston, surely it's not treason to study de Montfort's theories? After all –' he smiled thinly '– even the King himself has taken them as his own.' He gestured at Appleston. 'Come, let us dine together, I am sure Sir Hugh has other matters to pursue.'

'Oh, one other thing, Master Tripham?'

'Yes, Sir Hugh?'

'You talked about secrets. What is yours?'

'Oh, that's quite simple, master clerk. I did not like Sir Henry Braose, either his arrogance or his scrupulous doubts just before death. Nor do I like his waspish sister who should never have been allowed to stay at this Hall.'

'And Barnett?' Corbett asked.

'Ask him yourself!' Tripham snapped. 'Barnett has his own demons.'

Tripham opened the door, ushered Appleston out and slammed it behind him.

Corbett sighed and stared round the library. He remembered why he had come and went along the shelves looking for a Latin lexicon. At last he found one near the librarian's table. He pulled it out, sat down and found the place but groaned in disappointment. '*Passera*' was one of the Latin words for sparrow. Was that what Ascham had been trying to write? Was his death connected with Sparrow Hall itself? Or perhaps the dead bursar had simply been scrawling a passage in his own name? Corbett put his chin in his hands. His eye caught the small box of implements the librarian must have used. He pulled this over and went through the tawdry contents: a soft piece of samite, probably used as a duster, quills, ink-horn, pumice stone and small, silken finger-caps which Ascham would have used to turn pages. On a stone shelf beyond the desk, Corbett glimpsed a leather-bound ledger. He took and opened this: it was a record of which books had been borrowed from the shelves. Corbett searched for Ascham's name but there was nothing: the dead archivist probably had no need to borrow books from the room he constantly worked in.

Corbett closed the ledger, put the lexicon away and left the Hall.

The lane was now thronged with scholars and their hangers-on making their way down to the last lectures of the day. Corbett glanced across and glimpsed Barnett: the pompous Master was standing at the top of the alleyway talking animatedly to the same beggar Corbett had met. The clerk stepped back into a doorway and watched Barnett hand a coin over. The beggar fairly jumped with glee. Barnett leaned down and whispered in the man's ear; the fellow nodded and pushed himself off in his barrow. Corbett waited for the master to cross the lane and stepped out to block his path. Barnett seemed to ignore him but Corbett held his ground.

'You are well, Master?'

'Yes I am, clerk.'

'You seem out of sorts?'

'I do not like to be snooped and pried upon.'

'Master Barnett,' Corbett spread his hands, 'I merely watch you do good works, helping the lame, feeding the hungry...'

'Get out of my way!' Barnett snapped and, pushing by, opened the door to Sparrow Hall.

Corbett let him go and returned to his own chamber in the hostelry. He could tell, as soon as he opened the door, that someone had been there though, when he looked, nothing was missing. Corbett sat down at his table. He felt hungry but decided to wait until the evening to eat. He knew Ranulf and Maltote would soon return. He took out his quill and ink-horn and wrote a short letter to Maeve. He told her about his arrival in Oxford; how good it was to return to the place where he had studied as a youth, how both the city and University had changed. His quill sped across the page, telling her the usual lies he always told whenever he was in danger. At the end he wrote a short message for Eleanor, forming huge, round letters. He put the quill down and closed his eyes. At Leighton, Maeve would be in the kitchen supervising the maids for the evening meal or perhaps in the chancery office studying accounts or talking to bailiffs. And Eleanor? She would just have finished her afternoon sleep. Corbett heard a sound in the passage outside. He opened his eyes, quickly folded the letter and began to seal it. There was a knock on the door and Maltote and Ranulf came in.

'I thought you'd be joining us?' Maltote asked as he sat on the bed.

'I said I might do. I am not too hungry yet.'

'Then we should dine before we leave.'

'Leave?' Corbett asked.

'Tonight,' Ranulf replied. 'Maltote and I believe that our good friend David Ap Thomas and his henchmen will be leaving the city after dark.'

'How do you know?'

Ranulf grinned. 'This hostelry is a rabbit warren. You can hide in nooks and crannies and, when you are deep in the shadows, it is wonderful what you overhear.'

'You are sure?'

'As sure as I am that Maltote can ride a horse.'

Corbett handed the letter to Maltote. 'Then take this to Master Sheriff at the castle and ask him to send it to Lady Maeve at Leighton. Tell him I need his help and assistance on an urgent matter.'

Maltote put his boots on, grabbed his cloak and hobbled off. Corbett then told Ranulf what he had discovered on his visit to Sparrow Hall.

'Do you think Barnett,' Ranulf asked, 'is involved in the death of these beggars? I mean, he is a wealthy, flabby Master of the schools. Such men are not usually famous for their alms giving?'

'Perhaps. But what about Appleston and our Vice-Regent? Either man could be the Bellman. There again, the same could be said of our good friend David Ap Thomas.'

'What does concern me, Master,' Ranulf said, 'is the one question to which there appears to be no answer. Oxford is full of clerks –' he grinned '– such as ourselves, and scholars and students. Some of them come from abroad where their

135

lords and rulers are the enemies of our King. Others come from the Scottish march or Wales and have no great love either for our sovereign lord. There must be many who would love to be the Bellman?'

'And?'

'So why does the Bellman identify himself as living at Sparrow Hall?'

Corbett shook his head. 'I can't really answer that except to say the Bellman must hate the Hall.'

'Another question,' Ranulf continued, 'is that although we know the King is beside himself with fury at the Bellman's appearance, who else really cares about his proclamations?' Ranulf spread his hands. 'I agree that there must be people in Oxford, as there are in Cambridge or in Shrewsbury, who'd follow any madcap rebel but – today, forty years after de Montfort's death – what does the Bellman hope to achieve?'

'Are you saying that the King should just leave it alone?'

'In a way, yes,' Ranulf replied.

Corbett chewed the corner of his mouth.

'I hear what you say, Ranulf. It might be that the King was first advised that the antics of the Bellman were merely some scholar's prank and so that's why the murders took place. There was no real reason for them otherwise. How do we know Ascham or Passerel suspected the Bellman's identity? Perhaps he just killed them, as in some game of hazard, to raise the odds so that the King was forced to take notice? But again the question is, why?'

Ranulf got to his feet. 'I'm going across to the Hall,' he declared. 'Maltote will be some time hobbling to the castle and back. And, talking of hazard, I'll wager that he stops at the Sheriff's stables to have a look at the horses.'

'What do you want from the Hall?' Corbett asked.

'A book,' Ranulf replied abruptly, becoming offhand.

'What book, Ranulf?'

'The . . .' Ranulf stammered.

'Oh, for the love of God!' Corbett exclaimed.

'*The Confessions of St Augustine*,' Ranulf replied in a rush.

'Augustine of Hippo? What interest do you have in him?'

Ranulf sighed in exasperation and leaned against the door.

'When I was at Leighton Manor, Master, I often spoke to Father Luke. He heard my confession and told me about St Augustine.' Ranulf closed his eyes. 'Father Luke gave me a quotation from the *Confessions*: "Late have I loved thee, Lord." And again: "Our hearts are never at peace until they are at rest with Thee." They are the most beautiful words I've ever heard.' Ranulf opened his eyes.

Corbett sat, mouth open, eyes staring.

'I suppose you think it's funny?' Ranulf retorted.

Corbett just shook his head. 'Can I ask why?' he stuttered.

'As a young man,' Ranulf answered, 'Augustine was a scapegrace, a rascal, who consorted with whores and courtesans. Father Luke told me he even had an illegitimate son. But then he converted, and became a priest and a bishop.'

Corbett nodded, fascinated. 'And you think you can do the same?'

'Don't laugh at me, Master.'

'Ranulf, I have cursed you, I have complained about you, I have prayed for you, I have even had the urge to shake you warmly by the neck,' Corbett replied, 'but I have never laughed at you and I never will.'

His manservant let his arms fall to his sides.

'During our long stay at Leighton,' he stammered, not meeting Corbett's eyes, 'I started to think about the future.'

'And you wish to become a priest?' Corbett asked.

Ranulf nodded. 'If that's what it means . . .'

'Means to do what?'

'I am not too sure, Master.'

'But you are Ranulf-atte-Newgate,' Corbett exclaimed. 'The terror of maidens from Dover to Berwick. A street fighting man! My bullyboy!'

'So was Augustine,' Ranulf replied hotly. 'So was Thomas à Beckett. And Father Luke said that, even amongst Jesus's followers, there was a knife man.'

Corbett held his hand up. 'Ranulf, God forgive me, I don't doubt what you say but you must admit it comes as a surprise.'

'Good!' Ranulf lifted the latch. 'Father Luke said that when Augustine changed, it surprised everyone.' He opened the door and went out.

Corbett sat as if poleaxed. 'Ranulf-atte-Newgate!' he whispered. 'Who has lifted more petticoats than I have had hot dinners.'

Corbett closed his eyes and tried to think of Ranulf as a priest. At first he found it amusing but, the more he thought, the less surprised he became. Corbett lay down on the bed and stared up at the ceiling, wondering about the vagaries of the human heart. Ranulf was no longer a stripling. He was a man with a mind of his own and a steely determination to do what he wanted. He'd applied himself ruthlessly to his studies and his recent questions about the doings at Sparrow Hall showed a sharp mind as well as a quick wit. Somehow, Corbett realised, Ranulf's questions lay at the heart of the mystery. Why was the Bellman doing what he did? And why proclaim himself as a Master or scholar at Sparrow Hall?

He dozed for a while. When Ranulf returned, the manservant pushed open the door.

'The Vice-Regent gave me a copy,' he called in.

138

'Good,' Corbett murmured.

A short while afterwards Maltote limped back.

'The Sheriff will see you now,' he declared, still nursing his bruised shin. 'Oh, by the way, Master, they've got some fine horses in the castle stables.'

'Yes, yes, I'm sure they have.' Corbett swung his legs off the bed, put his war belt on and went to tell his companions to do the same.

They took their cloaks and walked out into the lane. They crossed Broad Street, taking the road which led up to the castle. At the corner of New Hall Street and Bocardo Lane they had to stop: the street markets and shops were closing. Peasants pushed handcarts and barrows, the wealthier ones leading ox-drawn carts, out towards the city gates. All had stopped before the open space before the gallows; a hideous, three-branched scaffold against which ladders had been placed. Bailiffs were tightening nooses round the necks of three felons whilst the town crier loudly proclaimed 'the horrible homicides, depredations and rapes of which these three had been found guilty'. He finished bawling and clapped three times. The red-masked executioners slid down the ladders as nimble as monkeys. The ladders were pulled away and all three felons danced and jerked at the end of their ropes. A collective sigh rose from the crowd, as a bailiff shouted that the King's justice had been done. Corbett glanced away. The crowd dispersed and they were allowed through up a lane that skirted the old city wall and led into the castle. The bailey was deserted. A groom told them the garrison was preparing for the evening meal. Only a little boy with a chicken under his arm staggered about, the bird squawking raucously. The stables and outhouses were quiet as the groom led them across and up outside stone stairs into the castle solar. This was a soldier's room: the walls whitewashed, the roof beams blackened by numerous fires. A few shields and rusting swords hung on either side of a battered crucifix, placed slightly askew, whilst the rushes on the floor were dry and crisp, and smelt rather stale.

Bullock was sitting in a window seat with a large, beautiful peregrine falcon on his wrist, its jesses tinkling like bells. The Sheriff was tenderly feeding it succulent pieces of meat; every so often he would murmur quietly to the bird, stroking the ruffled plumage under its throat.

'A beautiful bird, Master Sheriff!'

'I love hawks,' Bullock replied. 'Corbett, when I see this peregrine fly I truly believe in God and all his works. There, there, Raptor.' He spoke softly to the bird. 'Tomorrow, perhaps, amongst the marshes.'

Bullock sighed, got up and put the falcon back on its perch. He then led Corbett and his companions into a small adjoining chamber where he offered them stools whilst he leaned against the table, looking down at them.

'Your messenger said you needed my assistance?'

Corbett explained what Ranulf had told him. Bullock rubbed his chin.

'What do you want me to do?'

'Ideally, Sir Walter, I would like a cordon of steel around Sparrow Hall and the hostelry. On second thoughts—' Corbett paused. 'Perhaps just around the Hall itself; at least it will keep the Bellman under careful surveillance.'

'And the hostelry?'

'As I said, Ap Thomas is a leader of a coven. He may, or may not, be connected with the murder of the beggar men. If he leaves Oxford tonight, and we try to follow him, he will lead us a merry dance like some will-o'-the-wisp.'

Sit Walter sighed and loosened the belt round his ponderous girth.

'The King has arrived at Woodstock,' he explained. 'Half of my garrison has gone there. The few horsemen I have will be sent out to patrol the roads. I can't help you with Sparrow Hall. It has a garden, windows, postern gates and rear doors. It would take a small army to watch every bolt hole.' He sensed Corbett's anger. 'However,' Bullock added hastily, 'as regards Master David Ap Thomas, we have some verderers attached to the castle garrison. Sturdy buggers who like nothing better than a brawl – their leader is just the man to help.'

And, without a further word, Bullock left. He was gone for some time and when he returned a small, nut-brown man, dressed in shabby Lincoln green, accompanied him. The fellow entered the room so quietly Corbett hardly knew he was there.

'Let me introduce Boletus,' Sir Walter said. 'They call him that because it's the Latin for mushroom.'

Boletus stared unblinkingly at Corbett who noticed that the verderer had no eyelashes.

'Boletus patrols the royal hunt runs in the forest between here and Woodstock. He can move amongst the trees as quietly and as swiftly as a sunbeam. Isn't that right, Boletus?'

'I was born in the forest,' the verderer replied, his voice hardly above a whisper. 'The trees are my friends. Better a wooded glade, eh, than the dirty streets of the city?'

'Boletus,' Bullock explained, 'will watch Sparrow hostelry like a hawk. If David Ap Thomas and his henchmen leave, and I suspect they will after dark, Boletus will pursue like the Angel of Death and come back to inform us. In the meantime –' the Sheriff smacked his lips '– I intend to fortify the inner man. Sir Hugh, you are welcome to join me.'

Corbett excused himself but Ranulf and Maltote followed the Sheriff and his sinister companion out of the room. Corbett waited until they had gone. He would have liked to sleep, the night would be a long one, but he could not get Barnett's meeting with that beggar out of his mind. He left the castle and made his way through the emptying streets and alleyways towards St Osyth's Hospital. The sun was beginning to set: houses and shops were now closing, lamps being lit and hung on the hooks outside each door. The dun-collectors were out with their stinking carts, continuing their unequal battle to clear the sewers and sweep up the offal and mounds of rubbish left after a day's trading. The taverns were beginning to fill and, because the evening air was warm, windows and doors were flung open. A young man was singing the '*Flete Viri*' which Corbett recognised as a lament on the death of William the Norman. Further down, on the steps of a church, a small choir sweetly carolled Goliard songs and Corbett recognised his favourite, '*Iam Dulcis Amica*', so he stayed and listened before walking on.

On the corner of a street, just opposite the hospital, four scholars danced wildly to the sound of rebec and pipe. Corbett dropped a coin into their dish and crossed the street and into the main gateway of St Osyth's. The yard was packed with beggars thronging there for an evening meal of broth, rye bread and a stoup of watered wine. Brother Angelo stood in the centre shouting orders, greeting many of the beggars by name. He glimpsed Corbett and his smile faded.

'I am sorry, Brother,' Corbett apologised. 'I appreciate you are busy so I'll be blunt. Do you know Master Barnett of Sparrow Hall?'

'Why, yes.' Angelo turned to roar at a beggar who had taken two pieces of bread. 'Put that back, Ragman! You greedy little bugger!'

Ragman jumped, dropped the offending piece of bread and scurried off.

'Do you want something to eat, Corbett? You look pale-faced.'

'No, just information about Barnett.'

'Well, he's a strange one,' Brother Angelo replied. 'He likes the wine and the wenches, does Master Barnett, yet he also comes here, and brings money for the hospital. Sometimes he helps with the distribution of food. Some of the beggars talk highly of him, a kindly man.'

'Don't you think it's strange?' Corbett asked.

'Yes, on reflection, I suppose I do,' Brother Angelo replied. 'But, there again, he does no harm and who am I to refuse any help? And that's all I know.'

Corbett prepared to leave.

'Master clerk!'

Corbett came back. Brother Angelo's eyes had grown soft.

'Sir Hugh, you probably think I am just a suspicious Franciscan. However, I have heard the confessions of many men, and sometimes, when I shrive them, I detect an air of menace. Last time you were here, I felt that.'

'You mean from us, Brother?'

The Franciscan shook his head. 'No, not the stink of sin. More of danger.' He clasped Corbett's shoulder. 'Be careful.' Brother Angelo smiled. 'Keep your faith – and your backs to the wall!'

Chapter 9

Corbett, the friar's dire warning still chilling him, returned to the castle. Ranulf and Maltote were playing a desultory game of dice, Ranulf showing Maltote the finer points of cheating. Corbett sat in a window seat. He daydreamed about Leighton and quietly prayed that Maeve would be well. He felt agitated so he made his way up to the castle chapel, a simple, narrow chamber with the wooden altar at the far end. In a niche to the left of this was a statue of the Virgin and Child; with Mary smiling, showed the Baby Jesus to an oblivious world. Corbett took a taper and lit one of the candles. He knelt and said a Pater Noster, an Ave Maria and the Gloria. He heard Ranulf calling his name so he hurried down. Bullock was there with Boletus jumping in the air like a frog beside him. The Sheriff waved Corbett back into the solar.

'Shut up!' Sir Walter yelled at the verderer. 'Shut up and stop dancing about!'

Ranulf and Maltote gathered round.

'Your information was correct, Sir Hugh.' Bullock's face widened into a smile. 'I'm going to enjoy this. Master David Ap Thomas and his henchmen have left the city by stealth. They've broken the curfew, climbed over part of the wall and made their way to the forest south-west of the city.'

'Tell him the rest! Tell him the rest!' Boletus screeched.

'They have company,' the Sheriff continued, glaring at his

verderer. 'They are accompanied by a cross-biter, a pimp called Vardel, and half a dozen whores from a city brothel.'

'And I know where they are!' Boletus yelled triumphantly.

'Get your cloaks!' Bullock ordered. 'Boletus, I want four of your companions, six hobelars, fully armed, and about ten archers. We'll go by foot.'

A short while later the party of armed men, Boletus running ahead like a hunting dog, left the castle. As they tramped through the narrow streets, the beggars and tricksters saw the glint of chain mail, heard the clash of sword and drew back into the alleyways. Tavern doors were abruptly shut. Whores, their bright orange wigs like beacons in the darkness, saw them coming and fled like the wind. Now and again a shutter would open wide and a voice shouted abuse. Bullock, thoroughly enjoying himself, bawled back.

They left the city by a postern gate, following a dry, dusty path out past a straggling line of cottages and vegetable gardens. The darkness gathered round them. Soon all the noise and clamour of the city was left behind. The evening was cool, the sky clear and there was little sound, except the clink of arms or the odd flurry of some animal in the hedgerow or ditch. Some of the soldiers began to complain, but when Bullock turned, fist raised, they fell silent. At length they left the path and followed a trackway into the forest. The trees closed round them. The sounds of the forest became more intense: the hoot of a screech owl, the cry of a night hawk, quick thrusting rustles from the undergrowth. Corbett and Ranulf, with Maltote hobbling behind them, tried to keep up with Bullock's striding gait. The forest grew deeper, branches extending like stark fingers to catch the ghostly moonlight. Boletus came hopping back, moving soundlessly. He held his hand up and whispered to

Bullock who ordered his soldiers to fan out. The line of men moved forward slowly. Corbett sniffed the air. He smelt wood smoke, the rather unsavoury smell of burning meat, and glimpsed the glow of fire amongst the trees. The beat of a drum came faintly through the night air. As they drew closer, the trees thinned, the ground dipped and they looked down into a glade. Corbett watched fascinated as Bullock whispered rebukes to his men who were beginning to laugh and make obscene remarks. The glade was full of dancing, naked figures. Four fires had been lit and around these naked men and women cavorted. The musicians couldn't be seen, though Corbett glimpsed a group cooking meats over another fire at the far end of the glade.

'It's like some mummers' play,' Ranulf whispered.

'In God's name, what is that?'

A cowled, masked figure walked forward, dressed in a grey robe on which had been painted a large human eye.

'Master,' Ranulf had to stop himself laughing, 'I don't think this is what we thought it was.'

Beside Corbett, Bullock rose, drawing his sword.

'I don't give a bugger!' he said. 'I'm hungry: there's wine down there and some of those young ladies are very attractive.'

Bullock began to run forward, his men following. They were into the glade before the dancing stopped.

Corbett, who had motioned Ranulf and Maltote to stay behind, realised Bullock had underestimated his opponents. The dancers may have been drunk and caught unawares but they were well armed. Swords and daggers were drawn, staves produced and the glade became a battleground. Even the women joined in: Corbett saw one burly lady, a quarterstaff in her hand, send two of Bullock's men crashing to the ground.

'I suppose we had better help,' Ranulf whispered.

Corbett reluctantly agreed. However, by the time they

had reached the glade, the masked figure had been knocked to the ground and his crudely fashioned satyr mask pulled off his face. David Ap Thomas glared up at Corbett.

'You bloody, snooping crow!'

He vainly kicked out at the two archers now lashing his thumbs together behind his back.

All round them the sound of fighting began to die. There were about fourteen scholars and two whores; the rest, including the pimp Vardel, having decided that discretion was the better part of valour, had fled deeper into the forest. Some of Bullock's men were complaining of cuts and bruises. Nevertheless, they helped themselves to roasted strips of meat and drank greedily from the jugs of wine. Once they were finished, they led their prisoners off in single file back along the forest path.

Bullock was a cruel captor. Most of the prisoners had been allowed to don some form of dress but boots and shoes had been thrown into a bag and the night air was riven by curses, oaths and a stream of filthy abuse from the ladies of the town. The soldiers shoved and taunted back. Ap Thomas was loud in his protests.

'There is no law against it!' he cried.

'What exactly were you doing?' Corbett asked.

'Oh, kiss the Devil's arse!' Ap Thomas snarled.

They entered Oxford by a postern gate and made their way up into the castle. Bullock, now full of himself and eager to tell the University authorities of what he had found, declared they were all his prisoners and must spend time in the castle dungeon. The students, led by Ap Thomas, loudly protested; the whores, more pragmatic, began to smile and wink at their captors. Bullock led his line of prisoners away. Corbett and his companions watched them go, listening to the shouts fade on the night air, before they made their way back to Sparrow Hall.

The doorkeeper let them into the hostelry, loudly grumbling at the late hour. Corbett ignored him. He knew the fellow had probably been bribed by Ap Thomas to wait up to let the scholars back in so he let the man remain innocent of what had happened.

Once back in Corbett's chamber, Ranulf washed and bathed the bruise on his right hand. Maltote sat on the floor, nursing his shin, grumbling at how the night march had aggravated the injury.

'It was a waste of time,' Corbett declared, pulling off his cloak and unbuckling his war belt. 'Our good friend Ap Thomas is probably guilty of nothing more than being involved in petty pagan rites which are, I suppose, as good an excuse as any for debauchery.'

'There was nothing remarkable in the glade,' Ranulf remarked. 'Bread, wine, some meat: a yellowing skull which probably belonged to someone who was long in his grave when my grandfather was born.' He shook his head. 'And I thought Ap Thomas might have been guilty of more serious crimes.'

'I wonder?' Corbett sat down on the bed. 'I wonder if the Bellman knows what happened tonight because, if he does, I think he'll strike. He knows we are tired and weary after our wild-goose chase. Our good Sheriff, on the other hand, will spend the night thoroughly enjoying himself interrogating Ap Thomas and the other scholars whom he detests.'

'Shouldn't we watch Sparrow Hall?' Ranulf asked. 'Or, at least, the alleyways at the back? See who comes and goes? We could draw lots,' he suggested.

'I'll go.' Maltote, face pulled long, clambered to his feet.

'But your ankle?' Corbett said.

'I slept well this morning,' Maltote replied. 'And I don't think I can sleep now, not with this pain. What hour do you think it is?'

149

'About midnight, perhaps a little earlier.'

'I'll take the first watch.'

Maltote hobbled out of the room, his war belt slung over his shoulder.

'Should one of us go with him?' Ranulf asked.

'He'll be safe,' Corbett replied. 'Go after him, Ranulf. Tell him to stand and watch, keeping deep in the shadows and, if he gets tired, to return. Our doorkeeper will think he is one of Ap Thomas's companions.'

Ranulf left and Corbett lay down on the bed. He meant to keep awake but his eyes grew heavy and he slipped into a dreamless sleep.

Ranulf returned and pulled off his master's boots. He placed the cloak over him, blew out the candle and went to his own chamber. He struck a tinder, the meagre oil lamp flaring into light, and opened the *Confessions of St Augustine*.

'Thou has made us, O Lord, for Thyself and our hearts can find no rest until they rest with Thee.'

Ranulf closed his eyes. He would remember that. He would quote it the next time that Master Long Face entertained some pompous prelate or knowledgeable priest. Oh yes, everyone would shake their heads in silent wonderment at the change in Ranulf-atte-Newgate.

In the alleyway behind Sparrow Hall, Maltote squatted and wondered how long Sir Hugh would keep them in Oxford. Unlike Ranulf, Maltote could have lived and died at Leighton. Up at dawn, Maltote would happily stay in the stables until darkness fell and he dropped with exhaustion. He glanced up at the dark mass of Sparrow Hall and saw the faint pinpricks of candlelight. The wall around the hall garden was high and Maltote kept his eye on the postern gate. If anyone left, he was certain it would be through that door. A hunting cat slipped by. Maltote watched it climb the midden-heap next to the wall: a furry shape shot out, and both that and the cat disappeared into the darkness.

Maltote stared up at the stars and grinned. He'd enjoyed this night's foray into the forest. He could not believe his eyes at the sight of some of those ladies! Maltote licked his lips. He'd not told even Ranulf that he was still a virgin. He'd once loved a girl, a miller's daughter, who lived near Leighton Manor, and he'd taken some flowers to her but she had laughed when Maltote became red-faced and tongue-tied. Perhaps, when he returned, he'd go and visit her again? Maltote heard a sound and opened his eyes. The postern door was still firmly shut. He got to his feet, narrowing his eyes at the dark shape shuffling towards him: his hand fell to the dagger on his belt.

'Who's there? Who are you?' Maltote called.

A clack dish rattled, and Maltote relaxed. The beggar drew near, dish out. Maltote fished in his purse – he had a coin somewhere. Perhaps the man would be company to while away the night hours? He looked up and the dish hit him straight in the face. Maltote staggered back, hitting his head against the wall. He lurched forward but his assailant was too quick, the dagger came up, sharp and cruel, ripping into Maltote's belly. The groom screamed at the pain, one hand clutching his stomach, the other clawing the air. He fell, his head smashing against the cobbles, as the beggar shuffled off into the darkness.

The next morning Corbett was awakened by a pounding on the door. He pulled it open, to find Norreys standing there. Ranulf also came out of his room, tugging his boots on.

'Sir Hugh!' Norreys swallowed hard. 'You have got to come to the Hall, it's Maltote!'

151

Corbett cursed.

'He never came back,' Ranulf groaned. 'I was supposed to take over.'

'He's dying,' Norreys declared. 'Sir Hugh, your servant is dying. Master Churchley has him in the infirmary but there's nothing we can do.'

Corbett gaped at him. He crossed his arms against the cold he felt. Ranulf, however, had already pushed by them, pounding down the stairs. Corbett put his boots on, grabbed his cloak and went down with Norreys across the lane to Sparrow Hall.

Churchley was waiting for them in the parlour, the other Masters grouped around him. He opened his mouth to explain but then beckoned at them to follow and led them up the stairs to a white-washed chamber. Maltote was lying on a bed just inside the door. His face was as white as the sheet tucked under his chin, his eyes were half-closed and a faint trickle of blood snaked out of the corner of his mouth. Ranulf pulled the blankets down and groaned at the sight of the soggy, bloody mess of bandages Churchley had tied round Maltote's stomach.

'I did my best,' the physician explained.

Maltote turned, his eyes flickering open. He spluttered, his arms flailing feebly beside him. Corbett leaned down to hear the words he gasped.

'I'm thirsty. Master, the pain . . .'

'Who did it?' Corbett asked.

'The beggar. No face. Silent as a shadow.'

Corbett fought back the tears of rage.

'I'm dying, aren't I?'

Corbett grabbed Maltote's hand, which was icy cold to the touch.

'Don't lie,' Maltote whispered. 'I am not frightened or, at least, not yet.' His face tightened as a spasm of pain caught him.

'I have given him an opiate,' Churchley declared. He beckoned Corbett away from the bed. 'Sir Hugh, you must have seen such belly wounds on battlefields. The opiate soon wears off and when it does the pain will be terrible and he'll have a raging thirst.'

'Is there anything you can do?'

Churchley shook his head. 'Sir Hugh, I am a physician not a miracle worker. He will literally bleed to death and do so in great agony.'

Corbett closed his eyes, breathing in slowly. He went back to Maltote.

'Do you want a priest?' he asked.

Maltote struggled to answer. 'Father Luke shrived me before I left Leighton but if I could have the sacrament?'

Tripham came into the room. 'Sir Hugh, I apologise for disturbing you but there's a royal messenger waiting for you at the hostelry with messages from the King at Woodstock. I have already sent for Father Vincent,' he added. 'He's on his way.'

Corbett went back to the bed. He squeezed Maltote's hand and kissed him gently on the forehead. He then wiped the tears from his own face and hurried out, whispering at Ranulf to stay.

A short while later Father Vincent arrived, a little boy walking in front of him carrying a lighted candle and bell. Over the priest's shoulders hung a gold-fringed silver cope with an *Agnus Dei* in the centre. Churchley left the room but Ranulf remained. The service was short: Father Vincent gave Maltote the final absolution and administered the small Eucharistic wafer from a silver pyx. He then took a golden phial out of his pocket and anointed with holy oil Maltote's eyes, mouth, hands, chest and feet. The little boy stood like a waxen statue. The priest never even looked at Ranulf but, immersed in the sombre liturgy for the dying, finished the anointing. Afterwards he knelt by the bed and recited the *De Profundis*: 'Out of the depths, O Lord, have I cried unto Thee.'

Ranulf found himself echoing the words. Only when this was finished did Father Vincent turn and acknowledge Ranulf's presence.

'I am sorry.' He grasped Ranulf's hand and looked back at the bed where Maltote, the opiate now wearing off, was beginning to twist and turn in pain. 'Is there anything more I can do?'

Ranulf blinked back his own tears. He took off his boot and pulled out a gold piece from the hidden flap.

'Say Masses for him,' Ranulf whispered. 'Say Masses until Michaelmas.'

The priest would have given the coin back but Ranulf insisted he took it.

Father Vincent, with the little boy ringing his small hand-bell, made his way down the passageway and out of the hall. Others came – Appleston and Dame Mathilda – but Ranulf turned them away, bolting the door behind them. He crouched by the bed and grasped Maltote's hand. The groom turned. Ranulf's heart lurched at the agony in the cornflower-blue eyes.

'Will there be horses in heaven?' Maltote asked.

'Don't be stupid!' Ranulf replied hoarsely. 'Of course there will be!'

Maltote opened his mouth to laugh but the pain was too intense, and his body arched.

'I'm frightened, Ranulf. In Scotland . . . remember?' he gasped. 'That archer who had a spear thrust in the belly? He took days to die!'

'I'm here,' Ranulf replied.

He pulled back the blankets. Maltote's stomach was now a vast red puddle, blood soaking into the sheets and mattress beneath. Ranulf closed his eyes. He recalled one of Augustine's maxims, when the philosopher had been quoting from the Gospels: 'Judge all others, treat all others as you would want them to judge and treat you.' Ranulf got up, walked to the door and beckoned Churchley in.

'You are a physician, Master Aylric,' Ranulf whispered. 'I'll be blunt. I have heard of apothecaries who can distil a powder which gives eternal sleep.'

Churchley glanced at Maltote who was now thrashing about on the bed, moaning softly.

'I can't do that!' he declared.

'I can,' Ranulf retorted. 'There's no dignity in bleeding to death.' Ranulf's hand fell to his dagger.

'Don't threaten me!' Churchley snapped.

'I never make threats, only promises!' Ranulf snarled. He took off his boot, plucked out a gold piece and pressed this into the Master's hand. 'I want you to bring it now!' he ordered. 'A small cup of wine and the powder I need. I know you must have it.'

Churchley was about to refuse but then he scuttled off. Ranulf went back and knelt by the bed, holding Maltote's hand, making soothing noises as he would to a child. Churchley returned, a pewter cup in one hand, a small pouch in the other.

'No more than a sprinkling,' Churchley whispered. He thrust both into Ranulf's hand and fled from the room.

Ranulf bolted the door. He opened the pouch and poured half the contents into the wine, swirling it round. He went back to the bed and lifted Maltote up by the shoulders.

'Don't say anything,' Ranulf murmured. 'Just drink.'

He put the cup to Maltote's lips. Maltote sipped, coughing and retching. Ranulf brought the cup back and his friend drank greedily. Ranulf lowered him back on the bed. Maltote grinned weakly.

'I know what you have done,' he whispered. 'And I would have done the same. Ranulf...?' he paused, tightening his lips. 'Ranulf, yesterday when I went to the castle...' he gasped. 'I passed a group of scholars... They were arguing... one of them asked if there was a divine intelligence?'

'People without intelligence always ask that,' Ranulf replied smoothly.

He bent down and stroked Maltote's cheek. The young man's eyes were already becoming glazed, his face slack. Maltote grasped Ranulf's hand and held it. Maltote shuddered once and closed his eyes, his face turned away and his jaw fell slack. Ranulf leaned down and felt for the blood pulse in his neck but it was gone. He turned Maltote's face, kissed him on the brow and then pulled the blanket up over the corpse.

'God speed you, Ralph Maltote,' he prayed. 'May the angels welcome you into Paradise. I hope there is a divine intelligence,' he added bitterly, 'because there's bugger all down here!'

For a while Ranulf knelt by the bed and tried to pray but found it impossible to concentrate. He kept remembering Maltote grooming the horses and his friend's total inability to handle a weapon without hurting himself. He cried for a while and realised this was the first time he had done so since the city bailiffs had tossed his mother's corpse into the burial pits near Charterhouse. Ranulf dried his eyes. He emptied the rest of the wine into the rushes, put the small bag of powder into his wallet and left the chamber.

Ranulf thrust the cup into Churchley's hand.

'He's dead. Now, listen!' He snapped his fingers at Tripham. 'I speak for Sir Hugh Corbett and the King. I don't want Maltote buried here, not in this bloody cesspit! I want his body embalmed, placed in a proper coffin and sent back to Leighton Manor. The Lady Maeve will take care of it.'

'That will cost money,' Tripham bleated.

'I don't give a fig!' Ranulf retorted. 'Send the bill to me. I'll pay whatever you ask. Leave the body for a while: Sir Hugh will wish to pay his respects.'

Ranulf left the hall and crossed the lane. Corbett was in the yard talking to a horseman wearing the royal livery. The fellow was splattered in mud and dust from head to toe. Corbett took one look at Ranulf's face and dismissed the courier, telling him that Norreys would give him refreshment and look after his horse.

'Maltote's gone, hasn't he?'

Ranulf nodded. Corbett wiped his eyes.

'God rest him.' He thrust the letters he was holding into Ranulf's hand. 'I'll meet you in my room.'

Corbett went across to the Hall. He suspected, and secretly agreed with, what Ranulf had done. For a few minutes he knelt by the corpse and said his own requiem, Tripham and Churchley standing at the door behind him. Corbett crossed himself and rose. He put one hand on the crucifix above the bed and the other on Maltote's brow.

'I swear by the living God,' he declared, 'here, in the presence of Christ and of he who was slain, that whoever did this will be brought to justice and suffer the full rigours of the law!'

'Your manservant has already given us orders on what to do with the corpse,' Tripham broke in, now terrified by the harsh, white face of this powerful, royal clerk.

'Do what he asked you!' Corbett snapped.

He pushed by them and returned to Ranulf in his chamber at the hostelry. Neither talked about what had happened. Instead, Corbett opened the letters he had received from the King and Maeve.

'And there's one from Simon for you.'

He handed Ranulf a large, square parchment sealed in the centre with a blob of red wax.

Corbett opened his letters. The message from the King was predictable. He had arrived at Woodstock with his entourage and would wait there until his 'good clerk' had resolved matters to his satisfaction. The second letter was from Maeve. Corbett sat down at the table and studied it carefully. Most of it was chatter about the manor, the prospect of a good harvest and the depredations of certain poachers who had been raiding the stew pond. Maeve then went on to say how both she and Eleanor missed him and how Uncle Morgan was still full of the King's visit.

'I wish he would not tease Eleanor,' she wrote, 'with his stories about Wales and the way we Welsh terrified our enemies by displaying heads taken in battle. Eleanor, I think, encourages him.'

Corbett read on, then glanced over his shoulder at Ranulf.

'The Lady Maeve sends her regards. What news do you have?'

'Oh, just gossip about the chancery,' Ranulf refused to meet his eye and pushed the letter into his wallet.

Corbett returned to Maeve's last paragraph.

'I miss you dearly,' she wrote, 'and every day I visit the chapel and light a candle for your swift return. My deepest love to you and my good wishes to Ranulf and Maltote. Your loving wife, Maeve.'

Corbett took a piece of parchment and began to write his reply. He described Maltote's death, then paused as he recalled the groom taking Eleanor for a ride on her pony, and how she would shriek and laugh. Maltote would lecture her on horse lore, most of which Eleanor could not understand, but she'd sit in her special saddle and nod solemnly. Corbett blinked away the tears and in terse sentences described his sense of loss. He paused.

'Ranulf,' he asked, 'Maltote's body is to be sent back to Leighton, yes?'

'Of course, I told Tripham that I would cover any expense.'

'I'll do that,' Corbett replied.

'No, Master, let me. I had two friends, now I have only one.'

Corbett turned to face Ranulf squarely.

'Am I guilty?' he asked. 'Did I cause Maltote's death?'

Ranulf shook his head. 'The dance we are in is a deadly one. It could happen to any of us at any time. We are like hunters,' he concluded. 'We hunt in the dark and it's easy to forget that those we hunt also hunt us: a knife in the back, a cup of poisoned wine, an unfortunate accident.'

'And who do you think *was* responsible?'

'Well, it can't be David Ap Thomas. He and his henchmen were locked up in the castle. It must be the Bellman.'

'Which means,' Corbett replied, 'that either Maltote was killed as a warning to us or the Bellman was going about his business, and Maltote happened to be in his way. He was killed by the oldest trick in the book: a beggar pleading for alms.' Corbett stood up. 'I am going to trap him, Ranulf, I am going to catch Maltote's murderer and, God forgive me, I am going to watch him hang!'

Ranulf glared defiantly back.

'I mean that,' Corbett insisted. 'He will be caught and tried by due process of law. He'll die on the scaffold!'

Ranulf got up, his face only a few inches away from Corbett's.

'Now, that's very good, but let me tell you about Ranulf-atte-Newgate's law which makes sure there is no slip between cup and lip or, in this case, between prison and the gallows. Eye for eye! Tooth for tooth! Life for life.'

Chapter 10

Corbett was about to reply when there was a knock on the door. Dame Mathilda stood there, with Master Moth like a shadow behind her. The old lady was leaning on a stick, breathing heavily.

'I came to express my condolences.'

She extended her hand and Corbett raised it and kissed her fingers. She promptly snatched her hand away. Corbett looked at her in surprise.

'I am sorry,' she apologised. 'But all this business . . .'

'Corbett!'

He turned. There was a crashing on the stairs and Bullock came lumbering up, his face red as a plum.

'Oh, Lord save us!' Lady Mathilda whispered. 'Not him.' She turned, sniffing the air. 'He's a disgusting man.'

She put her arm out for Moth who took it, his eyes never leaving hers. They walked down the passageway, forcing Bullock to flatten himself against the wall. The Sheriff watched them go, narrow-eyed, his rubicund face glistening with sweat.

'I've come as fast as I could!' he bawled. He jerked his head at Dame Mathilda now going down the stairs. 'What did that old bitch want?'

'She came to offer her condolences,' Corbett snapped. 'My friend Maltote was stabbed last night. He's dead.'

161

Bullock groaned, slapping the leather saddlebags he carried against his leg.

'God have mercy on him!' he breathed. 'And may Christ and His Mother give him good rest!' He followed Corbett into the chamber. 'And who is responsible?'

'We don't know. Reportedly a beggar – but probably the work of the Bellman.'

Bullock nodded at Ranulf who stood up to greet him.

'Well, this is also the work of the Bellman.'

The Sheriff opened the saddlebags and threw on to the floor the faded, battered corpse of a crow, a piece of twine round its neck. Ranulf picked it up and, before anyone could object, pushed it out through the arrow slit window.

'What else has the bastard done?' he asked.

Bullock handed Corbett a scroll of parchment.

'Two of these were posted last night,' he replied. 'One on the door of an Oxford Hall, the other at the Vine. I had two bailiffs patrolling the city just before dawn. They found these and the dead crow.'

Corbett undid the scroll and read the words which seemed to leap from the page:

'So the King's crow has come to Oxford. Caw! Caw! Caw!

So the King's crow, La Corbière, sticks his yellow beak

In the midden heap of the city. Caw! Caw! Caw!

The Bellman says this: cursed be Corbett in his sleeping.

Cursed be Corbett in his waking.

Cursed be Corbett in his eating.

Cursed be Corbett in his sitting.

Cursed by Corbett in his shitting.

Cursed be Corbett in his pissing.

Cursed be Corbett naked. Cursed be Corbett clothed.

Cursed be Corbett at home. Cursed be Corbett abroad.'

'I don't think he likes you.' Ranulf remarked, peering over Corbett's shoulder. He pointed to the last few lines:

'When the crow comes,' the proclamation shrilled, 'it is to be driven away by stones. The crow has been warned! Signed the Bellman of Sparrow Hall.'

Corbett looked at the vellum. The ink and the writing were the same as before, with a crude bell painted at the top where a pin had been driven through to attach it to a door.

'So the Bellman was out last night?' Corbett remarked, tossing the scroll on the bed. 'That's why Maltote died. Sir Walter, as of tonight, from curfew till dawn, I want your best archers to guard all the approaches to and from Sparrow Hall. I order that on the King's authority.'

Bullock agreed.

'Do you have anything else to report?' Corbett asked.

'Well, our prisoners at the castle are not as bold and brave as they were last night,' the Sheriff replied, mopping his face and slumping down on a stool. 'But I think you should question them.'

'And have you told anyone at Sparrow Hall about Ap Thomas?' Corbett asked.

'Oh, yes, on my way up. I left Tripham looking as white as a sheet.' Bullock slapped his hand against his thigh. 'I'm enjoying this. I am going to take you back to the castle, Sir Hugh. Once we are done, I'm off like a whippet to lodge a formal complaint with the Proctors of the University and then I'm back to Sparrow Hall. I am going to rub their arrogant faces into the growing shame of their so-called college.'

Bullock ticked the points off on his fingers. 'Firstly, they house a traitor who is also a murderer. Secondly, someone

163

there has slain a royal servant. Thirdly, a group of their so-called scholars are guilty of debauchery and God knows what else. Finally, somehow or other that damnable place is linked to the deaths of these beggars on the roads outside Oxford.'

'Don't tell them about the button,' Corbett warned. 'Though, I have seen so many buttons on the gowns and clothing of the masters and scholars, it would be difficult to trace,' he added ruefully.

'What will happen to Ap Thomas and the others?' Ranulf asked.

'Oh, they'll appear before the Justices,' Bullock replied. 'They will be fined, and maybe given a short stay in the stocks, and then the University will probaby tell them to piss off for a year to face the fury of their families in Wales.'

'Are you sure they are innocent of the activities of the Bellman or the deaths of these beggars?' Corbett asked.

'I am certain,' Bullock replied. 'But, as I have said, Ap Thomas is more amenable now. He may answer further questions.' The Sheriff lumbered to his feet and tapped Corbett gently on the chest. 'Sir Hugh, you're the King's clerk. When I post my guards not a mouse will be able to fart in Sparrow Hall without our permission.' He pointed to the scroll lying on the bed. 'But the Bellman is a vicious bugger. I would heed his warning. Now, you'll come back with me to the castle?'

Corbett agreed. Bullock put his hand on the latch then turned.

'I'm sorry about the lad,' he said softly. 'I am sorry he died. Do you know what I'd do?' The Sheriff stuck his thumbs in his sword belt, puffing his chest out. 'If I were you, Sir Hugh, I'd get on my horse and go out to the King at Woodstock. I'd have this bloody place closed down and the Masters taken into the Tower for questioning.'

'You don't like Sparrow Hall, do you?' Corbett asked.

'No, I don't, Sir Hugh. I never liked Braose. I don't like to see a man profit from the pain and humiliation of others. I don't like his bloody sister either – constantly petitioning me to ask the King whether her brother's memory could be more hallowed. Braose was no saint but a bloody warlord who turned to religion and study in the twilight years of his life.'

Corbett watched fascinated as this fat, little man let his anger flow.

'I don't like the Masters either!' he spat out. 'Either here or elsewhere in the city. I resent their so-called scholars swaggering around, who are responsible for more crime than any horde of outlaws.'

'I was a scholar once.'

Bullock relaxed and smiled. 'Sir Hugh, I'm in a temper. Many Masters and their scholars are good men, dedicated to a life of study and prayer.'

'It's Braose you don't like, isn't it?' Corbett asked.

Bullock raised his head – there were tears in his eyes.

'When I was young,' the Sheriff replied, 'a mere lad, a stripling, I was my father's squire in de Montfort's army. Did you ever meet the great Earl?'

Corbett shook his head.

'He spoke to me once,' Bullock replied. 'He got down off his horse and clapped me on the shoulder. He made you feel important. He never stood on ceremony and, when he talked, it was like listening to music – your heart skipped a beat and the blood began to pound in your veins.'

'And yet you are now the King's good servant?' Corbett asked.

'Some of the dream died,' Bullock replied. 'Part of the vision was lost but the good of the commonality of the realm is still a worthwhile idea. Of course, there's Edward our

King – well, that's the tragedy, isn't it?' Bullock continued. 'In his youth, the King was like de Montfort. But come, I'm gossiping like an old crone – we should go.'

Corbett and Ranulf followed Bullock down and out of the hostelry. The lanes and streets were thronged but Bullock marched purposefully, the people parting like waves before a high-prowed ship. The Sheriff looked neither to the right nor the left. Corbett was amused at how quickly scholars, beggars, even the powerful tradesmen, kept well out of the little Sheriff's path. They paused on the corner of Bocardo Lane where the bailiffs were putting street walkers into the stocks. Corbett seized Ranulf's sleeve.

'Maltote? He died peacefully?'

'I did what was necessary, Master.' He glanced sideways at Corbett. 'And, when that happens to me, I expect you to do the same.'

They continued, following Bullock out of the town, across the drawbridge and into the castle. Sir Walter led them into a hall, and told them to sit behind the table on the dais whilst he waddled off into a corner where he filled cups of white wine.

'I'm sorry about the mess,' he apologised, bringing the wine back and clearing away the chicken bones and pieces of bread from in front of them. 'Bring the prisoners up!' he bawled at a soldier on guard just inside the door. 'And tell them I want no insolence!' Bullock sat down between Corbett and Ranulf. He picked up a napkin and started cleaning his fingers. He saw Corbett watching him. 'It's the grease,' he explained, gesturing at the mess on the table.

'No, no,' Corbett replied. 'Sir Walter, you've ...' Corbett shook his head. 'It's nothing, just something I have seen.'

He glanced up as the doors were flung open and Bullock's soldiers dragged a line of sorry-looking scholars into the hall.

'I've released the whores,' Bullock whispered. 'Smacked them on the bottom and let them go. They were causing dissension amongst my men.'

The scholars were lined up; their faces were dirty, and some bore red, angry bruises on the cheek or round the mouth.

'Well, you're sober now, are you? David Ap Thomas, step forward!'

The Welshman, still dressed in a grey, shabby gown, his hands tied securely before him, shuffled forward. He had lost his arrogance, and there was a cut on the side of his mouth, whilst his left eye was half-closed and beginning to bruise. Nevertheless, he began with a protest.

'I am a scholar at Sparrow Hall,' he declared. 'I am also a clerk. I can recite the psalm, I claim benefit of clergy. You have no right to try me before a secular court.'

'Shut up!' Bullock growled. 'You are not being tried.' He jabbed a finger. 'When I have finished with you, I am handing you over to the Proctors' court. It'll be back to Wales for you, my lad!'

Ap Thomas's bluster faded. Corbett snapped his fingers and beckoned him forward.

'Master Ap Thomas,' he began quietly. 'Last night one of my men was murdered by the Bellman. That's treason and you know the sentence for a traitor?'

Ap Thomas licked his lips. 'I know nothing about the Bellman,' he muttered. 'Put me on oath.'

'After having watched you last night, I know that would mean nothing!' Bullock snapped.

'Put me on oath,' Ap Thomas repeated. 'I know nothing.'

'But you hounded poor Passerel to death?'

'That's because we thought he'd killed Ascham.'

'And why, oh why –' Ranulf jibed '– did David Ap Thomas care for a poor old librarian?'

'Ascham favoured us,' Ap Thomas replied.

167

'Yes, yes,' Corbett interrupted. 'He told you about the ancient lore?'

'He also gave us money,' Ap Thomas replied. 'He gave us silver for our festivities.'

'Why should he do that?' Corbett asked. 'Ascham wasn't a wealthy man.'

Ap Thomas shrugged. 'It wasn't much. Just after he died, I received a purse of silver coins with a short note stating that Ascham wished it to be mine.'

'Where's the note?'

'I destroyed it. It was in a scrawled hand.'

'But who delivered it?'

'Actually, Passerel himself did.'

'Ah, I see,' Corbett replied. 'I suppose the letter was sealed?'

'Yes, it was. Passerel handed it over with the small purse of silver; he claimed to have found it amongst Ascham's possessions.'

'You realise, of course,' Corbett asked, 'that the money probably came from the Bellman and you fell directly into his trap? Your favourite Ascham, the source of knowledge for your pagan rites, had been brutally murdered, and then even in death proves his generosity with his gift of money. The Bellman knew exactly how you'd react: you'd drink, you'd mourn and then you'd look for a scapegoat. Passerel was no more guilty of Ascham's murder than I am,' Corbett continued remorselessly.

'Did you leave the poison for Passerel?' Ranulf asked.

'Of course not. The night he died we were . . .' Ap Thomas's voice trailed off.

'Out in the woods?' Ranulf asked.

'I am sorry,' Ap Thomas mumbled.

'You'll be sorrier yet,' Bullock spoke cheerfully. 'Do you know anything about the murders of these poor beggar men?'

Ap Thomas flailed his bound hands. 'Nothing,' he protested. 'Brakespeare and Senex were sometimes seen near Sparrow Hall but I know nothing of their murders.'

'Oh, take them to the stocks!' Bullock shouted to the captain of his guard.

'Sir Walter,' Corbett intervened, 'Master Ap Thomas has been helpful. His crimes are due more to foolishness than treason or any malice. Let him and his companions be handed over to the University Proctors.'

Bullock sipped from his cup. 'Agreed. Take the buggers away!' he bawled. 'I've had enough of them!'

The guards pushed Ap Thomas and his companions through the door. The Sheriff got to his feet and drained his cup.

'I'll have the guards around Sparrow Hall by tonight. Sir Hugh?'

Corbett looked up. 'I apologise, Master Sheriff. My mind was elsewhere.' He got to his feet. 'I was thinking,' Corbett looked down at his boots. 'You could tell from their clothing that Ap Thomas and his companions had been out in the countryside.' He paused. 'But these corpses which were brought in, Sir Walter – did you notice any mud, soil or grass on them?'

Bullock shook his head.

'Now these beggars,' Corbett added, 'were old but I doubt if they would give up their lives lightly. Moreover, if a man was pursued through a wood, his legs, hands and certainly his face would be scored by brambles and gorse.'

'I never saw any of that,' Bullock replied. 'But come, Sir Hugh, Ranulf, I still have the clothes and belongings of these beggars: they are kept in the store room next to my private chamber.'

The Sheriff led Corbett out of the hall and up a narrow, winding, stone staircase. Now and again Bullock grasped the ropes alongside, stopping to catch his breath. At last they reached a broad stairwell and Bullock took a ring of keys from his belt and opened the chamber on the right. Corbett fought to hide his surprise. The Sheriff's private chamber was clean and spacious: the floor was scrubbed and covered with woollen rugs. Above the diamond-shaped window was a triptych of Christ's Passion, with Mary and St John on either side. A four-poster high bed dominated the room; there was a desk under the window with a large box chair, and stools and covered chests. However, what caught Corbett's gaze were the shelves from floor to ceiling on either side of the window, all well stocked with books.

'Never judge a book by its cover,' Bullock joked. 'You are looking at my pride and joy, Sir Hugh. Some of the books I have bought myself but quite a few were a legacy from my uncle, who was Prior of Hailes Abbey.' He went to a bookshelf and pulled out a tome, dusting it carefully before handing it to Corbett.

The clerk recognised the title: *Cur Deus Homo – Why God Created Man*; a work by the great Norman scholar Anselm.

'The jewel of my collection,' Bullock breathed, coming up beside him. He pointed to the cursive calligraphy and beautiful small pictures which marked the beginning of each paragraph. 'Copied direct from the original,' the Sheriff whispered. 'Those bastards at Sparrow Hall know I own it. Tripham offered me gold by the ounce but I refused to sell.'

He put the book back on the shelf, took a key from a hook on the wall and led Corbett to the store room, which was a long, narrow place, full of chests and wooden boxes. It was dark and musty. Bullock grabbed a box and pulled it out on to the stairwell.

'If you don't mind,' he explained, 'I prefer if these are

kept out of my room.' He stirred the contents, raising a cloud of stale dust.

The Sheriff went back to his chamber whilst Corbett began to take out the pathetic rags.

'I ordered the bodies to be stripped,' Bullock shouted. 'Those poor bastards could not afford coffins but I made sure they were buried in proper shrouds.'

Corbett laid the different pieces of clothing on the ground: some battered, old boots; torn and patched hose; a leather jerkin; a jacket, rather moth-eaten, the mole fur on its edge eaten away; a woollen shirt, holed and dirty. Corbett tried to ignore the smell as he carefully examined the boots and hose.

'Not a blade of grass,' Corbett murmured, looking at Ranulf. 'Or a leaf. Nothing! I don't think these men were killed where they were found.'

Ranulf picked up one piece of hose and examined the worn woollen threads.

'Look, Master.' Ranulf pointed to the small, grain-like pebbles caught there.

'We have the same here.' Corbett pointed to another pair of faded, bottle-green hose. He then examined the boots: again there was no mud or anything to indicate the beggars had been killed in a field or wood.

'Put them back,' Corbett ordered.

He helped Ranulf do so, and Bullock came out.

'You are finished?'

'Yes.'

The Sheriff kicked the box back into the store room and slammed the door shut.

'Well, Sir Hugh, what do you think?'

'I suspect,' Corbett replied, 'that these men were not killed in some Satanic rite. I doubt if they were lured out on to some desolate heath or lonely field: they were killed here in Oxford. Perhaps in some street or alleyway?'

'But why?' Ranulf asked.

'Perhaps for pleasure,' Corbett replied. 'Some sick soul who liked to see an old man beg for his life before he is killed? That's why they were chosen. Who'd ever miss a beggar?'

'Sheer malice?' Bullock exclaimed. 'A simple lust for killing.'

'Something like that,' Corbett replied. 'A devil's hunt. Someone who goes out into the streets at night, chooses his victim and stalks him like you would a rabbit or a pheasant.'

'Yet no one has heard or seen anything,' Bullock retorted.

'Think of all the lonely places in the city,' Corbett replied. 'There's the old Jewish cemetery, not to mention the great open spaces of common land.'

'But what happened to the blood?' Ranulf asked.

'We have had summer rains, which could have washed it away,' Corbett replied.

'But, if that's the case,' Bullock intervened, 'why weren't the corpses left where they were killed? Why does the assassin risk capture by taking them outside the city and leaving the heads tied to the branches of some trees?'

'I don't know,' Corbett replied. 'But, Sir Walter –' he extended his hand '– from now on, Sparrow Hall is to be guarded every night until this business is finished.'

The Sheriff agreed and Corbett and Ranulf left.

'Have you told the Lady Maeve that Maltote's dead?' Ranulf asked as they made their way along an alleyway to Broad Street.

'Yes, I have,' Corbett murmured. He stopped and stared up at the blue sky between the row of houses. 'I am sorry, Ranulf. I am deeply sorry that Maltote's dead but I will grieve for him when this is over and his killer is punished.' He rubbed the side of his face. 'His corpse will be sent out to some abbey for embalming and then back to Leighton. There's an old yew tree in the graveyard. He can be buried beneath that.' Corbett walked on. 'What puzzles me now,' he continued, 'are the deaths of these beggar men. I always thought Ap Thomas was responsible.'

Ranulf was about to reply when he heard a sound behind him. The alleyway was a lonely, narrow thoroughfare and he heard the slither of a boot. He grabbed Corbett, dragging him towards the wall, and as he did so, something smacked into the side of a house where it jutted out a bit further along. Ranulf peered up the alleyway – nothing, though he noticed a cat leap across as if it had been disturbed. Then he glimpsed a dark shape move out of a doorway, and an arm being brought back and again he pulled Corbett aside. Once more there was the smack of a stone hitting a wall deeper down the alleyway.

Ranulf pulled out his dagger and edged forwards but, by the time he'd reached the place he'd glimpsed the figure, there was nothing except the sound of the faint patter of feet down the narrow runnel which led off the alleyway. Ranulf crouched and picked up some small, well-smoothed pebbles. Corbett came up.

'Slingshot,' Ranulf explained, getting to his feet with one of the pebbles in his hand. He threw the pebble up and caught it, allowing it to smack against the palm of his hand. 'If one of these had caught us, Master . . .?'

'Would it have killed?' Corbett asked.

'I've seen it happen,' Ranulf declared. 'Have you forgotten the bible story: David slaying Goliath?'

'No,' Corbett replied, taking the pebble from Ranulf's hand. 'I have also seen boys at sowing time, following their fathers, armed with a slingshot to drive away the marauding crows.' He stared down the narrow, darkened runnel. 'And that's how the Bellman regards me,' he continued. 'A noisy, interfering crow that should be brought down.'

They continued on their way. Corbett paused where the jutting wall of a derelict house had stopped the first pebble: he noticed how the slingshot had pierced deep into the plaster.

'That's it!' he declared. 'Unless we have to go out, Ranulf, we'd best stay indoors.'

'It could have been Bullock,' Ranulf remarked. 'He knew we had left the castle.'

'Aye,' Corbett replied. 'Or the Bellman. Or, indeed, one of Ap Thomas's friends.'

Corbett was relieved to reach Carfax, crossing the busy thoroughfare, shouldering his way past the crowds; he kept one hand on his wallet, the other on his dagger, wary of the pickpockets who clustered there. Ranulf followed behind. Now and again he'd turn, standing on tiptoe to look over the crowd but he could glimpse no one who appeared to be following them. They reached the hostelry, entering by the rear entrance because the front was thronged with scholars and Corbett wanted to avoid any confrontation over Ap Thomas. Norreys was in the yard, standing by the well, cleaning out some casks.

'Ah Sir Hugh.' He came over. He smiled but his eyes looked anxious, his face haggard and white. 'The news about Ap Thomas's arrest is now all over Oxford,' he stammered. 'Master Tripham and his colleagues have asked to meet you in the library.' Norreys wiped his hands on his leather apron. 'They asked if you'd be so kind as to go across immediately?'

'We noticed the scholars in the lane,' Corbett remarked. 'So we decided to come this way.'

'Oh, there'll be no trouble,' Norreys explained. 'Ap Thomas and his henchmen were not well liked. They are now more a source of laughter than anything else.' He returned to the cask he was cleaning, put the lid firmly back on, hammering in the wooden pegs. He took off his apron. 'I'll fetch my cloak and follow you.'

Corbett walked through the hostelry. This time he found the atmosphere much lighter and the scholars more respectful, the bachelors and commons standing aside as he passed. They crossed the lane to the hall where a servitor ushered them into the library. A short while later they were joined by Tripham, Master Barnett, Churchley and Appleston. Dame Mathilda came in last, her black polished cane tapping the floor, her head held as regally as a queen's. Ranulf watched as Moth helped her into the high chair at the top of the library table; he then glanced curiously at Corbett who seemed to be lost in a reverie. Norreys came over, huffing and puffing, wiping his hands on his gown. Tripham told them to take their seats.

'I would offer you some wine, Sir Hugh, but,' he added sardonically, 'Master Churchley has told us how wary you would be of eating or drinking anything here.'

'I think the same applies to all of you,' Corbett replied. 'There's no rhyme nor reason for the deaths of Ascham or Passerel. Or, indeed, that of my good servant Maltote. The Bellman strikes when he wishes, not just to safeguard himself but to heap insult upon injury. You asked to see me?'

'I . . .' Tripham stammered. 'We would like to protest – the Sheriff has informed us that Sparrow Hall is to be placed under curfew from dusk till dawn. Is that really necessary?'

Corbett shrugged. 'That is a matter for you and the University,' he replied. 'But Maltote was a king's servant and was brutally murdered. Furthermore, a number of your scholars, Master Tripham, are to face serious charges of debauchery, and perhaps even dabbling in the black arts.'

'We are not responsible,' Tripham snapped, 'for the private lives of each individual scholar.'

'And neither am I,' Corbett replied, 'For every royal

official. Moreover –' Corbett's voice rose '– on my way back here I was attacked yet again. A piece of slingshot narrowly missed my head.'

'We have all been here,' Tripham expostulated. 'Sir Hugh, all this morning no one has left the hall. We have sat in close council in the parlour discussing what should be done with Ap Thomas and his cronies.'

Corbett hid his surprise. 'You are sure, Master Tripham?'

'We would all take oaths on it,' Dame Mathilda snapped. 'And you could interrogate the servitors who brought us wine and sweetmeats. Since we rose this morning and heard Mass in our chapel, no one has left Sparrow Hall. And, Sir Hugh, to my knowledge nobody left the hall last night when your servant was murdered.'

'I don't want Maltote's body to be dressed here,' Corbett replied, ignoring the outburst. 'It is to be sent to Osney Abbey for embalming.'

'Norreys will take it there,' Tripham replied. 'But, Sir Hugh, how long will you stay here? How long will this go on?'

'How long will you continue to pry into our lives?' Barnett snapped.

'Until I find the truth,' Corbett, stung by their arrogance, retorted. 'What about you, Master Barnett, and your secrets?'

The sneer faded from Barnett's fat, smug face.

'What secrets?' he stammered.

'You are a man of the world,' Corbett continued, wishing he had kept better control of his tongue. 'Yet you feed the beggars and are well known to Brother Angelo at St Osyth's hospital. Why should a man like you bother with the under-dogs of this world?'

Barnett stared down at the tabletop.

'What Master Barnett gives to the poor,' Tripham murmured, 'is surely a matter for him alone?'

'I am tired,' Barnett replied. He glanced round the library. 'I am tired of all this. I am tired of the Bellman. I'm tired of attending the funerals of men like Ascham and Passerel: of lecturing to students who neither comprehend nor like what you say.' He stared at Corbett. 'I'm glad Ap Thomas has been arrested,' he continued, ignoring the gasps of his colleagues. 'He was an arrogant layabout. I don't need to reply to your question, master clerk, but I will.' He got to his feet, knocking away Churchley's restraining hand. He undid the buttons of his long gown and then the clasps of the shirt beneath. 'I have spent my life in avid study. I love the taste of wine, the dark passion in a bowl of claret, and young girls, full-breasted, slim-waisted.' He continued to unfasten the clasps of his shirt. 'I am a wealthy man, Corbett, the only son of a doting father. Have you ever heard the phrase in the Gospels: "Use money, tainted though it be, to help the poor so, when you die, they will welcome you into eternity"?'

Barnett pulled open his shirt and showed Corbett the hair-cloth beneath. Barnett sat down on a stool, his arrogant face now downcast.

'When I die,' he murmured, 'I don't want to go to hell – I have lived in hell all my life, Corbett. I want to go to heaven so . . . I give money to the poor, I help the beggars, I wear a hair shirt in reparation for my many sins.'

Corbett leaned across and pressed his hand.

'I am sorry,' he murmured. 'Master Tripham, I have told you what I know: soldiers from the castle will guard every entrance from Sparrow Hall until this business is finished.' He got to his feet. 'Now I would like to pay my last respects to my friend.'

Tripham led him out of the room and along to the corpse chamber.

'We have done what we could,' he murmured as he opened the door. 'We've washed the body.'

177

Corbett, followed by Ranulf, stood by the bed and looked down.

'It's as if he's asleep,' Ranulf whispered, staring at the boyish, ivory-white face.

'We dressed the wound.' Tripham stood behind them. 'Sir Hugh, did you know about the terrible bruise on his ankle?'

'Yes, yes,' Corbett replied absentmindedly. 'Master Tripham, leave us for a moment.'

The Vice-Regent closed the door. Corbett knelt beside the bed and wept as he quietly prayed.

Chapter 11

Corbett and Ranulf returned to their own chamber, passing
Norreys on the stairs. He offered some food and drink but
they refused. Ranulf said he wanted to go for a walk so
Corbett went and sat in his chamber: deeply upset by
Maltote's death, he tried to distract himself. He took out the
proclamations which Simon had given him at Leighton and
sifted through them. They were all similar: the shape of the
bell at the top through which a nail had been pierced; the
broad, clerkly brushes of the quill; the phrases full of hate
for the King. At the foot of each was the same phrase:
'Given by our hand at Sparrow Hall, The Bellman.'

Corbett pushed them away. He wiped the tears from his
face and picked up Maeve's letter from his chancery bag,
going carefully over the phrases. One sentence caught his
eye. Maeve's complaint about how uncle Morgan teased
Eleanor with stories of decapitated corpses and heads hanging by their hair from branches.

'That's it!' Corbett breathed.

He put the letter down and recalled the clothing he had
examined at the castle: no grass, no soil, not a leaf or a piece
of bark.

'If they weren't killed there . . .?'

He got up and walked to the window. He missed Maltote
more than he would admit and he knew Ranulf would never
be the same again. He thought of his young friend's corpse

and Tripham's words about the bruise on the ankle. As Corbett stared down into the yard at a great cart, fear chilled his stomach. He gave a shout of exasperation and banged his fist against the open shutter. Going to the door he threw it open.

'Ranulf!' he shouted.

His words rang like a death knell down the lonely corridor. It was early afternoon: the students, already subdued by Ap Morgan's capture, were now dispersed to their school rooms and lecture halls. Corbett's unease grew. He felt lonely, suddenly vulnerable. There were no windows in the gallery, apart from an arrow slit high on the wall at each end, so the light was poor. Corbett edged back inside the doorway. Was there anyone there, he wondered? He was certain he was not alone. He drew his dagger and whirled around at the soft, scuffling sound behind him. A rat? Or someone lurking in the darkness?

'Ranulf! Ranulf!' Corbett shouted. He sighed as he heard a pounding on the stairs. 'Take care!' Corbett warned.

Ranulf came on, running along the gallery, dagger out.

'What's wrong, Master?'

Corbett looked over his shoulder. 'I don't know,' he whispered, 'but we are not alone, Ranulf. No, no!' He seized the servant's arm. 'We will not go hunting. At least not here!'

Corbett almost dragged Ranulf into the chamber.

'Put on your war belt,' he ordered as he did likewise. 'Bring a crossbow and a quiver of bows.'

'Where are we going? What are we doing?'

'Have you noticed,' Corbett replied, 'that since we came to Oxford, no headless corpses have been found on some lonely trackway? I know where those poor beggars were killed.' Corbett jabbed a finger at the floor.

'Here?' Ranulf exclaimed.

'Yes, here, in the hostelry. In the cellars below! Remember, Ranulf, these buildings once belonged to a wine merchant. You visited the houses of such merchants in London?'

'They have huge cellars and long galleries,' Ranulf interrupted. 'Some in Cheapside could house a small village.'

'And there are the legends,' Corbett added, 'of the woman who lurked in the cellars here with her child, when Braose founded his Hall. I wager our noble founder had to hunt them out.'

Ranulf watched him anxiously.

'I'll come with you.'

'No, you won't,' Corbett replied. 'But you will watch the cellar door. If anyone comes in after me, follow them down. No, no!' Corbett shook his head. 'Maltote didn't die in vain, Ranulf.' He stared round the chamber. 'An old priest once told me how, at least for a while, the dead linger with you.' He smiled. 'I used to put my findings down to intuition or logic but, for this, I give thanks to Maltote. Count to a hundred!' he ordered. 'Then follow me!'

Corbett went down the stairs. On the ground floor he went along to Norreys's counting office. The man was writing in a ledger and Corbett realised that, if anyone had been in the top gallery, it hadn't been him.

'Sir Hugh, can I help?' Norreys got to his feet, wiping ink-stained fingers.

'Yes, I would like to search the cellars, Master Norreys.'

The man pulled a face. 'What do you expect to find down there? The Bellman?'

'Perhaps,' Corbett answered.

'There's nothing there; just barrels and supplies but . . .'

Norreys took a squat, tallow candle from a box and, jingling the keys on his belt, led Corbett out along the passageway. He stopped to light the candle then unlocked the cellar door.

'I'll go by myself,' Corbett said.

He went down the steps towards the cellar, which was dark, musty and cold.

'There are torches in the wall sconces,' Norreys sang out.

At the bottom Corbett lit one of these as Norreys slammed the door behind him. Corbett made his way carefully into the darkness. Every so often he would stop to light a sconce torch and look around. The wall to his left was of solid brick, but on his right were small caverns or chambers. Some were empty, others contained bric-a-brac, broken tables and benches. He turned a corner and coughed at the thick staleness of the air. Corbett lit more torches and quietly marvelled at this sprawling underworld.

'These must run the entire length of the lane,' he murmured.

Now and again he paused to go into one of the chambers or crouch and look into the caverns. He was glad he'd lit the torches: they would show him the way out. He must have wandered for some time before he made his way back, following the line of torches. He espied another narrow passageway. He went down but the end was blocked off. Corbett remembered those beggar men: he knew they had died here. He could feel an eerie stillness, a sense of evil. He heard a sound further along the passageway and crouched down, examining the brickwork and ground carefully. He could find nothing but small pools of water. Corbett dipped his fingers carefully into one of the puddles and rubbed small pieces of gravel between his fingers. He lifted the candle and stared up at the vaulted ceiling but he could find no trace of any leak or water seeping through. Corbett closed his eyes and smiled. He'd found the killer!

He went back into the passageway where the torches were still alight, making the shadows dance. Corbett wanted to get out. He felt as if the place was closing in around him. His heart began to quicken and his mouth ran dry. He turned a corner and stopped. The passageway was in darkness. Someone had extinguished the sconce torches. Corbett heard a click and immediately stepped back just as a cross-bow bolt whistled through the air, smacking into the brickwork. Corbett turned and ran.

He avoided the narrow passageway, the blind alley. At one point Corbett stopped, drew his dagger and crouched down to catch his breath. He looked back and saw a figure silhouetted against the light. Corbett licked dry lips. His attacker could not see so clearly and a second bolt whirred aimlessly through the darkness. Corbett rose and ran as fast as he could before his assailant could insert another bolt and winch back the cord. The man saw him coming. In the flickering light Corbett watched those fingers pulling back the cord but then he crashed into him and both men rolled on the ground, kicking and jabbing at each other. Corbett grasped the small arbalest and sent it smashing against the wall. His assailant broke free. Corbett made to rise but the man's sword was out, the point under his chin. The figure, half stooping, pulled back his cowl.

Master Richard Norreys.

Corbett pulled himself up to lean against the wall. His hand stole to the dagger in his belt but the sheath was empty.

Norreys crouched down, pushing the tip of his sword into the soft part of Corbett's neck. Corbett winced and held his head further back.

'Don't struggle.' Norreys wiped the sweat from his face with one hand, though the other, holding the sword, didn't even quiver. 'Well, well, well,' Norreys mused.

He edged closer into the pool of light; his eyes had a soft, dreamy look. Corbett fought to control the fear. He decided not to lash out – Norreys was as mad as any March hare. If he struggled or resisted Norreys would plunge that sword into his throat, then sit and watch him die.

'Why?' Corbett tried to move his head away. He kept glancing down the passageway behind Norreys. Where in God's name, he thought, was Ranulf?

'Why what?' Norreys asked.

'Why the killings?'

'It's a game, you see,' Norreys replied. 'You were in Wales, Sir Hugh, you know what it was like. I was a speculator, a spy. I used to go out with the others at night. Along those mist-filled valleys. Nothing –' Norreys's voice fell to a whisper '– nothing moved, only the murmuring of the trees and the call of an owl. But they were always there, weren't they? The bloody Welsh, creeping like worms along the ground.' Norreys's face was suffused with rage. 'Soft! Soft!' His eyes opened wide. 'We'd always go out in a group of five or six. Good men, Sir Hugh, archers, with wives and sweethearts back home. We'd always lose one, sometimes two or three. Always the same! First we'd find the corpses. Then we'd go looking for their heads. Sometimes the bastards would play games with us. They'd take a head and leave it like some apple bobbing in a breeze.' Norreys paused, clasping the sword with both hands. 'You think I'm mad, witless, possessed by a demon. I tell you this, master clerk,' he continued on in a rush, 'when the King's army disbanded at Shrewsbury, I began to have dreams. Ever the same. Always the darkness, camp fires amongst the trees, footsteps slithering beside or behind me. And those heads – always the heads! Sometimes during the day, I'd see little things – a leaf on a branch, a ripe apple hanging down –' Norreys sighed '– and I'd dream again. Then I came here.' He smiled. 'You see, Sir Hugh, I am an educated man: trained as a clerk, a student of the horn book. I was also a good soldier so the King gave me the sinecure here.'

'Are you the Bellman?' Corbett asked.

'Bellman!' Norreys sniggered. 'Bellman! I couldn't give a fig about de Montfort or those fat lords across the lane. I was happy here and the dreams became less frequent... but then the Welsh came.' He closed his eyes but abruptly opened them as Corbett stirred. 'No, no, Sir Hugh, you have got to listen. As I had to – to those voices. Do you remember, Sir Hugh, how the Welsh used to call out in the darkness? They'd get to know our names, and as we hunted them they hunted us. And, if they took one of our company, they'd call out: "Richard has gone! Henry has gone! Tell John's wife she's a widow!" Norreys's voice rang through the vaults. He looked round. 'I'll have to go soon,' he whispered. 'The scholars will be back from the schools. They'll be knocking on my door for this or that.'

'The old men?' Corbett asked quickly.

'It was an accident,' Norreys replied, shaking his head. 'Mere chance, Sir Hugh. An old beggar came here, wanting work so I sent him down to the cellar to collect a tun of wine. Of course, the stupid, old man had to broach a cask. Quite drunk he was when I came down. He was frightened and ran away. I followed.' Norreys chewed the corner of his lip. 'Here,' he whispered leaning forward, 'here in the darkness, Sir Hugh. It was like being in Wales again. I was hunting him. He'd call out, saying he was sorry. I caught up with him and he struggled so I slit his throat. I left his corpse here but that night I had a dream.'

'So you cut his head off, didn't you?' Corbett interrupted. 'You put the corpse and the head in a barrel, and took it out of Oxford by this gate or that to dispose of.'

'That's right,' Norreys agreed. 'I'd throw the corpse into the woods and tie the head to a branch. Do you know, Sir Hugh, it was like being exorcised or shriven in church? The dreams stopped. I felt purified.' Norreys smiled, a gleaming look in his eyes. 'I felt like a boy jumping off a rock into a deep, clear pool: washed clean.' He paused, staring at a point above Corbett's head.

Corbett breathed in deeply, straining his ears. Oh God, he prayed, where's Ranulf? He looked down the passageway behind Norreys but he could see nothing.

'Then you killed again?' Corbett asked.

'Of course I did,' Norreys smirked. 'It's like wine, Sir Hugh. You drink it, you taste and feel the warmth in your belly. The days passed and I needed that warmth again. And who cared? The city is full of beggars – men with no past and no future: the flotsam and jetsam of this world.'

'They had souls,' Corbett replied, wishing Norreys wouldn't press so hard with the sword. 'They were men and, above all, they were innocent: their blood cries to God for vengeance.'

Norreys shifted and Corbett knew he had made a mistake.

'God, Sir Hugh? My God died in Wales. What vengeance? What are you going to do, Sir Hugh? Cry out? Beg for mercy?'

'I'll be missed.'

'Oh, of course you will be. I'll take your corpse out. I promise I'll do it differently. There are marshes deep in the woods. The fires of hell will have grown cold by the time your corpse is found. I have thought it all out. Your death will be blamed on the Bellman. The King's soldiers will come into Oxford and those pompous, arrogant bastards across the lane will take the blame. Sparrow Hall will be closed but the hostelry will continue.' He saw Corbett shift his gaze. 'Oh, what are you waiting for? Your cat-footed friend? I locked the cellar door. You are alone, Sir Hugh.' He cocked his head sideways. 'But what made you suspect me?'

'My servant, the one who died, is his blood on your hands?'

Norreys shook his head.

'He said he'd knocked his shin against a bucket,' Corbett continued as he glimpsed a shadow move further down the passageway. 'I wondered why the Master of the hostelry, a place not known for its cleanliness, should be washing the cellar floor. You were removing the blood stains, weren't you? And then I began to reflect how the corpses bore no mark of being hunted through the forest, how beggars might come here seeking alms, bread and water, how the cellars were deep; and I recalled your work as a speculator in Wales. Of course, as a steward, you had every right to go out in your cart to buy produce in the surrounding villages. No one would be suspicious, no one would stop you.'

Norreys pointed a finger at him. 'You are a good hunting dog!'

'You took the corpses out and left them with the heads dangling from branches. No one would notice the dark stain in a barrel built to contain wine, the lid firmly nailed down. Whilst I, the King's hunting dog, was here, you stopped your slaughter. You knew I was curious so you washed the killing places and Maltote hit his shin against a bucket.'

'Anything else?'

'You dropped a button . . .'

'Ah! I wondered . . .'

'And there's thin gravel here. I found traces of it on the beggar's clothing.'

'I thought you had found something,' Norreys jibed. 'I followed you down here . . .'

'I will make you an offer,' Corbett interrupted, for Ranulf was not very close.

Norreys's eyes widened.

'In the passageway behind you,' Corbett continued, 'is my servant, Ranulf-atte-Newgate. Before he became a clerk,

Ranulf was a night stalker. He can open any lock and move like a ghost.'

Norreys shook his head, his sneer dying at the click of a crossbow behind him.

'You can take your sword away,' Corbett said softly, 'and stand trial before the King's justices.'

'I could kill you.' Norreys smiled but his gaze faltered.

Corbett brought his hand up slowly, pressing against the sword blade: he relaxed – it wasn't sharp, merely a sticking iron.

'You can accept my offer,' Corbett remarked.

Norreys, however, was more concerned at Ranulf behind him.

'Or Ranulf can kill you!'

Corbett suddenly knocked the sword away, rolling forwards. Norreys was up. Ranulf came into the light. Corbett heard the whirr of a crossbow bolt and Norreys staggered, dropping his sword, clutching at the bolt in his chest. The look of surprise was still on his face even as Ranulf seized his hair, pulled back his head and, with one swift slash, cut his throat. Ranulf knocked Norreys to the ground and crouched down beside Corbett. The clerk closed his eyes and drew nearer to the wall, drawing deep breaths, trying to calm the pounding of his heart.

'I came as quickly as I could,' Ranulf grinned. 'The lock was rusty and stiff and, for a few moments, I lost my way.' He helped Corbett to his feet. 'Do you know what I would do, Master? I'd leave this bloody place!' He kicked Norreys's corpse with his boot. 'I'd ride like the wind to Woodstock and obtain the King's warrant to arrest everyone in both the hostelry and the Hall until this matter is finished.'

Corbett pushed him gently away and leaned against the wall.

This is a nightmare, he thought, glancing around. Dark,

slimy passageways, flickering candlelight, the blood-soaked corpse of a murderer. Was this how it would end? Would Ranulf, one day, not be at hand? Or would he meet an assassin unlike the others, who killed silently and speedily, not bothering to boast about his exploits? Corbett picked up his dagger and re-sheathed it. Ranulf wiped his own blade on Norreys's jerkin, picked up the crossbow and helped Corbett down the passageway. At the foot of the steps Corbett paused. He felt calmer though very cold.

'You are right,' he murmured. 'Pack our bags, Ranulf. We'll leave here and go to the Merry Maidens. Hire a chamber but don't tell anyone where we are.' He staggered up the steps and pulled open the door. 'I'm not going back to that room.'

For a while Corbett sat on a bench, his face in his hands. A servitor came to ask if all was well, and whether Sir Hugh knew where Master Norreys was ...

Corbett lifted his head and the man took one look at the clerk's pale, angry face and hurried off. Ranulf came down, saddlebags over his shoulder and arms. They walked out into the lane. Corbett felt as if he was in a dream. He allowed Ranulf to guide him through streets, pushing away beggars. On one occasion Corbett had to stop because the sound and smells made him feel dizzy. However, by the time they reached the Merry Maidens, Corbett had regained his wits. Still cold and tired he sat in front of a weak fire in the taproom whilst Ranulf hired a chamber, and some food, roast pheasant in an oyster sauce. Ranulf remained silent and just watched as Corbett ate sparingly, drank two bowls of claret and told him about Norreys.

'I'll sleep for a while,' Corbett concluded. 'Go back to Sparrow Hall, Ranulf and tell Master Tripham what has happened. Wake me just as the bells ring for Vespers.'

Corbett went up to his chamber. A tapster went before

him carrying the fresh sheets and bolsters Ranulf had ordered. The room was a simple, whitewashed cell with a rickety table and two stools, but the beds were comfortable and clean. Once the tapster had changed the sheets, Corbett bolted the door, crawled into the bed, pulling the blankets over him, and fell into a deep sleep.

Corbett slept for an hour. When he woke, his hand went to the dagger on the floor until he remembered where he was. He tossed the blankets off, got up and washed. He felt better and, going down to the taproom, found Ranulf engaged in a game of hazard. His servant winked at him, pocketed his winnings and followed Corbett out into the small herb garden behind the inn.

'Do you feel better?'

'Aye.' Corbett stretched. 'It happened so quickly, Ranulf. You are hunting a murderer and, before you know it, the bastard's hunting you. You have told Tripham?'

'There's chaos at Sparrow Hall,' Ranulf replied.

'Chaos!'

'Bullock has removed Norreys's corpse to the market cross in Broad Street. He's hung it on a gibbet as a warning to other would-be murderers.'

'And what are the rest of the Masters doing?'

'They are virtually prisoners in their own Hall. They remind me of sparrows caught in a cage.'

Corbett smiled at the pun.

'If I had my way . . .!' Bullock bellowed as he strode out into the garden.

'I told him where we were,' Ranulf whispered.

'If I had my way,' the Sheriff repeated, hitching his great, leather belt further up his ponderous girth, 'I'd have all the buggers arrested and thrown in the dungeons!' He stared at Corbett. 'That was stupid, Sir Hugh. You could have ended up pickled in a barrel!'

'I needed to search for proof and I suspected Norreys would follow me.' Corbett shrugged. 'But that's over now and we must concentrate on Sparrow Hall.'

'Once the curfew sounds,' Bullock retorted, 'there'll be more soldiers round Sparrow Hall and that hostelry than flies on a dung heap. I'm also leaving men in the street outside; I thought I'd tell you.' The Sheriff spun on his heel and walked back to the tavern.

'What now, Master?'

'I don't know, Ranulf.'

Corbett looked up at the sky, which was still shot red from the setting sun. He wafted his hand against the gnats which had begun to swarm despite the bowls of vinegar that had been placed along the garden path.

'The Bellman will not strike again, at least not against us. Old beggars will no longer be slaughtered in the cellars of the hostelry.' He heard laughter, followed by the sound of a young boy breaking into a carol in a chamber high in the tavern. 'You were playing hazard?'

Ranulf threw the dice from hand to hand. 'Yes, and I wasn't cheating.'

Corbett placed his hand on Ranulf's shoulder. 'I owe you my life.'

His servant glanced away.

'How are you finding the *Confessions of Augustine*?'

'Difficult but thought-provoking.'

'So, we'll see a new Ranulf, eh?' Corbett steered him back towards the tavern door. 'No more maidens in distress. And the aged goldsmiths of London will sleep more peacefully in their beds, eh?'

They entered the taproom and Corbett called across for wine. Ranulf thought Corbett would go up to his chamber but, surprisingly, the clerk joined a group of scholars sitting in the far corner. One of them had a tame badger and was busily feeding it drops of mead which the creature greedily guzzled.

'Have you had it long?' Corbett asked.

The scholar looked up. 'Since it was a cub. I found it wandering in Christ Church meadows. They say it brings luck.'

'And has it?' Corbett asked, sitting down.

'Well, it's drinking my mead.' The scholar looked enviously at Corbett's brimming cup so the clerk called the tapster over.

'The same for my companions!' he ordered.

'You are not interested in badgers, are you?' the scholar asked slyly.

'No, I'm not,' Corbett replied. 'Tell me, have you heard of the Bellman and his proclamations?'

'I have heard a lot of things, sir: of deaths at Sparrow Hall and in the hostelry.'

'But you have read the Bellman's proclamations?' Ranulf asked.

'I've glanced at them.' The scholar waved round to his companions. 'As have we all.'

'And?' Corbett asked.

The fellow gathered the tame badger into his arms and sat stroking him gently.

'It's much ado about little, sir. What do we care for de Montfort? It's the work of some trickster or madman. You'll not get the scholars arming themselves and marching on Woodstock.'

'And that's the general feeling?'

'I read the proclamations only because they were posted on the door of Wyvern Hall,' the scholar replied. 'But, to answer you bluntly, sir, I couldn't care whether the Bellman lives or dies.'

Corbett thanked him, placed a coin on the table to buy

more mead for the badger and, followed by a curious Ranulf, returned to his chamber.

'What was all that about?' Ranulf asked, slamming the door.

'It's something we've overlooked,' Corbett retorted. 'Let's go back to that day at Leighton Manor. Edward arrives full of rage at the Bellman's proclamations, all the nightmares about de Montfort springing fresh in his soul. The King cares so we have to care – after all we are the King's most faithful servants, his royal clerks. We come to Oxford and we make the mistake of entering the Bellman's world. However, as I was standing out in the garden, staring up at the sky, I recalled something you said at the hostelry. What does it really matter? Who really cares? And the scholar downstairs, the young man with the badger, proves it.' He glimpsed the look of puzzlement in Ranulf's eyes. 'Read your Augustine: reality is only what we perceive. Augustine perceived God, and suddenly all his former realities – lechery, revelry, drinking and women – disappeared.' Corbett settled further back on the bed. 'Who knows, the same might happen to Ranulf-atte-Newgate. It is the same with the King: De Montfort is a demon that haunts his soul – to him the Bellman poses a terrible threat to his crown and his rule.'

'But in reality?'

'The reality,' Corbett continued, 'is that people don't care. De Montfort's been dead for almost forty years: the Bellman is aiming directly at the King. We have got to pose Cicero's question: "*Cui bono*?" What is the profit to the Bellman for all his hard and dangerous work? What is he trying to achieve? He won't excite rebellion. He'll not have armies marching on London and Westminster. So what is his purpose?'

'To settle scores?' Ranulf queried.

'But why? Why now? Why the murders? The attack on me? The growing chaos at Sparrow Hall?' Corbett picked at a loose thread on the blanket. 'They have had their warning,' he added softly.

'Warning, Master?'

'Chaos,' Corbett replied. 'The Bellman seems bent on bloody mayhem and, if that's the case, believe me, Ranulf, before we are much older, there will be another murder at Sparrow Hall!'

Chapter 12

Ranulf sat just inside the church of St Michael. He crouched at the base of a pillar and stared across at the side chapel, disturbed by the colourful painting there. The church was dark except for two lighted candles, which glowed like the eyes of some beast lurking in the gloom. The candles lit up the lurid wall painting of Christ at the Last Judgement, coming with his angels to pronounce eternal doom, life or damnation. Ghostly skeletons, clothed in shrouds, lifted their hands in supplication to angels swooping above them, swords raised. On Christ's left, goats ridden by fleshless hags mixed with demons, swarming for the last harrowing of souls before the doors to eternity closed for ever.

'Remember, man, that thou art dust and into dust thou shalt return!'

Ranulf looked over his shoulder at the small chink of light from the anchorite's window.

'For death shall come!' the anchorite intoned. 'Sprung like a trap upon every living soul upon the earth!'

'Go to your prayers, old woman!' Ranulf shouted back.

'And I pray for you,' Magdalena retorted. 'Passerel prayed here but he died: the assassin slid in like a viper, with not a sound, even when he stumbled against the iron boot bar just within the door. So pray!'

'I need your prayers,' Ranulf briskly replied.

He stared down the long nave of the church at the huge

cross which hung above the high altar. He was reflecting on
what the anchorite had said when he heard a sound and
turned, but it was only a rat climbing out of the parish coffin
that stood on a set of trestles in the transept. Ranulf ran a
finger round his lips. He found it difficult to pray for himself,
never mind poor Maltote. He shifted slightly to the left so he
could see the statue of the Virgin and Child where it stood
before a lighted oil lamp to the left of the high altar. Ranulf
found it hard to recite the Ave Maria: what memories did he
have of motherhood except of a foul-tempered woman who
slapped him on his face and threw him out into the streets?
One day Ranulf had returned and found her dead of the
pestilence. He had just stood and watched as the corpse
collectors came and took her off in a barrow to join the rest
of the bodies in the great lime pits outside Charterhouse.

The sacristy door opened and Father Vincent came out.
He genuflected before the rood screen and came down the
church. Ranulf rose to meet him, not wishing to startle the
priest.

'Who is it?' Father Vincent stopped, peering through the
darkness.

'Ranulf-atte-Newgate!'

'I thought I heard a noise,' Father Vincent said. He
jingled the keys in his hands. 'I must lock up now.' He came
closer and saw the book Ranulf was carrying. 'You are at
your devotions, sir?'

'He's praying!' Magdalena shouted. 'He's praying for
God's judgement on Sparrow Hall!'

'It's the *Confessions*,' Ranulf retorted. '*St Augustine's
Confessions*. I borrowed it from the library at Sparrow Hall.'

The priest took the book and weighed it in his hands. 'Will
this help you catch the assassin?' he asked quietly.

'I'm not here for that, Father. I came to pray.'

'And do you want me to hear your confession?' The

priest's tired, old eyes held those of Ranulf's. 'Do you want to be shriven, Ranulf-atte-Newgate?'

'I have many sins, Father.'

'Nothing can be refused absolution,' the priest replied.

'I have lusted. I have wenched. I have drunk.' Ranulf took the book back. 'And, above all, Father, I have killed. I killed a man this afternoon.'

The priest stepped back.

'It was in self defence,' Ranulf explained. 'I had to kill him, Father.'

'If that is so,' Father Vincent replied, 'there is no sin.'

'And I intend to kill again,' Ranulf added. 'I intend to hunt down my friend's assassin and carry out an execution.'

'That must be done by the due process of law,' the priest hastily replied.

'I will kill him, Father.'

The priest crossed himself. 'Then I cannot give you absolution, my son.'

'No, Father, I don't suppose you can.' Ranulf genuflected and, without a backward glance, walked out of the church.

Corbett sat at his desk and pulled the two fat tallow candles closer so they bathed the piece of parchment in front of him in their light. Outside in the yard, dogs yapped at the moon. Now and again the sounds of revelry and drinking could be heard from the taproom below. Corbett had opened the shutters. The night air was soft, warm, mingling the smell of the yard with the more fragrant odours from the kitchen and herb garden. Corbett felt uneasy. He stared down at the blank piece of vellum and tried to marshal his thoughts.

'What have we here?' he whispered. He dipped his quill into the ink pot.

Item – The self-proclaimed Bellman nails his letters to

the doors of churches and Halls all over Oxford. Vicious attacks on the King but who, apart from the King, really cares?

Item – which of the masters from Sparrow Hall could move so quickly round Oxford? Tripham? Appleston? Surely not Barnett who seems to spend his life torn between sin and penance for it? Or the Lady Mathilda, with her cane tapping on the cobbles? Or the silent Master Moth? Yet he seems witless and unable to read?

Item – Ascham knew something. What book was he looking for? Why did he write 'PASSER...' in his own blood as he lay dying? And why was Passerel killed so silently in St Michael's church?

Corbett lifted his quill. Ranulf had gone there, saying he needed to pray. Corbett hoped he'd be safe. He smiled grimly as he recalled Ranulf's cold ruthlessness when dealing with Norreys.

Item – Langton? Why was he poisoned? And why was he carrying a warning letter to myself?

Item – All these deaths are the work of the Bellman. But why?

Corbett put the pen down and rubbed his face. He looked at the hour candle but it was so battered Corbett could hardly distinguish the hour marks. He rose, took off his jerkin, crossed himself and lay down on the bed. He would rest for a while and, when Ranulf returned, continue with his work. He thought of Maeve, Eleanor and Uncle Morgan at Leighton. Perhaps Maeve would be in the solar talking to her uncle? Or in her bed chamber? Maeve always took so long to come to bed, her mind constantly busy, getting things ready for the following day. Corbett closed his eyes, determined to sleep only for a short while.

When he awoke the shutters were closed and the candles doused. Ranulf lay fast asleep in his bed near the door. Corbett heard sounds from the yard below. He opened the shutters and was momentarily dazzled by the sunlight.

'God have mercy,' he murmured, 'but I slept well and deep.'

'Gone into the west,' Ranulf joked as he threw his blankets off the bed. 'I was back before midnight, Master. The taproom was empty. You were sleeping like the dead.'

Ranulf realised what he had said and apologised. He went down the passageway and came back with a fresh jug of water. Corbett decided not to shave but washed himself hurriedly. He changed his shirt and linen and, leaving Ranulf to his own ablutions, went down to the deserted taproom. He was half-way through a bowl of hot broth when Bullock strode into the room snapping his fingers.

'Sir Hugh, you had better come! And you!' he barked at Ranulf who had just come down the stairs. 'We've found the Bellman!'

Corbett pushed away the bowl and jumped up.

'The Bellman? How?'

'Follow me!'

They hurried after him into the street, Ranulf running back for their war belts. He caught them up just as they entered the lane leading to Sparrow Hall.

'Who is it?' Corbett clutched at the Sheriff's sleeve.

'It's Appleston. You know, de Montfort's bastard son!'

'And you have proof?'

'All the proof in the world,' the Sheriff retorted. 'But much good it will do either him or you.'

Tripham, Churchley, Barnett and Lady Mathilda were waiting for them in the small parlour.

'We found him just after dawn,' Tripham bleated, getting to his feet, wringing his hands together. 'So many deaths!' he wailed. The Vice-Regent's face was white and haggard. 'So many deaths! So many deaths! The King will not accept this.'

'Another murder,' Corbett asked, staring round the group.

'No murder,' Lady Mathilda replied. 'Appleston took the coward's way out. Master Alfred Tripham will show you.'

The Vice-Regent led them up the stairs. On the first gallery two servants busily folding cloths from a chest stood up and flattened themselves against the wall as if they did not wish to be seen. Bullock pushed open a door. The chamber within was luxurious: it contained a four-poster bed with the curtains pulled, shelves laden with books, pewter plates and cups, stools and a cushioned chair before the elegant writing table under the window. On either side of it stood half-open coffers. Bullock pulled back the curtains of the bed. Appleston lay there, so serenely Corbett thought he was asleep. Bullock, grumbling under his breath, went and pulled back the shutters.

'Don't touch the cup on the table,' he warned as Corbett picked it up and sniffed at it.

He caught the acrid tang beneath the claret.

'What is it?' he asked.

'I am a sheriff, not an apothecary!' Bullock snapped. 'But Churchley claims it's a form of sleeping potion, the kind which provides eternal sleep.'

Corbett sat on the bed. He gently eased back the blankets and loosened the buttons of Appleston's nightshirt.

'Is all this really necessary?' Tripham asked.

'Yes, I think it is,' Corbett replied.

Pulling up the nightshirt he studied the corpse. Corbett could find no mark of violence. The skin was slightly clammy, the face pale, the lips half-open and turning purplish, but nothing significant. If it had not been for the cup, Corbett would have thought Appleston had died silently in his sleep.

'And why do you think he's the Bellman?'

'Look at the desk,' Tripham replied.

Corbett did so. A piece of parchment, neatly cut, caught his eye: the writing on it was the same as on the Bellman's proclamation. He also noticed the ink jar and quill lying beside it.

'"The Bellman cometh and goeth,"' he read aloud. '"He sounds his warnings and proclaims the truth yet the darkness always comes. Who knows when he will return?" Slightly enigmatic,' Corbett observed.

He went back to the bed and picked up Appleston's hand and noticed the black ink stains on the fingers: flecks of ink also stained the white linen nightshirt.

'And there's more,' Bullock declared.

He began to open chests and coffers, taking out rolls of vellum, pots of black ink. He also pushed scraps of yellowing parchment and thrust them into Corbett's hand.

'Draft copies of the Bellman's proclamations.' He pointed to a roll of vellum lying beside the desk. 'Extracts from the chronicles about de Montfort's life. And, more importantly— '

Bullock went into a coffer and rummaged about. He brought out what looked like a small triptych. However, when Corbett opened it, instead of a picture of the crucifixion in the centre with Mary and John on the side panels, there was a crudely depicted portrait of de Montfort portrayed as a saint; on either side stood hosts of people, hands outstretched, scrolls coming out of their mouths which bore the words, '*Laudate*!' '*Laudate*!' Praise! Praise!

Corbett joined in the search. Tripham stood by the door

bleating protests. Bullock relished turning over coffers and chests. In the end Corbett piled all that they'd found on the desk.

'So Appleston was the Bellman,' he concluded. 'We knew him to be the illegitimate son of de Montfort and there is no doubt he had a special love for the Earl. The scrolls, the writing implements all seem to indicate he was the Bellman.'

'You are not so sure?' Ranulf asked.

'Oh, I may accept that he's the Bellman,' Corbett replied. 'But why did he commit suicide? For that's what the verdict will be, yes? Appleston realises he could no longer continue his subterfuge. Accordingly, he draws up a small memorandum proclaiming the truth, takes a potion and dies peacefully in his sleep.' He glanced at Tripham. 'Was the door locked or unlocked?'

'Unlocked, Sir Hugh.'

Corbett sat down on a stool and scratched the end of his nose.

'Here's a man who is going to commit suicide,' he declared. 'He's written his death warrant – you see the ink stains on his fingers. Most of the wine has been drunk. Appleston does not bother to die dramatically but climbs into bed.' Corbett stared at the candlestick, he noticed how the wax had burnt down. 'If you could all leave. Master Sheriff, you too.'

Bullock was about to protest.

'Please,' Corbett added. 'I promise I will not keep you long.'

Bullock followed Tripham out of the chamber. Ranulf closed the door behind them.

'You don't believe it was suicide, do you, Master?'

'No, I don't,' Corbett replied. 'It's not logical. Most assassins value their lives. The Bellman has enjoyed the game. He has killed in secret under the cloak of darkness. So why should he go so quietly into the night? Oh— ' Corbett nodded. 'There's a lot of evidence against him. His parentage, the documents in this chamber. But there again, Ranulf, if you were the bastard son of de Montfort, you'd be proud of it too, wouldn't you?'

'Yes, yes, I would.'

'So, tell me, Ranulf, if you were going to commit suicide, if you were going to write the last note of your life, you'd want to do it undisturbed surely? You'd lock and bolt the door. But Appleston did neither. He climbed into bed without dousing the candle. Above all, if a man was about to die, why change into his night attire?' Corbett walked across to the door. On one peg hung a Master's cloak bearing the badge of the Hall and, on the other, a shirt, jerkin and hose. Corbett examined these carefully.

'They are all clean,' he murmured.

He looked round the room and glimpsed a straw basket in the far corner under the lavarium. He went across and pulled this out, emptying the contents on to the floor. He picked up a soiled shirt and hose.

'This is what Appleston wore yesterday.' Corbett put them back in the basket. 'Appleston also arranged fresh clothes for the morrow.'

'Perhaps he's a man of routine,' Ranulf replied. 'I have heard of a similar case in Cripplegate when a mother baked bread, even though she had decided to take her life before morning.'

'Perhaps.' Corbett walked round the room. He sat at the desk and sifted through pieces of parchment. 'But let's say –' he waved a piece of vellum in his fingers '– *Causa Disputandi*, that Appleston was the Bellman. Bullock came in here and immediately found the evidence. Why make it so apparent?'

'Appleston was past caring,' Ranulf replied. 'Don't

forget, Master, he must have calculated we were closing in. We'd found out his secret . . .'

'But I'm not closing in,' Corbett commented drily. 'I'm stumbling around in the dark as much as ever.'

'Yes, yes. But, Master, let's say we left Oxford and took horse to Woodstock and told the King what we knew. What would have happened?'

'The Masters here would have been arrested.' Corbett nodded. 'I follow your drift, Ranulf. The King would have been deeply interested in Appleston. He would have been tempted to lodge him in the Tower with the Torturers until the truth was out. Indeed, Edward would have been beside himself to learn that a bastard son of the great de Montfort might have been plotting against him.'

Corbett saw Ranulf's boots scuff the bed tapestries and, going across, he lifted the sheets and blankets. Beneath the mattress, built into the wooden bedstead, was a small drawer. Corbett told Ranulf to move and they both crouched and tried to open it. The drawer was locked but Ranulf took a small pin out of his purse and inserted it carefully in the lock. At first he had no luck but, drawing it out, he inserted it again more carefully. Corbett heard a click and Ranulf pulled the drawer open. They took it out and placed it on the bed. Ranulf glimpsed Appleston's dead face and, feeling guilty, pulled the sheet over it. The small drawer contained a few items: a lock of hair in a leather pouch; a ring bearing the insignia of a white lion rampant; a pilgrim's medal from Compostella in Spain; an ivory-handled dagger in a clasp bearing the same escutcheon as the ring.

'De Montfort's arms,' Corbett remarked. 'Probably relics of the great Earl.'

He took out the book and opened it. Bound in calf-skin, with small glass jewels embedded in the brown leather cover, the pages inside were stained and marked, the writing in different hands. Corbett took this over to the light.

'It's a collection of tracts,' he remarked, 'collected and bound together in one volume.' He turned to the front of the book. 'And this did not belong to Appleston, it's the property of the hall.'

'Is that what Ascham was studying?' Ranulf asked.

'Perhaps?' Corbett replied, leafing through the pages. 'They are tracts,' he declared, 'written and circulated in London during de Montfort's civil war with the King. They are written by different people, most of them are anonymous.'

'Anything from the Bellman?' Ranulf asked.

'No, but one writer calls himself Gabriel, taking the name of Heaven's chief herald,' Corbett replied. 'Ah!' He smiled. 'They are savage criticisms of the King's government,' he continued. 'Nothing original – the usual list of royal abuses and expressions of support for de Montfort.'

'So?' Ranulf asked.

'What is interesting, my dear Ranulf, is that they are the source of the Bellman's proclamations. He simply copied them out, transcribing them for his own use.'

'And did Appleston do that?'

'I don't know. But one thing we can establish is how long Appleston has had this book. We must look in the library at the register of books that have been borrowed.' Corbett turned the pages of the book over. On the back of the various tracts was scribbled: '*Ad dominum per manus P.P.*'

Ranulf came across and looked over his shoulder.

'What does that mean, Master?'

'Nothing,' Corbett replied. 'I suspect that these tracts were collected by royal adherents in London and sent to

Braose. He collected them and later had them bound in one volume.'

'More evidence against Appleston?'

'I don't know,' Corbett replied. 'Ranulf, go down to the library and ask to see the register. Tell them not to disturb us as yet.'

Ranulf hurried off. Corbett put the book back on the table. Was Appleston the assassin? He closed his eyes and put his face in his hands. Think, he urged: Appleston is the bastard son of de Montfort. He hates the Braose family and the King. He decides to resurrect the memory of his dead father. He takes a book from the hall library, assumes the anonymous name of the Bellman and begins to write tracts. At night he slips out of the Hall and posts these round Oxford. He enjoys himself, baiting the King and bringing Sparrow Hall into disrepute.

Corbett took his hands away from his face and stared at the corpse stiffening under the sheets on the bed. Ascham must have grown suspicious, perhaps he had missed the book. He let his suspicions show so, one evening, Appleston goes out into the garden and sulks between the line of bushes and the library wall. He taps on the shutters. Ascham opens them and Appleston puts a crossbow bolt straight into the man's chest. But what about the scrawled word 'PASSER' . . .? Corbett recalled the library window and felt a tingle of excitement in his belly.

'Of course,' he whispered. 'Appleston was athletic, vigorous. He could have climbed in, taken Ascham's finger, dipped it into a pool of blood and written those letters himself, so that the poor bursar took the blame. After all it was Appleston who told Passerel to flee to the church. Did Appleston go back, late at night, with a poisoned jug of wine? And what of Langton?' Corbett didn't know why the murdered master would have been carrying a letter from him to the Bellman. However, it would have been easy for anyone in that library to slip a potion into Langton's wine cup.

Corbett got to his feet. And the slingshot fired at them? Hadn't Appleston spent his youth in the countryside? Perhaps he had grown quite skilled in the use of the sling? Appleston knew that Corbett had learnt about his parentage and, fearful that all would be discovered, had he decided to take his own life? Corbett heard footsteps outside and Ranulf returned.

'Well?' Corbett asked.

'The book is in Appleston's name,' Ranulf declared. 'But listen, Master, the entry is only for yesterday morning. It was two entries down from mine.'

Corbett sighed in disappointment. 'And there's no other sign?'

'No. The title of the book is *Litterae atque Tractatus Londoniensis, Letters and Tracts from the city of London.* I looked through the register very quickly. No one else has signed it out.' Ranulf jabbed a thumb over his shoulder. 'And Master Tripham is getting restless. He wants to know what to do with the corpse.'

'Tell him to send up a servitor,' Corbett ordered. 'The one who looked after Appleston.'

Ranulf left. A short while later he returned with the servitor; a lanky, cadaverous-faced individual with strands of red hair across his bald pate, and a face as white as a sheet. His cheeks and crooked nose were savagely pitted with pimples and sores. His lower lip trembled and Corbett had to sit him down and reassure him that he had nothing to fear. The man gulped, his bulbous eyes constantly watching Ranulf as if he feared he was going to be tried and executed on the spot.

'I did nothing to frighten him, Master,' Ranulf said as he

leaned against the door. 'Apparently his name is Granvel. He was Appleston's servitor.'

'Is that true?' Corbett asked gently.

The man nodded.

'And how long have you served him?'

'I have been two years at Sparrow Hall.' Granvel's voice had a broad, rustic twang. 'Master Appleston was a good man. He was always kind; he never beat me even when I made a mistake.'

'Did he talk to you?' Corbett asked. 'I mean, about what he did?'

'Never, never, always please and thank you. Presents at Easter, mid-summer and Christmas. Now and again the occasional shilling when the fair came to Oxford. And he took me once to see a mummers' play in St Mary's Church. That's all I know, Master. I always cleaned his room and he told me never to touch his papers or books.'

'And last night?'

'All was normal, Master, except Master Appleston came back very irate. It was dark . . .'

'Excuse me,' Corbett interrupted. 'Did Master Appleston ever leave late at night? I mean, go out into the city?'

'Not that I know of.' The man's head went back. 'He wasn't like that, sir. Not like that Master Churchley, hot as a sparrow he is and lecherous to boot. Master Appleston was a gentleman and a scholar. He loved his books, he did. I mean a real gentleman, sir. He even emptied his own chamber pot out of the window. Didn't leave it full for some poor servant to do, like the others.'

Corbett tried not to look at Ranulf who, head bowed, was laughing quietly to himself.

'But last night something was wrong?'

'Oh yes. Master Appleston came back after dark. I think he'd been out somewhere to eat.' Granvel lowered his voice. 'All those strange doings, Master, at the Hall.' He tapped the side of his nose. 'And, before you ask, I know nothing about it nor do any of the servants.' He winked slyly. 'Oh, we've heard all about the Bellman, sir. But how could someone leave the Hall at night? All the doors are locked and bolted.'

Corbett pulled a face but Granvel was quick.

'Oh, I suppose, Master, if someone wanted to leave they could do. I am just saying it's difficult to do so without being seen by someone.'

'You mean the Bellman?'

'Of course! We've all heard about the proclamations but we can't read. I've wondered, like the rest, how on earth someone could enter and leave Sparrow Hall at their will?'

Corbett looked at Ranulf who shook his head. Corbett dipped into his purse and handed a coin over. Granvel, now relaxed, warmed to his task.

'The same goes for the poisoning of old Master Langton. How could the wine be poisoned? Everyone drank from the same jug. Anyway,' he continued almost at a gabble, 'as I said, last night Master Appleston comes back, angry he was. Some of the soldiers round the Hall were fairly rough. They seized Master Appleston by the cloak and knocked that sore on his mouth. Well, Master Appleston comes into the parlour, breathing thunder he was: with the sore beside his mouth reopened and bleeding. He complained to Master Tripham: said he knew there had to be soldiers but that being manhandled was another matter.'

'And then he had something to eat?' Corbett asked.

'Oh no, Master,' Granvel gabbled on. 'That's what I said earlier. Strange doings here. Everyone frightened of every one else. No, he came up to his room and prepared for bed. I brought him some fresh water and he changed. He had his shift and furred robe on when I came up with a goblet of wine.'

Corbett pointed to the goblet on the table beside the bed.

'That goblet?'

'Yes, sir, that's the one. There are plenty in the kitchen. Master Appleston was sitting at his desk. I put the wine down and left.'

'And that was it?'

'Oh no, Master.' Granvel smiled in a fine display of the only two teeth in his head. 'Master Tripham came up to see him.'

'And who else?'

'Master Churchley brought a tincture, some camomile, I believe, for the sore on Appleston's mouth.'

'And there was someone else, wasn't there?'

'Oh yes, yes, that fat Sheriff comes into the hall, squat little toad he is. "I want to see Master Tripham!" he shouts. "Aye," Master Tripham replies, "And I want to see you, Sir Walter. There's a fair argument over Master Appleston's treatment".'

'And then what?'

Granvel shifted on his stool. 'Well, "Bugger it!" the Sheriff says. "I'll apologise to Master Appleston myself!"' Granvel shrugged. 'I took him up to the room then stayed in the passageway.'

'Oh come, Master Granvel! You did listen in?'

The man smiled, his eyes on the second coin in Corbett's fingers.

'Well, it was hard not to, Master. I didn't hear distinct words but voices were raised. And then – Bullock by name, Bullock by nature – the fat Sheriff fairly sweeps out of the room and nearly knocks me down.' Granvel spread his hands. 'After that, Master, I returned to my quarters below stairs. Except for my usual visit.'

'Usual visit?' Corbett asked.

'Well yes, sir, it's in the regulations of the Hall. You know how these Masters study by candlelight. After midnight, I, like the rest, go up to check on my master's chamber.'

'And?'

'Nothing. I tapped on the door. I tried the latch but it was bolted.'

'Was that usual?'

'Sometimes, when Master Appleston had a visitor in the room or did not want to be disturbed. So I went away.'

'But the room was locked?'

'Oh yes. So I thought, I'd leave it for an hour and when I returned the door was unlocked. I opened it gently and peered in. The candles were doused, there were no lights, so I closed the door quickly and went to bed myself.'

'And you know nothing else?'

'I knows nothing else, Master.'

Corbett handed over the coin. 'Then keep your mouth shut, Master Granvel. I thank you for what you have said.'

Ranulf opened the door and the servant scuttled out.

'So, Master?'

Corbett shook his head. 'When I was a boy, Ranulf, there was a murder in my village. No one knew who did it. A ploughman had been found in the great meadow outside the village, a knife between his ribs. My father and others took the knife out and brought the corpse back to the church. Our priest then made each of the villagers walk around the corpse. He was invoking the ancient belief that a corpse will always bleed in the presence of its murderer. I remember it well.' Corbett paused. 'I stood at the back of the church, watching my parents and all the adults walk slowly round the corpse. Candles flickering at the head and foot of the coffin made the old church fill with shadows.'

'And did the corpse bleed?'

'No, it didn't, Ranulf. However, as the men walked by, our priest, a shrewd old man, noticed that one villager was not wearing his knife sheath. He took him aside and, in the presence of the reeve, carefully scrutinised him. Blood which couldn't be accounted for was found on the man's tunic; moreover, he couldn't explain where his knife was. He later confessed to the murder and fled for sanctuary.'

'And you think the same will happen here?'

Corbett smiled and went up and pulled back the sheets.

'Study his face, Ranulf. What do you see? Examine particularly his lips.'

'There's a sore.' Ranulf pointed to the bloody scab. 'Not properly healed.'

'Yes, I thought of that when Granvel mentioned the tincture of camomile. It looks as if it has been rubbed.'

'But Granvel explained that?'

Corbett shook his head. 'Look at the cup, Ranulf – there's no blood mark round the rim. Would a man as neat and precise as Appleston go to sleep with a sore still bleeding? More importantly—' Corbett began to pull the bolsters away from underneath the dead man's head. There were four all together. Corbett turned these over and sighed in satisfaction: in the middle of one bolster were faint blots of blood, pieces of hardened scab still caught in the linen.

'Master Appleston didn't commit suicide,' Corbett declared. 'I'll tell you what happened, Ranulf. Late last night someone came here. A friendly visit – perhaps bringing a wine jug. Whoever it was filled Appleston's cup not only with wine but with a heavy sleeping draught. Appleston fell into a deep sleep and then the assassin, our Bellman, took a bolster, held it over Appleston's face and quietly smothered him: that's why the room was locked when Granvel returned.'

Chapter 13

Corbett told Ranulf to hold his peace as they went downstairs. Bullock was seated in the parlour with Tripham and Lady Mathilda, Master Moth standing like a ghost behind her. Churchley and Barnett sat apart in the window seat, heads together.

'Well?' Bullock asked, rising to his feet.

'Master Leonard Appleston was not the Bellman,' Corbett replied, 'nor did he commit suicide. I am not going to give you the evidence for this.' He caressed the book he had found in Appleston's room. 'Late last night someone came and killed poor Appleston and then made it look as if he was the Bellman.' He stared round at the assembled company. 'Sparrow Hall is a veritable nest of murderers,' he added.

'I protest!' Tripham bleated from where he sat beside Lady Mathilda. 'Sir Hugh, I must protest at such a description. We at Sparrow Hall cannot be blamed for the murderous antics of Master Norreys . . .'

'Murderous no longer,' Bullock broke in. 'His body's gibbetted in Carfax.'

'It was a royal appointment,' Churchley said. 'Norreys was the King's nominee: he had little to do with Sparrow Hall itself.'

'Why was Appleston murdered?' Barnett asked.

'Because the Bellman is scared,' Corbett replied. 'He

must realise the net is closing. Appleston was the suitable sacrificial lamb. I found this book in his room, which makes me wonder if he was also murdered because he entertained his own suspicions: we'll never know now, will we?'

'Talking of books,' Tripham intervened, desperate to assert his own authority. 'Your servant, Sir Hugh, has our copy of *St Augustine's . . .*'

'Appleston allowed me to take it,' Ranulf replied.

'Well, Appleston's dead and we want it back.'

'What now?' Lady Mathilda asked from where she sat with a piece of embroidery on her lap.

'A few questions first,' Corbett replied. 'Master Tripham, you went up to see Appleston last night?'

'Yes, I did. He was upset at the way Sir Walter's soldiers had manhandled him.'

'And, Master Churchley, you took him up a tincture of camomile?'

'Yes, for the sore on his mouth.'

Corbett stared at the sparrows carved on both sides of the fire hearth and then at Bullock who seemed to have lost some of his bombast.

'And you, Sir Walter?'

'I went to apologise for my men.'

'And the meeting was amicable?'

Bullock opened his mouth to reply.

'The truth!' Corbett demanded.

'It was far from amicable,' Bullock admitted. 'At first Appleston accused me of being a bullyboy, of enjoying the discomfiture of the Masters and scholars at Sparrow Hall. I told him not to be so stupid. I was about to leave when he also called me a traitor: he had seen my name amongst the adherents of de Montfort. I told him he was too young and too foolish to pass judgement on his elders.' Bullock shrugged. 'Then I left.' The Sheriff sat down on a stool. 'Why,' he added, 'can't de Montfort's ghost leave us alone?' He glanced up. 'Sir Hugh, what will happen now? I can't keep guarding Sparrow Hall for ever and a day. The King must be told.' A touch of malice entered his voice. 'He will order the dispersal of the Masters and this place closed.'

'The Proctors of the University and others will have something to say about that,' Barnett brayed. 'Our status and property are the same as Holy Mother Church. We are not puffs of smoke to be wafted away.'

'Why are you so sure Appleston is not the Bellman?' Churchley asked. 'We have only conjecture for your conclusions.'

'In a while, in a while,' Corbett murmured. 'Master Alfred, I would like to look in your library. I'll take this book back myself. Ranulf here will return *The Confessions*. He can always study the work at the royal libraries in Westminster.' Corbett, followed by Ranulf, walked to the door. He turned. 'But none of you is to leave,' he warned. 'The fire still burns,' he added, 'and the pot has yet to come to the boil.'

'What did you mean by that?' Ranulf asked as they walked down towards the library.

Corbett stopped. 'I don't know, but it will make them think. Perhaps the Bellman will make another move and, this time, may not be so clever. Go back and collect their book. I'll wait for you in the library.'

Corbett pushed open the door of the library and went in. The arrow slits high in the walls provided some light but he opened the shutters at the far end, which gave him a view out over the garden. He went to the archivist's desk and opened the register. He noted the entries for Ranulf and afterwards Appleston for the book he had just brought back. Corbett walked round the library. Each shelf had its own mark and these were copied on the inside folio of every book. He found the place for Appleston's book, then carefully removed and studied other works on the same shelf. Many of them were similar, writings from the time of the great civil war as well as extracts from chronicles about de Montfort. One folio, thicker than the rest, contained the private papers of Henry Braose, the founder of the college. As he leafed through these, Corbett's heart skipped a beat. Certain pages had been neatly cut out with a knife. Corbett did not know whether this was recent or had occurred when the book was first bound. There was no index. Corbett took the book to a seat underneath the window and scrutinised it. Most of the contents were letters between Braose, the King and members of the Royal Council. Some were from Braose's beloved sister Mathilda; three or four to Roger Ascham his friend. Corbett closed the book and examined the cover: there was no dust so someone had quite recently taken it out. The door opened and Ranulf came in.

'I'll put it back, Master,' he offered, holding up *The Confessions*. 'I know where it goes. Have you found anything interesting?'

'Yes and no,' Corbett replied. He showed Ranulf the book with the pages ripped out.

They went back to the shelves and continued their searches. Servants came in to ask if they wanted anything to eat or drink but they refused. Tripham and then Lady Mathilda also entered to see if they needed further assistance. Corbett murmured absentmindedly that they did not and he and Ranulf returned to their searches. Now and again a bell rang and they heard the sound of feet pattering outside.

'Nothing,' Corbett concluded. 'I can discover nothing.'

He paused as the door opened and Master Churchley came in.

'Sir Hugh, Appleston's corpse must be dressed and prepared for burial. Master Tripham also asks if your servant has returned our book; it is quite costly.'

'The corpse can be removed,' Corbett replied. 'And Ranulf has brought your book back.'

'How much longer will you be?'

'As long as we want, Master Churchley!' Corbett snapped. He waited until the door closed. 'But if the truth be known,' he whispered, 'there is little more we can do here.'

'Monica!' Ranulf declared abruptly.

'I beg your pardon?'

'Monica,' Ranulf explained, beaming across the table. 'I was thinking about Augustine's mother, St Monica, who prayed every day that her son be converted.' His eyes grew soft. 'She must have been a woman of great strength and patience,' he added. 'I wish . . .' Ranulf paused. 'Is there anything we know about her?'

Corbett clapped Ranulf on the shoulder. 'A true scholar, Ranulf,' he declared, 'never leaves a library without learning something. This place must have a book of hagiography: *The Lives of the Saints*,' he explained, seeing the puzzlement in Ranulf's face.

Corbett went along the shelves and took down a huge calf-skin tome which he laid gently on the table. He opened it, pointing to the titles.

'You see, St Andrew, Boniface, Callixtus.' He opened the pages.

'The writing's beautiful,' Ranulf muttered. 'And the illuminations . . .'

'Probably the work of some monastic scribe,' Corbett explained. He turned back to the cover of the book where Henry Braose's name was boldly etched.

'Henry must have been a very wealthy man,' Ranulf remarked.

'After the civil war ended,' Corbett replied, 'De Montfort

and all his party were disinherited. Their lands, manors, castles, libraries and treasure chests were all deemed spoils of war. Edward never forgot those who supported him: de Warrenne and de Lacey were lavishly rewarded. It was wholesale plunder,' Corbett continued. 'And Braose was one of the principal beneficiaries. Now, St Monica—' He sifted through the pages to the chapter which began with 'M', the letter being painted in blue and gold. Corbett looked down the page and gasped. Ranulf came round so he turned the page over quickly. He found the place for St Monica and pushed the book over. Ranulf seized it eagerly and began to read the entry, his lips moving soundlessly. Corbett walked to the window, so Ranulf would not glimpse his excitement. He stood, breathing in deeply, calming the excitement in his belly. But how, he thought? How could it be done? He stared into the garden. The assassin came here, slunk along the walls with an arbalest. But why did Ascham open the shutters? And what of the other murders?

'Master, I'm finished.'

Corbett went back, picked up the book and placed it back on the shelf. He was sure it would be safe there: that and the book found in Appleston's chamber were all the proof he really needed.

'We'd best go.'

Ranulf caught Corbett by the shoulder. 'Master, what is it?' He smiled. 'You've found something, haven't you?'

'A faint suspicion.' Corbett winked. 'Suspicion but not proof.'

'So what now?'

'*Doucement*, as the French would say,' Corbett replied. 'Gently, gently, lad. Come, let's walk.'

They left the library. Corbett became infuriatingly quiet as he walked round the Hall, upstairs and along the galleries. At one point near a back door, Ranulf stopped and pointed to an iron boot bar cemented into the floor.

'Just like the one in St Michael's Church,' he observed.

'It's to clean boots,' Corbett absentmindedly replied.

'According to Magdalena the anchorite,' Ranulf replied, 'Passerel's assassin tripped against the one in St Michael's.'

'Did he now?' Corbett replied slowly and he stared down at the boot bar.

'We must go there,' he added enigmatically.

Corbett then went outside, staring up at the different windows, particularly those at the back of the hall. Before he left, Corbett plucked a red rose, still wet with the morning's dew. When they went out into the stinking alleyway where Maltote had been fatally wounded, he ignored the curious stares of Bullock's soldiers and placed the rose in a niche on the wall.

'A memento mori,' he explained. 'But come, Ranulf, it is time for prayer.'

They went out into the streets and made their way through the thronging crowds of hucksters and traders into St Michael's Church. Corbett walked up the nave and stood in the mouth of the rood screen.

'So, a Daniel has come to judgement!' The anchorite's voice echoed down the church. 'You have come to judgement, haven't you?'

'How does she know?' Ranulf whispered.

'A matter of faith rather than deduction,' Corbett replied. 'I wager that poor woman has prayed every day for vengeance on Sparrow Hall. Oxford is a small community – Appleston's death must now be known by all.'

Corbett genuflected towards the sanctuary lamp and walked to the side door where Passerel's assassin had crept in. He crouched down to examine the iron boot bar cemented into the paving stones. It was just within the door so people could scrape the mud and dirt from their boots.

'Passerel's assassin stumbled there,' the anchorite shouted. 'I saw him, like a thief in the night, but that's what Death is, the silent stealer of souls.'

Corbett ignored her. He then walked out of the church, not bothering to listen to the anchorite's fresh cry, 'The justice of God will shoot out like a flaming rod against sinners!'

He and Ranulf walked across the street, turned a corner and went down Retching Alley into a small ale shop. The room inside was no bigger than a peasant's hovel, with a mud-packed floor, some stools and large, overturned vats as tables. Nevertheless, the ale was tangy and frothy.

'Well?' Ranulf put his blackjack down. 'Are we going to walk round Oxford or sit here on our arses looking at each other?'

Corbett smiled. 'I was thinking about chance, Ranulf. Luck, the throw of the dice. Take Edward's great victory over de Montfort at Evesham – oh, Edward's a fine general but he was lucky. Or the outlaw we hanged at Leighton. What was his name?'

'Boso.'

'Ah yes, Boso. How did you catch him?'

'He decided to flee,' Ranulf replied, 'but took the wrong path. You can't run far when you are trapped fast in a marsh.'

'And if he had taken another path?'

'We'd have lost him. As you know, an army could hide in Epping Forest.'

'It's the same here,' Corbett replied. 'We can use logic and deduction but what brings results is luck.'

'Is it, Master?' Ranulf cradled the blackjack in his hands. 'In a few months it will be November, the feast of the Holy Souls. I keep remembering the story you told me about the murder in your parish when you were a boy. Think of all the

222

dead, all the victims of the Bellman crying to God for justice.'

Corbett toasted him silently with his own pot of ale.

'Quite the theologian, Ranulf. Divine intervention is a possibility but God also helps those who help themselves. Let's go through the list of victims.' Corbett put his ale down.

'Copsale died in his sleep, probably poisoned or smothered like Appleston.'

'And Ascham?'

'Was foolish enough to open the window shutters: he probably didn't even think.'

'And Passerel?'

'I don't know why Passerel was killed except that as he and Ascham were close friends, the Bellman might have feared that the archivist had shared his anxieties with him.'

'And Langton?'

'Again, very easy. People were gathered in the library and cups of wine stood on the table; an easy target. What I can't understand is how the dead man had a letter for me from the Bellman in his wallet?' Corbett stared at a chicken which was pecking at the mud-packed floor.

'And Appleston?' Ranulf asked. 'It must have been some-one strong to keep that bolster over his face.' Ranulf called across to the tapster to fill their blackjacks. 'But who, Master, and why?'

'According to Aristotle,' Corbett replied, 'man is natur-ally good. This confused your favourite philosopher Augustine: how could Man, who must be good if he is created by God, do evil?'

'Did he resolve the problem?' Ranulf asked.

'Yes, Augustine did: he said that when a man sins, he is seeking a selfish good. He is in fact saying, evil be thou my good.'

'And the Bellman is doing that?'

Corbett finished off his ale. 'Perhaps? Anyway, enough theory, Ranulf. Let me reflect for a while.'

Corbett rose and walked into the yard behind the small ale house: he sat on a turf-built bench, staring into the oval-shaped carp pond as if fascinated by the fish. Ranulf let him be. He supped his ale and, making himself comfortable in a corner, dozed for an hour. He was woken by Corbett tapping his boot.

'I am ready now.'

They returned to Sparrow Hall, where Corbett sought out Tripham.

'Master Alfred, I would be most grateful if you could keep your colleague Churchley under close supervision. However, I must first have words with Lady Mathilda.'

Corbett, followed by a still-mystified Ranulf, climbed the stairs. A servant directed them to Lady Mathilda's chamber at the far end of the gallery. Corbett knocked.

'Come in!'

Lady Mathilda was seated by the hearth, a piece of embroidery on her lap, needle poised in mid-air. On a stool opposite sat Master Moth, his ghost-like face and watchful eyes reminding Corbett of an obedient lapdog.

'Sir Hugh, how can I help?'

Lady Mathilda waved him to a chair. She dismissed Ranulf with a cursory glance.

'Lady Mathilda.' Corbett pointed to her writing desk. 'I need to see Sir Walter Bullock urgently. If I could borrow pen and paper, would Master Moth take my message to the castle?'

'Of course. Why, is there something wrong?'

'You are the King's spy at Sparrow Hall,' Corbett replied, sitting down at the desk, 'so, you should know before the others do; I believe that Master Churchley has a great deal to answer for as, perhaps, does his colleague Barnett.'

Corbett seized a quill, dipped it into the inkpot and wrote a short note asking the Sheriff to come as quickly as he could. He sanded the paper, folded and neatly sealed it with a blob of hot wax. Lady Mathilda made her strange hand signs to Master Moth who nodded solemnly.

'The Sheriff may not be at the castle,' Dame Mathilda pointed out.

'Then ask Master Moth to wait until he returns. Lady Mathilda, I have some questions, which I believe you may be able to assist me with.'

Corbett watched and waited as Moth took the letter, knelt, kissed Lady Mathilda's hand then quietly left the room. Once he was gone, Corbett locked and bolted the door behind him. Lady Mathilda looked up in alarm, placing the piece of embroidery on the small table beside her. Ranulf watched fascinated.

'Is that really necessary, Sir Hugh?' Lady Mathilda snapped.

'Oh, I think so,' Corbett replied. 'I don't want Master Moth coming back, Lady Mathilda, for I have never seen a man, anyone, being so close to a manifestation of someone else's soul.' Corbett sat down in the chair opposite and picked at the hem of his cloak. 'On any other occasion, Lady Mathilda, I would have gone back to my chamber, written out my conclusions and reflected on what I should do. But I can't do that here: with you, time is very dangerous!'

Lady Mathilda's face remained impassive.

'No one suspects you,' Corbett continued, 'old and venerable, resting on a cane. How could Lady Mathilda go out and stab someone in an alleyway or send a crossbow bolt into a man's chest? Or place a bolster over Appleston's face and keep it there?'

'This is preposterous!' Lady Mathilda protested.

225

'No, it's not preposterous,' Corbett replied. 'But, when you have someone like Master Moth to do your bidding for you . . .'

'Foolish!' Lady Mathilda cried. 'Your brains are addled!'

'Ah *mea Passerella* – my little sparrow – isn't that what your brother called you so many years ago, Mathilda, when you and he fought for the King against de Montfort? You, by your own admission, were a royal spy in London where you collected the tracts and broadsheets of de Montfort's followers and sent them to your brothers. "*Per manus P.P.*"' Corbett watched Lady Mathilda's pebble-black eyes. 'I noticed that on the back of various tracts in the book I found in Appleston's chamber was scrawled "*Per manu P.P.*" – "by the hand of his *parva passera*": "little sparrow", as your brother called you. I have been through the other books in the library,' Corbett continued, 'as Ascham did. 'But, although you tried to remove any letters which betrayed your brother's sweet epithet for you, his little sparrow, you missed one place.' Corbett paused. 'He had a book of the *Lives of the Saints*, in which Ranulf wanted to read about the life of Monica, mother of Augustine. The first saint to appear under 'M' was "Mathilda"' and beside the name your brother had written "*Soror mea, Passerella mea*": my sister, my little sparrow. Ascham knew that, didn't he? And when he was dying, his mind confused, he tried to scrawl the word on a piece of parchment.'

'Sir Hugh.' Lady Mathilda picked up the piece of embroidery. She jabbed the needle as if it were a dagger. 'Are you accusing me of being the Bellman? Of trying to tear down what my brother built? Are you saying that I – feebled, resting on a cane – killed my colleagues here at Sparrow Hall?'

'That's exactly what I'm saying, Lady Mathilda: that's why I asked Master Moth to leave. In my note to Bullock, I wrote that he should keep Master Moth with him and take his time getting here. Master Moth is more dangerous than he looks: the silent assassin. You don't even need to make those strange gestures at him; he would know, just by watching your face, that you were in grave danger and act accordingly. By the time he returns with our good Sheriff I will be finished and you, Lady Mathilda, will be under arrest for high treason and murder.'

'This is nonsense!' Lady Mathilda spat back. 'I am the King's good friend. His most loyal subject.'

'You *were* the King's good friend and loyal subject,' Corbett declared. 'Now Lady Mathilda, your soul seethes with malice. You want revenge: revenge on the King; revenge on those here at Sparrow Hall who, when you die – and die you shall – will soon forget your brother's memory, change the name of your precious Sparrow Hall and obtain royal confirmation of different statutes and regulations. In a way, the mad anchorite's curse will be fulfilled.'

'A witless harridan,' Mathilda interrupted. 'I should have dealt with her years . . .' She paused and smiled.

'You were going to say, Lady Mathilda?'

'What proof?' she asked quickly. 'What proof do you have of this?'

'Some. Enough for the Royal Justices to begin their questioning.'

Corbett studied this small, passionate woman. Years ago, at St Paul's, a priest had attacked him in the confessional with a knife. Corbett knew that Lady Mathilda, despite her apparent frailty, was just as dangerous. Murder didn't always need brute strength – just the will to carry it out.

'I asked for proof, Sir Hugh?'

'I'll come to that by and by, Lady Mathilda. Let's go back to the root and cause of it all, forty years ago when Henry Braose and his sister Mathilda decided to support the King.

Both of them were skilled, ruthless and determined. Henry was a brave soldier and Mathilda, who adored her brother as if he were God himself, was also accomplished: a woman of great cunning and deception, well versed in writing and reading, she acted as the King's spy in London. She and her brother were opportunists with the ambition of eagles, to climb and soar as high as they could. The only obstacle was de Montfort. Glorious days, eh, Mathilda? While Henry fought with the King, you spied upon the King's enemies. God knows how many men paid with their lives for trusting you.'

Lady Mathilda smiled but she bowed her head and continued to sew.

'At Evesham it all ended,' Corbett continued. 'De Montfort's defeat was final and the Braoses came forward to collect their reward: land, tenements, treasure and the King's personal favour. Men like de Warrenne and de Lacey were content just to grab and hold, but not the Braoses. Brother and sister shared a dream – to found a college, a Hall in Oxford.'

Lady Mathilda looked up. 'Golden years, Sir Hugh. But those who gambled and won . . .?'

'You, Lady Mathilda, were the source of your brother's energy and ambition. He shared everything with you, didn't he?'

Lady Mathilda gazed back unblinkingly.

'And you ensured that his dream was fulfilled. Land was bought here and across the lane, people were cleared out, and your lavish treasure was spent on building Sparrow Hall.'

'It was our right,' Lady Mathilda intervened. 'Those who bear the sweat of the plough have every right to reap the harvest.'

'And so you did,' Corbett replied. 'Your brother's dream

became a reality. But, towards the end of his life, he began to regret his avaricious acquisitions. Your brother died and, to your fury, you realised that what he had built had passed into the hands of others who wanted Sparrow Hall to break from the past. The King, your old master and friend, was no longer concerned, was he? There were no more grants, no more preferment. And the Masters here not only wanted to forget your brother, but heartily wished you elsewhere.'

'You've still not mentioned any proof!'

'Oh, I'll come to that by and by. What I want to establish –' Corbett rose and pulled his chair closer '– is why you did it? I think I know the reason. Like a child, Lady Mathilda, you felt that others should not possess what you could not have. You decided to destroy what you and your brother built up and, in so doing, waged a terrible war against your former friend the King. Revenge was your motive, the evil you called your good!'

Chapter 14

Corbett looked at Ranulf, who just stood with his back to the door, arms crossed, staring down at the floor. There was no excitement, none of his usual desire to participate in the questioning. Corbett hid his unease.

'Are you going to tell me the rest?' Lady Mathilda broke in, 'Or should I pass you a piece of embroidery, Sir Hugh, so you can help me?'

'I will weave you a tale,' Corbett retorted, 'of treason and bloody murder. Full of malice, Lady Mathilda, and angry at the King's lack of support, you sat and brooded. You, above all, know the nightmares which haunt our King's soul. You chose your tune and played it skilfully. You studied that book I found in dead Appleston's chamber: all the old claims and challenges of de Montfort and his party. You became the Bellman.'

'And, if I did, why should I name Sparrow Hall?'

'Oh, that was the heart of your plot – to teach the King a lesson, never to forget you or Sparrow Hall. The crisis began: at the same time, you offered yourself as a spy to the King.'

'And what did I hope to gain?'

'Royal attention. Perhaps the removal of certain Masters who had plans to change the name and status of the Hall. To create suspicion and distrust, to strengthen your hand here.'

'And I suppose I just slipped out of Sparrow Hall to post my proclamations on church doors?'

'Of course not. Your servant did that – the ever silent Master Moth. I have seen where your chamber is positioned, it would be easy for him to slip out of a window, cross the yard and over the wall.'

'But Master Moth can't read or write.'

'Oh, I think he was perfect for your plans,' Corbett replied. 'He's young, able and vigorous. He could steal like a shadow along the streets and lanes of Oxford. And if he wanted to, be dressed for the part, act the beggar . . .'

'Whatever he is, Sir Hugh, he still cannot read or write!'

'Of course he can't: that's why you drew the bell at the top of each proclamation. He would understand that, and know where to pierce it with a nail.' Corbett paused. 'Every proclamation had the same symbol: each proclamation was pinned through that symbol. I wondered why. Now I know the reason.'

Corbett was pleased to see he had gained Lady Mathilda's attention: her needle no longer stabbed the piece of embroidery.

'Murder is like any game,' Corbett continued. 'As in chess, you begin the game and you plan your moves. I doubt if your mind was bent on murder at first: more on catching the King's eye and getting your own way here at Sparrow Hall . . . until Ascham became suspicious, God knows why or how? He was your brother's friend. He, too, remembered the tracts and writings of de Montfort's faction. He knew you were a trained clerk.' Corbett pointed to her stained fingers. 'That's why you snatched your fingers away when I tried to kiss them once. A busy scribbler, eh, Lady Mathilda? Ascham was perceptive. He knew the Bellman was in Sparrow Hall with ready access to de Montfort's writings. Perhaps he voiced those suspicions? And so you decided to kill him. On the afternoon he died, you were with Tripham – or so you said – but I suspect you murdered Ascham before you met the Vice-Regent. You, and Master Moth, had to move quickly before Ascham's suspicions hardened into certainty. You went down into the deserted garden and there, hidden by the line of bushes, you and Moth committed dreadful murder. Moth tapped on the shutters, and when Ascham peered through, he did not see him as any danger and so opened. But you were there, as well, hidden beneath the sill or to the side. Anyway, you killed him with a crossbow bolt and then threw in that piece of parchment. Ascham, his mind drifting, tried to write down the name of his murderer with his own blood on that same scrap of parchment. He was still thinking about Henry Braose and Mathilda, his sister, the *"Parva Passera"*. He never finished.'

Corbett glanced towards Ranulf who was staring at Lady Mathilda. Corbett hoped Moth would not return though he was confident that, if he did, Moth would be no match for Ranulf. Corbett wetted his lips.

'Now, as in a game of chess, mistakes can occur when you make your moves. Ascham should have died immediately: however, you seized on his dying message as a stroke of good fortune – Passerel would take the blame. But then you started to brood: Ascham and the bursar had been friends, perhaps Ascham had voiced his suspicions about you to Passerel. So you arranged for a little legacy to be handed over to David Ap Thomas and his students, and the rest was easy. They blamed Passerel and he fled for sanctuary, but you knew the King was sending one of his clerks to Oxford, and that Passerel must not have the chance to talk with me. So, out went Master Moth with a jug full of poisoned wine and Passerel was no longer a danger. I know it was Master Moth, for when he entered St Michael's by the side door, the anchorite saw him hit his leg against the iron boot bar but he did not cry out. Being a deaf mute, Moth would simply have to bear the pain.'

'And Langton?' Lady Mathilda asked.

'Before I left for Oxford,' Corbett replied, 'I hanged an outlaw called Boso. Before I sentenced him to death, I asked him why he killed? His answer had its own strange logic: "If you have killed once," he replied, "the second, the third and all other murders follow on easily enough." You, Lady Mathilda, have a great deal in common with Boso. You are the Bellman, the avenger of all the insults over the years. You would carry out sentence of death against those Masters who had dared even to consider changing the Hall founded by your beloved brother. At the same time, you would prick the King's conscience.'

Lady Mathilda smiled and put the embroidery on the side table.

'You talked of chess, Sir Hugh. I enjoy a good game: you must visit me some day and play against me.'

'Oh, I'm sure you enjoyed your game,' Corbett replied. 'You were once the King's spy: you like the cut and thrust of intrigue. Anyway, after you returned the book Ascham was studying, you felt safe; after all, you have been through your brother's papers and removed any reference to his "*soror mea, parva passera*". You had the run of Sparrow Hall, access to the papers and manuscripts of the dead men, Churchley's poisons, all the time in the world to prepare, plot and protect yourself. Did you ever think that the deaths of the old beggar men might be connected to Sparrow Hall?'

Lady Mathilda simply grimaced.

'No,' Corbett continued. 'I suppose you were locked into your own foul and murderous plans. Perhaps you forgot your original purpose – to have the Masters of Sparrow Hall disbanded and the college closed down, only to be re-founded after you won favour with the King – and became more interested in the game than the outcome? The death of Langton was merely to increase the grip of terror,' Corbett continued. 'As the Bellman, you wrote me a letter before that dinner party, which you gave to Langton to hold. He was very biddable and would accept any story you told him, and you instructed him only to hand it over once the evening's business was finished.'

'Things might have gone wrong,' Lady Mathilda mused.

'In which case you would have asked for it back,' Corbett replied. 'It was a gamble but you enjoyed it. It would increase the fear and perhaps make me panic, as well as make the Bellman appear more sinister and powerful. We adjourned to the library. The servants brought in cups of white wine. You knew I was going to visit the library after the meal. Perhaps you handed Langton the letter as we left the refectory: I followed Tripham, and the rest, including my servants, had drunk deeply. During the conversation there, you picked up Langton's cup, poured the potion in and ensured it wasn't far from his hand. Langton drank, died and the letter was delivered.'

'Is that how Copsale died?' Ranulf interrupted brusquely. 'Did you give him a sleeping draught to ease him into eternity?'

Lady Mathilda didn't even bother to acknowledge the question.

'We can never prove that,' Corbett replied. 'But I am convinced that his murder was a sentence carried out against a man who had dared to question and plan changes at Sparrow Hall.'

Corbett was about to continue when there was a knock on the door. He nodded at Ranulf to open it, and Tripham came in.

'Sir Hugh, is there anything wrong?'

235

'Yes and no,' Corbett replied. 'Master Alfred, I would prefer it if you stayed downtairs. Oh, and if Master Moth returns, detain him on some pretext.'

Tripham was about to protest but Corbett held up his hand.

'Master Alfred, I shall not be long. I promise you!'

Ranulf locked the door behind him. Lady Mathilda made to rise but Corbett stretched across and pressed her back in the chair.

'I think it's best if you stay where you are. God knows what this room holds; knife, crossbow, poison? There's plenty of poison, isn't there, in Sparrow Hall? And it was not difficult for you to gain access to Master Churchley's stores as, of course, you've got a key to every chamber.'

'I have listened, Sir Hugh.' Lady Mathilda breathed in deeply.

Corbett marvelled at her poise and equanimity.

'I have listened to your story but you have still offered no proof.'

'I shall come to the evidence soon enough,' Corbett replied. 'You are like all the assassins I have met, Lady Mathilda – arrogant, locked in hatred, full of contempt for me. Hence the mocking messages, the rotting corpse of a crow.' He pointed a finger at her. 'Now and again, you made small mistakes: like snatching your fingers away when I attempted to kiss your hand lest I notice the ink-stains, or feeling safe to drink your wine just after Langton had died from drinking his poisoned wine. Moreover, you, amongst all those at Sparrow Hall, seemed the least perturbed by Norreys's killings.'

'I am of that disposition, Sir Hugh,' Lady Mathilda interrupted.

'Oh, I am sure you are. You really believed you would not be caught. If you felt threatened you'd remove me, like your assassin Moth killed Maltote. What did it matter? Anything to fuel the King's rage or suspicion. Nevertheless, you took precautions: the Bellman's days seemed numbered so you killed Master Appleston so that he took the blame.' For the first time Lady Mathilda's lower lip trembled. 'You really didn't want to do that, did you?' Corbett asked. 'Appleston was a symbol of your brother's magnanimity, his generosity of spirit. But someone had to take the blame. So, late last night, you and Master Moth paid him a visit with a jug of wine, the best claret from Bordeaux. Appleston would sit and talk. He then fell into a deep sleep and you and Master Moth held the bolster over his face, pressing down firmly. Appleston, drugged, unable to resist, gave up his life as easily as the others. Afterwards, with the door locked, you left enough evidence to make anyone think Appleston was the Bellman, then you disappeared back to your chamber.'

'If,' Lady Mathilda retorted, 'that did happen, how can you prove it?'

'Appleston had retired to bed. He was planning to go to the schools the following morning – he left out fresh robes. He also had a sore on his lip and when you pressed the bolster into his face, you touched the scab and made it bleed. You then turned the bolsters over and put the stained one beneath the others. In trying to depict Appleston as a suicide, you made a dreadful mistake.'

'Very shrewd,' Lady Mathilda taunted. 'But where's the real proof? The evidence for the Justices?'

'You have heard some of it.'

'Mere bird droppings!' Lady Mathilda scoffed. 'You can peck and poke to your heart's content, Master Crow, but you'll find no juicy tidbits.'

'Oh, I haven't started yet,' Corbett replied, looking round the room. 'I'll have you imprisoned in the cellar, Lady Mathilda. Then I and Master Bullock will go through this chamber.' He smiled into Lady Mathilda's face. 'We'll eventually find the evidence we need: pen, ink, parchment. Oh, and I forgot to tell you, the anchorite at St Michael's Church, the one you wished you'd dealt with—' Corbett stared boldly lest she detected he was lying. 'The anchorite saw Master Moth go into the church with the poisoned wine.'

Lady Mathilda brought back her head. 'It was too dark! Black as night. How could she see anybody in that gloom?'

'Who said the anchorite was in her cell?' Corbett lied. 'She was just within the doorway. She gave me a description which fits Master Moth. She then recalled,' Corbett continued remorselessly, 'the same person pinning the Bellman's proclamations to the door of St Michael's Church.'

'You are lying!'

'I'm not.' Corbett drew in his breath for his greatest lie. 'You see the night Moth went to St Michael's, he dropped the mallet. Magdalena, hearing the sound, came down from her cell above the porch. She peered through a crack and saw him: the same dark hood and cowl, that boyish, innocent face.' Corbett rose to his feet to ease the cramp in his legs. 'I shall tell you what will happen now, Lady Mathilda: I'll go before the Royal Justices and provide them with the same evidence I have laid before you. They may not issue a warrant for your arrest but they'll certainly be interested in Master Moth.' He sat back in his chair. Ranulf was still staring at Lady Mathilda with the same fixed look. 'You know the mind of the King,' Corbett continued. 'He'll show no mercy. Master Moth will be taken downriver to the Tower and into its dark, dank dungeons. The King's torturers will be instructed to apply their finest arts.'

'He's a deaf mute!' Lady Mathilda cried.

'He is an intelligent and malicious young man,' Corbett retorted. 'And your accomplice in murder.'

'He killed Maltote,' Ranulf declared, stepping forward. 'He killed my friend. You have my word, Lady Mathilda, that I will join the King's torturers. They'll question and question until Master Moth agrees to tell the truth.'

'Do you want that to happen to Master Moth?' Corbett asked quietly.

Now Lady Mathilda bowed her head. 'I'd forgotten about that,' she murmured. 'I'd forgotten about Master Moth.' Lady Mathilda glanced up. 'What would happen if I told you what I know?'

'I am sure that the King would be merciful,' Corbett replied, ignoring Ranulf's black looks.

Lady Mathilda pulled up the cuffs of her sleeves. She leaned back in her chair, turning sideways to stare into the cold ash of the fire hearth.

'Put not your trust in princes, Master Corbett,' she began. 'Forty years ago, I, and my brother Henry, were scholars here in Oxford. My father, a merchant, hired a master and I joined Henry in his studies. The years passed and Henry became a clerk at the royal court.' She smiled grimly. 'Something like yourself, Sir Hugh. I went with him. The old king was still alive but Prince Edward and my brother became firm friends. Then came the civil war with de Montfort threatening to tear the kingdom apart. Many of the court left to join him but my brother and I held fast. I went into London to spy for the King'. She turned in the chair. 'I risked my life and gave my body so the King could learn the secrets of his enemies. I listened to conversations, picking up information, for who would believe that the pretty little courtesan in the corner thought about anything but wine and silken robes? My brother stayed with the King. He was instrumental in organising Edward's escape and was always in the thick of the fight. After the war—' Lady Mathilda waved her hand. 'Oh, you know Edward. He showered us with gifts, anything we wanted: manors, fields, granges and treasures.' She looked at Corbett squarely. 'Brother Henry became sick of the bloodshed and the carnage. He didn't want to spend his life in some manor house, hunting, fishing and stuffing himself with food and wine. He had this vision of an Oxford college, a Hall of learning. What Henry wanted, so did I. I loved him, Corbett.' She glanced at Ranulf. 'I had more passion, Red Hair, in my little finger than you have in your entire body.'

'Continue,' Corbett said, wary lest Ranulf be provoked.

'The years passed,' Lady Mathilda continued. 'The college grew from strength to strength. My brother and I spent all our wealth. Then Henry grew ill, and when he died, this pack of weasels turned on his memory.' Her voice rose to a mocking chant: '"We don't want this and we don't want that!" "What a name for an Oxford college!" "Shouldn't its statutes of government be changed?" I watched them,' she added contemptuously. 'I could see what was going on in their heads: as soon as I died and my body was dumped in some grave, they'd begin to dismantle Sparrow Hall and refashion it in their own way. I appealed to Edward for help but he was too busy slaughtering the Scots. I asked for confirmation of my brother's foundation charter, only to receive a letter from some snivelling clerk saying that the King would attend to the matter on his return to London.' Lady Mathilda paused, breathing quickly. 'Where were the King's promises then, eh, Corbett? How could he ever forget what the Braose family had done for him? Never trust a Plantagenet! One afternoon I was in the library, leafing through that book you found in Appleston's chamber and the memories flooded back.' She shook her head, lips moving soundlessly, as if unaware of Corbett.

'And you decided to become the Bellman?' he asked.

'Yes, I thought I'd raise the demons in the King's soul. So

I began to copy out the proclamations. It took days, but about a baker's dozen were done and Master Moth was despatched to display them.' She smiled grimly. 'Poor boy! He didn't really understand what I was doing but he was the perfect weapon. If he was stopped he could act the beggar. Who'd ever be suspicious of a deaf mute? I showed him the mark of the bell and he carried a little bag of nails and a mallet.' She clapped her hands in glee. 'Oh, I felt such relief!' She smiled in satisfaction. 'Then I wrote to the King telling him about the traitor at Sparrow Hall and that I would search him out.' She pursed her lips. 'Oh, I had his attention then! The King was all ears! There were couriers and letters sent under the Privy Seal to his "dear and loyal cousin Mathilda". I never meant to kill,' she added as an afterthought, 'but I made a mistake. The King might have been frightened but Copsale wasn't. He was intent on changes here and he didn't like me. Everyone knew he had a weak heart so his death would not appear suspicious. I raided Churchley's store room of potions and helped Master Copsale to his higher reward.' She shrugged. 'I thought it would end there,' she continued in a matter-of-fact voice. 'I really did, but old Ascham was sharper than I thought. He was suspicious of both Appleston and me: he began to hint and make allusions, sometimes I would catch him watching me at the table. He had to die. It was so easy. I slipped into the garden with Master Moth. He tapped on the shutters, and when Robert opened them, I loosened the bolt, threw in that note, closed the window and slammed the shutters close: the bar, freshly oiled by Master Moth, fell into place.'

'And Passerel?'

Lady Mathilda smiled. 'At first I couldn't understand the meaning of what Ascham had written but then I saw how I could use it. I realised Passerel might have learnt something from Ascham. Our bursar was an agitated little man and forty days in a lonely church can be a powerful prick to the memory.' She shrugged. 'The rest you know. I really thought it would end with Appleston's death.' She wagged her finger at Corbett. 'But, of course, you changed all that: the King's clever, little crow hopping about, protected by his bullyboy.'

'Why did you kill Maltote?' Corbett asked grimly.

She raised her hand in a mock innocent gesture but her eyes showed no contrition.

'The Lord be my witness: I told Master Moth never to be taken.' She straightened in the chair, smoothing out the pleats of her dress. She breathed in noisily, her eyes never leaving Corbett. 'You have my confession, master clerk. So what will happen now, eh? Edward will not put me before the King's Bench. He'll remember the old days –' she preened '– and the good service I did for the crown: I am afraid it will be some nunnery for Lady Mathilda.'

'I need some wine,' Ranulf interrupted. 'Sir Hugh, a cup of claret?'

Corbett was only too pleased to have Ranulf out of the room.

'Yes,' he replied.

'And one for me, lackey!' Lady Mathilda snapped.

Ranulf glanced at Corbett who nodded.

'And don't worry,' Lady Mathilda called after him, 'there'll be no more poison.'

Ranulf left, and Lady Mathilda started to rise.

'Madam, I would prefer it if you sat.'

Lady Mathilda did so.

'Can I remind you, clerk, that the King addresses me as "His loyal and dearest cousin", not to mention your promise of mercy. I do not want to be arrested by that buffoon of a sheriff but taken to Woodstock. I'll go in black, and throw myself at the King's feet: he'll not forget Henry or his Mathilda.'

242

The door opened and Ranulf returned. He served the wine. Corbett sipped his and Lady Mathilda drank greedily as Ranulf sat down with his back to the door. She looked over her cup at Corbett.

'You'll take me to Woodstock, Corbett. You promised me mercy and I know that your word is your bond. You'll repeat your promise before the King: Edward will understand.'

'And Master Moth?' Ranulf interrupted.

'He will accompany me: he's my servant.' She didn't even bother to turn her head.

'Bullock is downstairs with Master Moth,' Ranulf announced. 'The sheriff wishes to have words with us; he said it was a most urgent matter.'

Corbett looked at Lady Mathilda. He felt uneasy. Ranulf's silence and grim face made the hair on the nape of his neck curl in fear.

'Take him with you,' Lady Mathilda said.

'Oh, don't worry!' Corbett rose to his feet. 'Ranulf is very particular about the company he keeps. We'll take the key out and lock you in.'

Ranulf looked as if he was about to refuse but rose to his feet. He took the key out of the lock and opened the door. Corbett was half-way through before he realised his mistake. Ranulf gave him a push, sending him hurtling across the gallery. The door slammed shut, and was locked and bolted.

'Ranulf!' Corbett threw himself against the door but the metal embosses on the outside only hurt his shoulder. 'Ranulf!' he shouted. 'For the love of God, I order you to open!'

Inside the chamber, however, Corbett might have been at the furthest end of the earth. Lady Mathilda half rose in alarm. Ranulf pushed her back in the seat. She watched his hand go to the hilt of his dagger.

'You'll not kill me?' she whispered. 'Not an old lady? The

King's dear cousin? You'll not draw your steel on me?'

'I'll not stab you,' Ranulf replied, coming to crouch beside her chair, his cup of wine still in his hand. 'I want to tell you, Lady Mathilda, that you are no woman! You have no soul! You seethe with malice and hatred.'

'And I toast you, Ranulf-atte-Newgate.' She put the cup to her lips and sipped. Her eyes rounded in alarm as Ranulf, with a vice-like grip, seized her hand. He stood up, pushed back her head, forcing more wine down her throat.

'And Ranulf-atte-Newgate toasts you!' he hissed. 'You asked for wine, you bitch, now drink deep of the poison!'

She struggled but Ranulf held her fast.

'You killed my friend, you malicious, murdering bitch! And, when I've finished with you, I'll settle with Master Moth as well!'

Ranulf ignored the pounding on the door and Corbett's yells from outside. He held the cup firm, his eyes glaring in fury.

'Never trust a Plantagenet,' he whispered. 'Drink the poison. Go down to hell and tell the Lord Satan that I, Ranulf-atte-Newgate, sent you there!'

He drew his hand back. Lady Mathilda let the cup fall to her lap, the remains of the wine splashing out in a sinister stain. She rose to her feet, a hand to her throat.

'There's nothing you can do,' Ranulf declared. 'There'll be no comfortable nunnery, no escape.'

Even as he went to the door, Lady Mathilda, hands clutching her stomach, sank to the floor. Ranulf looked round and he saw her jerk once or twice as he turned the key.

Corbett, Bullock and others were in the gallery outside. Ranulf stood aside and let them in. Corbett crouched by Lady Mathilda, feeling for the blood beat in her neck. He shook his head.

'She was the King's prisoner,' Bullock declared softly.

'You shouldn't have done it!' Corbett gripped Ranulf's shoulder.

'I carried out royal justice,' Ranulf retorted. He drew a parchment from the pocket of his doublet and handed it to Corbett. 'I received this from Simon the clerk,' Ranulf explained. 'I have done nothing but what the King has ordered though, I must admit, I enjoyed it.'

Corbett read the commission.

To the Sheriff and Bailiffs of the town and our city of Oxford and to the proctors of the University, Edward the King sends greetings. Know you that, what our beloved and trusted clerk, Ranulf-Atte-Newgate, has done in and around the city of Oxford, he has done for the wellbeing of the Crown and the good governance of our realm. Given under our own hand, *Teste me ipso*, Edward the King.

The writ bore the imprint of the royal Privy Seal. Corbett handed it to Bullock.

'So be it,' the Sheriff murmured. 'What the King wants, the King must have.' He handed the parchment back.

Corbett grasped Ranulf's elbow to lead him out of the room.

'What shall I do with her?' Bullock shouted.

'Bury her,' Corbett replied. 'Bury her fast. Let the priest sing a Mass.'

'And Master Moth?' Bullock got to his feet. 'I read your postscript, my men are holding him downstairs.'

'Take him to the castle,' Corbett replied. 'He's not to be manhandled or abused. You are to await the King's pleasure.'

He led Ranulf further down the corridor.

'Ranulf-atte-Newgate.' Corbett faced him squarely. 'Do you remember when I first met you? Dirty, starving and ready for the hangman's cart?'

'I remember it every day, Master. In my life I have had two friends: one I met that day, the other was poor Maltote. So, before you object, Sir Hugh, remember Maltote. That bitch,' he spat out, 'really had planned to spend the rest of her days in some comfortable nunnery! Justice has been done. Not according to your likes but, as Father Luke said when he hanged Boso, it's what God wanted. She had killed and she would have killed again. Do you think she would have forgotten you, Master? Do you really think she'd have let you walk away? '

Corbett nodded. 'Let's go Ranulf,' he replied. 'Let's go back to the Merry Maidens. Let's drink some wine and toast Maltote. Tomorrow we will make final arrangements for the transport of his corpse, and then go to Woodstock and thence to Leighton.'

They went downstairs, out into the lane. It was deserted but for Bullock's men guarding both entrances. Ranulf was still justifying what he had done when they heard a cry from behind them. Corbett turned. Master Moth, hair flying, had broken free from his captors and was speeding silently towards them. He'd grabbed a crossbow from somewhere. Corbett stared in horror as he brought it up: he pushed Ranulf aside but, even as he did, he heard the catch click, saw the hatred in Moth's face and knew he had mis-calculated. Too late. The crossbow bolt took him high in the chest. Corbett's body exploded in pain and he staggered back. Ranulf was now running forward, dagger drawn. Corbett collapsed to his knees. He watched Ranulf moving quickly, the macabre dance of the street fighter. He was heading for Moth. He suddenly switched the dagger from one hand to the other, swerved and, as he did, drove the blade deep into Moth's stomach. Ranulf then whirled round, sword drawn, bringing it down in a sweeping cut, slicing into Moth's neck. Corbett didn't care: the pain was terrible. He could taste the blood at the back of his throat. People were running towards him, slowly, as if in a dream. Maeve was there, with little Eleanor clutching her skirts.

'You shouldn't be here,' he whispered. 'But, there again,' he added, 'neither should I.'

And, closing his eyes, Sir Hugh Corbett, the Keeper of the King's Secret Seal, collapsed on to the mud-strewn cobbles of Oxford.